SHADOW RITE

THE QUEEN'S FAYTE
BOOK THREE

THE QUEEN'S FAYTE SERIES

SHADOW RITE

THE QUEEN'S FAYTE
BOOK THREE

D.D. CROIX

Fine Skylark Media
California

Fine Skylark Media
P.O. Box 1505
Lake Forest, California 92609-1505

Shadow Rite: The Queen's Fayte Book Three
Copyright © 2021 D.D. Croix
ISBN: 978-0-9908146-9-6
All rights reserved.

Cover provided by Karri Klawiter
Editing services provided by Katrina Roets

D.D Croix
Shadow Rite: The Queen's Fayte Book Three:
by D.D. Croix — 1st ed.
[1. Teen and Young Adult, Science Fiction and Fantasy, Historical — Fiction. 2. Teen and Young Adult, Mysteries and Thrillers, Fantasy and Supernatural — Fiction. 3. Science Fiction and Fantasy, Fantasy, Coming of Age — Fiction. 4. Science Fiction and Fantasy, Fantasy, Dark Fantasy — Fiction. 5. Science Fiction and Fantasy, Fantasy, Myths and Legends — Fiction.]

DEDICATION

For my family

CHAPTER ONE

FINGERNAILS STRUCK THE edge of the alabaster throne like knives striking flint. *Tap. Tap. Tap.* That insistent rhythm drew my attention to the throne's occupant and her inscrutable sapphire stare.

Who was this woman?

Not an earthly woman, to be sure. No human had flesh so smooth or so pale it practically shimmered. A moment shook loose from my foggy mind. This creature, whatever she was, had torn a hole between our worlds and dragged me through it. Only someone like Druansha could do that, or someone like Krol.

A slight tilt of her head confirmed my suspicion. Long teardrop ears poked through that silky curtain of snow-white hair. She was what the Fayte Guardians called an Ancient One. A fae.

Her fingernails, sharpened to points like tiny blades, tapped their impatience again. I shifted for a better view, but an icy cold stone pressed against my cheek.

Wait… why was I sprawled upon the floor?

In my confusion, another memory emerged. I'd been with Lucas and the other Fayte Guardians. The Converging Ceremony had been underway in Balmoral

Fayte Hall, or what was left of it after my battle with Krol, when this ethereal figure appeared in the mist. She'd spoken, but what had she said? I sat upright and pressed my temple. Something about the Brightlands. Something about me.

It's time for you to answer for your crimes against the Brightlands.

She'd delivered those words with the same vexed expression she wore now.

"Good, you're awake," she sneered. "Guards, get her to her feet." She snapped those preternaturally long fingers, and two armed guards standing with others along the room's perimeter stomped to my side. They aimed iron spears at my face.

I scrambled to my feet. "The weapons are hardly necessary." The words scratched over my coarse, dry tongue.

Where was I? A quick glance around revealed narrow windows slashed into glassy, opalescent walls that glowed with soft, white light and soared up to a single, crystalline point. Was this the Brightlands, as she'd said? Was this the palace I'd glimpsed from the Gray Woods?

Guards and attendants filled the sprawling room, with the throne at its center. No other chairs or tables or furnishings of any kind cluttered the floor, but upon the walls hung tapestries like those in the Fayte Sanctums. These, however, depicted a single figure, the one perched with feline grace upon the throne.

Her long, willowy limbs reminded me of Druansha, but the others weren't like her at all.

The guards were of a stockier build with bulbous noses, long beards, and arms and legs as thick as trees. I towered over them as if they were children, but their portly bellies and the crevices around their eyes suggested otherwise.

I tried to ignore them and adjusted the Fayte robe that covered my simple cotton dress and tugged at my gloves.

Everything was still in its proper place, which was a comfort. Instinctively, my fingers found my Faytling, still hidden beneath the robe and my bodice. Carefully, and as discreetly as I could, I worked it out from beneath my collar.

The movement earned me a jab of the spear. "Stand still when Queen Rhilasa speaks to you."

I scowled back at the guard but held my tongue.

He pulled the weapon back, but his sneer was a warning. *Don't try it again.*

On the throne, my captor's upper lip twitched with amusement. "Never mind the stone. It won't help you here."

How smug she was. Still, I pulled my hand away from my Faytling and addressed her with as much courage as I could muster. "I demand to know why you've brought me here."

She laughed. "Did you hear that, everyone? Jane Shackle, the human beast who killed my son, your dear, beloved Prince, says she *demands* answers. Tell me, human, is that fear that makes your voice tremble?"

My fingers curled into fists. "You had no right to bring me here. Take me back."

She touched her chest and feigned surprise. "Take you back? Why would I do that? Are you afraid to die here, so far from your home? So far from those you love?" That saccharin smile vanished, and she was once again staring daggers at me. "Do you think my son wanted to die so far from his home and those *he* loved?"

So, it was true. This was the Brightlands Queen, the mother Krol had been so eager to please.

From the row of guards behind her, I heard a cough and the clearing of a throat.

The woman leaned back and sighed. "Do you have something to say, Azender?"

Someone stepped between two husky guards, and I had

to blink twice to be sure my eyes weren't deceiving me. He was an astonishing figure with a thick sweep of gray hair styled into a pompadour over his left eye and bushy gray whiskers that covered his cheeks. From the waist up, he wore an elegant white doublet with a shimmering deep-blue cloak flung over one shoulder. From the waist down, however, his goat legs were clad only in thick, gray fur. "My Queen," the faun said, "I was only wondering if I might offer a suggestion."

She pursed her lips and bent her fingers like talons on the armrests. I expected an angry outburst, but her tension slipped away. "Fine," she said. "You may approach."

The creature straightened his velvet sleeves and stepped up to the throne, his cloven hooves making a quiet tap against the stone floor. When he reached her, he used a small footstool to speak into her inclined ear.

As he whispered, her mild irritation became curiosity. "Something new for the collection? Yes, perhaps you're right." A wicked gleam sparkled in her eye.

My mind raced. What collection? Then a thought: Krol had delivered Lucas's Sliver to her. It was the price he'd demanded from my beloved's father in their devil's bargain. Was that part of her collection?

She lifted a hand and snapped her fingers. "Where is my Master of the Guard? Where is Troxell?"

Behind her, the first guard obeyed the command, waddling with a side-to-side gait to avoid tripping on a golden beard so long it tickled the tops of his polished black boots.

"Take the human away," the Queen ordered.

Murmurs filled the air as Troxell's fingers toyed with one of the many silver bands worked into the braids embedded in his beard. I caught a gleeful shine in his eyes as he approached.

Was he taking me to the dungeon? Something worse? I turned to run, but where?

Troxell chortled. "You're no match for the Dwarven Guard, dearie. Come quiet like, and we can make this easy."

"Troxell," the Queen growled.

He turned and bowed, making his beard puddle on the floor. "Forgive me, Your Majesty. I misspoke. We shan't make it easy. Not at all."

"Better." Her glance jumped from the diminutive man to something behind us both.

"That will not be necessary, Troxell."

I whipped around, but I already knew it was Druansha in the doorway. She stood with her head high and her pale and wavy hair shrouding her shoulders, tamed only by a silver diadem resting on her forehead. She was an astonishing vision, as she always was. To the Order, she was the Lady of the Fayte, the guiding light to the Fayte Guardians who protected the Queen of the British Empire.

To me, however, she was so much more. She'd been a dragonfly, *my* dragonfly and my only true friend until I found the Guardians. That seemed so long ago now. I didn't know exactly what she was to me anymore, but the sight of her still filled me with hope.

The burly guards blocking her pointed spears at her slender midriff, covered only by the soft folds of her gauzy gown and a silvery cord wrapped around her hips, but I knew they'd never stand a chance against her.

When her gaze met mine, I saw stone-cold determination in her eyes. She lifted her hand and made a throwing gesture. At that instant, every spear aimed at her flew into the air and crashed against the far wall. The guards beside me cowered and tightened their grips on their own spears as she marched toward us.

When she passed me, her gaze communicated a silent question: *Are you hurt?*

I straightened and lifted my chin to show her I was

fine.

She nodded and continued toward the throne. "What have you done, Mother?"

Queen Rhilasa leaned back again and smirked. "I do not answer to you, child."

Druansha stood firm. "I am not a child."

The Queen shrugged. "You are still my child, whether you wish it or not."

"You're making a mistake. Krolaidh deserved what happened to him."

"What *happened* to him? You believe your brother deserved his death?"

"Jane only defended herself."

The Queen rose. In her right hand an alabaster staff with an aquamarine stone appeared, and she pointed it at Druansha's throat. Streaks of blue and white light shot from that crystal and connected with Druansha's flesh.

The younger fae stiffened and rose inches from the floor before lurching forward from the neck. She struggled to speak, but only a gurgle escaped. For what seemed an eternity, she dangled in midair.

Everyone in the room froze and held their breath, including me. After an agonizing moment, the Queen lowered her staff, and the lightning streaks retracted. Druansha dropped to the ground. She touched her throat but said nothing.

"You should be more careful with your words, Daughter. I am still your Queen, as much as that displeases you."

"Mother."

That simple word might have meant, "Mother, no, that doesn't displease me at all," but it clearly meant the opposite.

"He would have killed her," Druansha continued. "It was his intent. You know that as well as I."

Krolaidh was my father, and he had wanted to kill me.

He would have, too, if I hadn't killed him first. It was still a difficult truth to accept.

"That hardly matters to me," the Queen said. "She's nothing. She isn't our kind. Look at her. She's human."

Contempt oozed from the word.

"She is half-human, yes. The rest is just like you and me."

And what was that, exactly? I still didn't know. We called their kind by so many names: fairy, fae, sometimes elves or Ancient Ones. But I still hardly understood.

"Half makes no difference." Her disdain was still evident, but the venom had waned. She seemed to be growing weary of the argument.

"Perhaps not to you," Druansha replied. "But the Seilie High Court does not agree."

The low murmurs among the guards stopped. I could hear only the sound of my own pulse thundering in my ears as the Queen stared at her daughter. "I'm sure the High Court has no interest in such matters."

Druansha touched her lips thoughtfully. "I didn't think that would be the case, so I visited the Arbiter to inquire."

The Queen's spidery fingers tightened around her staff. "You've spoken to the Seilie Arbiter? You sought Court counsel behind my back?"

"It wasn't counsel," Druansha said. "I didn't even know your plans until this moment. I was merely wondering if the Law of Reckoning, in a general sense, would apply to Jane, considering her circumstances."

"You mean, considering she is not our blood," the Queen snapped. "I'm sure the Law does not apply at all."

"Considering she is *half* our blood," Druansha corrected, "I believe it does. The Arbiter agrees with me."

"Does he?" the Queen mused. "How wonderful for that little tadpole."

"On Jane's behalf," Druansha said, "I invoke the Law of Reckoning, so this matter may be considered by the

High Court."

"I do not accept your petition," the Queen shot back. "If the human beast wishes to invoke that right, she must do so herself."

With a look, Druansha urged me on.

The Queen leaned forward and fixed me with her glare. "Before you speak, human, let me be clear: The punishment you receive here will pale in comparison to the suffering you will endure if you insist on trying the Seilie Ministers' patience and mine with an unnecessary trial. I assure you, I will take personal delight in plucking you apart piece by piece once they determine what an unworthy wretch you are. So, please consider your next words carefully."

I should have been afraid, but a surprising calm stole over me instead. For the first time since I'd entered this chamber, she was defensive.

That gave me an advantage.

A moment of clarity settled over me, and I saw a life flash before me. Not my own life, but Lucas's. My poor, sweet Lucas. Never entirely happy and never entirely sad, but always trapped somewhere in between because a Sliver of his soul had been stolen from him. A betrayal by his own father and mine.

My father had caused unspeakable harm to Lucas, but maybe this was a chance to undo it. If Krol was to be believed, this Brightlands Queen now possessed that Sliver. Could I retrieve it?

Or was I only deluding myself?

A tiny voice within me, the one telling me to be brave and to try, was the only thing that made sense in this nonsensical place where dwarfs carried spears, fauns wore velvet, and vengeful fae queens stole human girls from their worlds. Truly, what did I have to lose?

I pulled back my shoulders and met the Queen's sneer. "Your Majesty, I will invoke the Law of Reckoning, and there's something else as well. I want Lucas Starwyck's Sliver."

Queen Rhilasa didn't twitch or even blink, yet the violence she wished upon me smoldered behind those sapphire eyes. I nearly lost my nerve when Druansha frowned.

The Queen's hand whipped upward. "Troxell!"

The small, round man trudged back to her. "Yes, Your Majesty?"

"Take the human's stone."

A malicious gleam sparked in his eye. "With pleasure, Your Majesty." He snapped his fingers, and the guard to my right reached up to my neck, hooked his stubby pinkie around the cord at my collar, and jerked my Faytling free.

I tried to grab it, but he was quicker than he looked. "Stop! That's mine." I reached again, but he pulled it beyond my reach.

"You won't be needing it," the Queen purred and spun her hand in a quick circle. When it stopped, I saw my Faytling resting in her upturned palm.

I stared at the guard's empty hand. "How…?" I didn't bother finishing the question. It was by some magical means, and I was powerless to stop it.

"Troxell, take her away."

The Master of the Guard motioned, and the minion beside me pushed the blunt end of his spear into my side.

I thought Druansha would rip the weapon from his hands, but she turned to the Queen instead. "Why are you doing this, Mother?"

The Queen rose with my Faytling dangling from her fingers and stepped down from her throne. She pushed back the long sides of her ivory coat, revealing matching trousers that fit like a second skin. "She must go somewhere, my dear."

Without another word, she crossed the floor in long, deliberate strides and disappeared into a side chamber with

Azender scurrying close behind.

A triumphant Troxell motioned to the guards. "You heard the Queen. I'll be taking the prisoner."

"Absolutely not!" Druansha stepped in front of me. "I will see to Jane's accommodation myself."

The guards beside me went pale and stepped back.

Troxell puffed out his chest and slid his fat fingers over his beard. "The Queen gave her orders. We will see to the human."

Druansha closed in on him, stopping within inches so he was forced to lean back to meet her gaze. "Are you not the Master of the Dwarven Guard, Troxell?" she asked calmly.

The shifting and chatter around the room fell silent. Only the whistle of air moving in and out of this diminutive man's nose rose above the sound of my own thundering heart.

Troxell squared his shoulders. "You know well enough I am, Your Highness."

"Do you think, then, that it's advisable for someone of your minor rank to ignore the explicit command of the Princess of the Realm?"

"But your own Queen Mother ordered—"

He stopped at the rise of her hand.

"Is she here now?"

"No, Your Highness, but—"

Her hand rose higher to stop him again.

"I said I would see to it, and if you object, you may take it up with my mother. For that matter"—she turned to address every one of the dozens of guards in the room—"is there anyone here who wishes to take this matter up with my mother?" Her gaze slid from one sullen, hirsute face to the next, daring any of them to speak.

Not a single one returned her look, let alone raised his voice.

"Well then," she declared, "I believe we're done here."

She shooed away the guards beside me, and with a soft touch on my cheek, she urged me to follow her to the door.

I did so with haste, before any guard found his courage, yet her touch startled me. I braced, waiting for the familiar disorientation that precedes a vision, but it didn't come. I touched the spot on my chest, where my missing Faytling should have been. Was its absence the reason?

The grand double doors stood open, held by two liveried faun footmen. Once we'd passed through, Druansha glanced back to see if anyone followed. No one did.

When we were a safe distance away, she whispered, "That Sliver, how do you know she has it?"

"I don't, to be honest. I only know my father gave it to her. That's what he said. He boasted of it."

She frowned, troubled. "My mother promised she was done with that. She won't like that you've accused her that way, so openly."

"I didn't realize it was an accusation. I only want it back. Do you think she has it?" The Queen had given no indication either way.

"I wouldn't have thought so, but I also wouldn't have thought her capable of doing what she's already done today. If she does have it, I doubt she'll admit it, let alone return it."

It wasn't the answer I'd wanted. Through the long corridor, we walked in silence. When we reached a wide, ivory staircase, we ascended to the upper floors, which were stacked like curved terraces as far as I could see.

"I had to do it," I mumbled as we took the second flight. I was trying to convince her as well as myself. "I promised Lucas I would help him get it back, and it was my father who took it, after all."

"I know," she said quietly. "It will make our path more difficult but not impossible."

11

Doubt cast a shadow over her and tightened the knot in my stomach. But it didn't matter. If Lucas's Sliver was here, I had to find it—I would find it—whatever the cost.

CHAPTER TWO

DRUANSHA LED ME deeper into the crystalline palace, up polished staircases of milky white stone and along stark corridors that glowed with their own radiant light. It was all so extraordinary, yet I couldn't help but worry what the Queen would do once she discovered her plans for me had been usurped.

I rubbed the spot on my arm where the guard had jabbed me with his spear and wondered how much worse it could be if the Queen had her way.

"Could we slow down a little?" After the third flight of stairs, I was feeling winded.

Druansha glanced down, bemused. "Of course. Sometimes I forget how small you are."

I straightened to my fullest height, which still placed my nose closer to her elbow than her shoulder. Mostly I'd grown used to how tall she was, but now it wasn't just her. The doors and the windows, even the chairs, the tables, and the rest of it, were all designed for people her size, not mine.

We turned down a narrow corridor and stopped at the last door. Druansha opened it.

Inside, golden sunshine filtered through gauzy, white

curtains pulled across a wide window, painting a warm glow over the chamber's velvet-covered chairs and settee, the richly carved tables and chests. But it was the mammoth canopy bed, with its silky, lavender pillows and matching blankets, that mesmerized me. It had been midnight when the Queen spirited me away. If I were still at Balmoral Castle, I would be fast asleep in my own little bed in the maids' quarters by now.

How wonderful it would be to rest my head on those pillows, even for a bit. But I knew sleep wouldn't come. My nerves were too frazzled for that.

"It's a lovely room," I whispered as Druansha closed the door behind us. I lingered at a stone table and traced the woven braid carved into its top with my gloved finger. The design was similar to the one adorning the floor around the divining pools in the Fayte Sanctums. Was that by design? Perhaps if I removed my gloves I could sense the—

"It will do no good," Druansha said, cutting into my thoughts.

My fingers went to my chest and brushed over the empty place where my Faytling should be. "Right. I forgot."

"No, the Faytling is not the cause. My mother wards every corner of the palace. They block all the Knowing Ways within these walls and a good distance beyond."

"Is that what you call my visions?"

She nodded.

Knowing Ways. It sounded magical. For so long, I had considered my visions a curse and would have done anything to stop them. Now, they were just part of me, like seeing, hearing, or any other sense.

"The pattern is the same, however. You might find other familiar markings as well." She gestured to a wardrobe and a dressing table.

I went to the bed posts, which were as wide as pillars

and held a canopy of soft, lavender fabric that puddled along the floor. Another woven braid encircled the posts in a spiral pattern. "It's a beautiful design."

"Yes, but its true beauty lies in its purpose."

I followed a tendril of the complex braid with my gloved finger. "What is its purpose?" As soon as I asked the question, I realized there could be only one answer. "They're wards, aren't they?"

She nodded, pleased. "My mother wards the palace against me, but I have ways of warding against her as well. When I'm here, I don't want her poking around in my thoughts."

"I know how you feel." I grinned to let her know I was only teasing. Mostly. "I've seen this design before too. Back home."

"They adorn your Fayte Halls."

Of course. These were carved into the pillars that flank the main door to Windsor Fayte Hall. "They're for protection?"

"They protect the Fayte Order."

"They didn't help against Krol." I immediately regretted the complaint. It wasn't her fault her brother had done what he'd done.

Still, a weight seemed to settle on her. "No, they didn't. But they weren't designed to protect against him."

"Your mother." It wasn't a question. It didn't have to be. I could feel it in my heart and my bones. The Fayte Guardians were protectors, but they were protected as well.

If Druansha read that thought, she chose to ignore it. After all that had happened, it was a subject I was happy to leave for another time. There was something I wanted to know, however. "Can your mother read my thoughts? I thought so for a moment before you arrived, but then I wasn't sure."

"It's difficult to say. She has always had that gift, most

of our kind do, but lately she's struggled with it, though she does everything she can to hide the fact. She despises any kind of weakness, but especially her own."

"She was strong enough to lift you from the ground." The image of that terrifying force flashed through my mind.

"Yes, that was new," she said.

"So, her wards don't limit her abilities, only ours?"

"They limit everyone except herself, yes. My mother prefers to have the advantage. As long as you're in here, however, these wards will protect you as they do me."

"That's reassuring. I've been wondering what will happen when she learns the guard didn't take me, though I have to admit, I'm happy to be here." I settled onto the violet settee and nearly swooned at the softness of its velvet cushions.

"I'm glad you approve." Her gaze drifted to the fireplace, which roared to life at her glance. "This is my room, or used to be. As you have probably guessed by now, my mother and I are estranged."

I wasn't cold, but I still welcomed the fire's warmth. "I'm sorry." I struggled at what to say. She had never spoken to me with such candor before. "Has it always been that way?"

"Not always." She lingered beside the dressing table, staring into the silver mirror and looking as though her thoughts were a million miles away. "But for a long time. She has kept this chamber just as I left it, however. She hasn't changed a single thing."

"Have you been away long?" Was it appropriate to ask something so personal? I was no longer sure where the boundaries were between us.

"Not long enough, I fear."

I rose from the couch to move closer to the fire, drawn by its warmth. "It must be a comfort to at least know you have a home to return to when you wish it."

"Home." The word slipped from Druansha like a sigh. "Sometimes I'm not sure I understand the word."

I scoffed, thinking she was making light of it, but her expression told me otherwise. I tried to cover the sound with a cough. Still, it was difficult to hear such a thing from someone who has always had a home, even if it wasn't ideal. It wasn't the same as having no home at all.

Druansha raised her head. "Is that how you feel? As though you've never had a home?"

Guilt warmed my cheeks. I hadn't intended to share that thought, but I suppose I wasn't sorry, either. "I've never had a home, not really. At least not one I can remember."

She watched me for a long moment, then shook her head. "Of course. Sometimes I forget that."

That my visions gave me glimpses into the memories of others often felt like a cruel joke since I couldn't remember my own childhood. For years, I'd used my ability to steal the memories of others, and for a time, that had dulled the pain of the loss.

Now, however, I found no comfort in it at all, only the guilt and shame of taking something that didn't belong to me. At least I had the Fayte Guardians. Mrs. Crossey had taken me under her wing and taught me what she could, and Mrs. Bellington, my mother's sister, had filled in some blanks, even sharing what she could of the circumstances leading up to my arrival at Chadwick Hollow School for Orphan Girls. I suppose it was a comfort to know my mother intended my stay there to be temporary while she negotiated our return to the Fayte Order.

Whatever happened to cause her to leave me at that school was not known to anyone, least of all me. I was sure it had to be something dreadful because she was never seen again, and my childhood memories disappeared with her.

None of these dark thoughts were going to bring back

those lost years, however. I turned back to Druansha. "If you dislike this place so much, why did you come back?"

"You, of course."

I should have known. Where would I be without her? She had been my savior in so many ways, I couldn't forget that. I swallowed hard to force back the lump in my throat. "Thank you."

The words only scraped the surface of my gratitude, and I hoped she knew it.

When she glided to the window and pulled aside the curtains, I saw it wasn't a window but a doorway to a balcony. In the distance, the sun dipped low in the sky, making the room's shadows stretch long and thin. As the sunlight dimmed from warm yellow to cool violets and blues, the chamber's walls began to glow, brightening as the sunlight waned.

Druansha pulled back from the window and returned to the couch where I sat. "You haven't asked about the Reckoning. You must be curious."

"Of course." Honestly, I'd almost forgotten about it. I'd been so distracted by everything else.

"It's a trial, of sorts," she explained, running her fingers over the soft velvet. "Taking my mother's complaints to the Seilie Ministers isn't ideal, but I've been assured you will be treated fairly. I'm afraid that's more than I can say for my mother."

"What I don't understand is that, if your mother is Queen, why would another court have authority over her?"

"The Seilie Ministers rule over all the lands. Kings and Queens serve only at their pleasure, and Rhilasa's place is more tenuous than most because she was born in exile. Her people lived beyond the Gray Woods. When my father died, no one thought the Ministers would allow her to rule, but my brother and I were too young and could not yet inherit the throne. She convinced them it was what my father wanted for us and for his people."

"You didn't agree?"

She turned away. "I don't believe my mother has ever troubled herself with the preferences of others. That was all a long time ago, however. It hardly matters now."

"You seem worried."

"Not worried, only cautious."

I wasn't feeling confident about this Reckoning to begin with, and now even less so.

"Is it far?" I asked.

"Only a day's journey. But I don't trust her."

"Why? Do you think she will still prevail?"

Druansha touched her lips and mulled the question. "I don't know. What I do know is she fears the Seilie. She must abide by the Ministers' rules or risk expulsion from their realms."

"Realms? How many are there?"

Druansha shrugged. "A number would be meaningless. They're forever merging and dividing, and new ones are always appearing. It's impossible to keep track of them all."

I had so many questions, but three hard knocks on the door cut me off.

Druansha stared at the door but didn't move. Did she fear it was the guards? Were they going to take me after all?

"Princess Druansha, may I enter?"

She sighed. "Yes, Azender."

When the door opened, the Queen's adviser entered. He stood with his human hands straight at his sides, his goat legs tensed, and his lips twisted into a disapproving frown. "So, it's true. You've taken our guest into your care."

She folded her arms, looking as ready for a fight as I've ever seen her. "Does Mother know?"

"Not at present, no."

She tilted her head. "I don't suppose I could persuade you to keep it that way."

The faun clasped his hands behind his back, just above the small tuft of his tail. "The Queen is indisposed at present. I won't be speaking with her again for some time."

Druansha crossed the floor, tapping her fingers on her folded arms, then turned back to him. "Would you be so kind as to arrange refreshment for our guest?"

He frowned. "Of course, and shall I send a handmaiden to help you settle in, perhaps make up an extra bed?"

"Yes, a handmaiden would be welcome," she said. "But there will be no need for an additional bed. I'm not staying."

CHAPTER THREE

AZENDER'S OBVIOUS SURPRISE quickly disappeared behind a gracious smile. "Very good, Your Highness. I'm sure your mother will be eager to hear your reasons."

"I'm sure she will," Druansha added. "Speaking of my mother, that thing she did in the Throne Room with her crystal, I don't recall seeing that particular trick before."

He chuckled but quickly tried to disguise it with a cough. "Pardon me, Your Highness. Much has changed in your absence. Her Majesty's mastery is quite impressive, isn't it? Utterly astonishing, really, and quite new."

"Is it?" She watched him, waiting for an explanation that didn't come.

The silence stretched between them until Azender broke it. "I shall go see about the refreshment. Again, it is so good to have you back, Your Highness. The palace really isn't the same without you." He smiled halfheartedly and retreated from the room.

I waited for the door to close before assailing Druansha. "What do you mean you're leaving? You can't do that. I won't stay here alone."

The shake of her head told me she expected my tirade. "It's necessary. Now that we've challenged my mother, I'm sure she's plotting how to sway the proceedings. She may already have dispatched emissaries to speak on her behalf. I must get back to be sure they don't taint the Reckoning before it even begins. But you needn't worry. You will be safe here. My mother knows she will be held accountable if any harm comes to you now. If you need anything, Azender will see to it. You are my guest."

That was hardly reassuring. "What should I do while you're gone? Sit around like a caged bird?"

Druansha glanced around at the luxurious bed, the cozy fireplace, the balcony overlooking the Brightlands' verdant hills. "It's not such a bad cage, is it?"

She could be so frustrating. It reminded me of the dragonfly she had been, my sassy, usually arrogant dragonfly friend. Then, just like that, my anger gave way, replaced by too many fond memories to count. I shook my head. "Perhaps it would be, under better circumstance."

"Yes, I suppose so. I'm sure it's better than the alternative, however."

I had to agree with her. I envisioned a dank dungeon and a shiver ran through me. I moved closer to the fire and stared into the dancing flames. "Couldn't I come with you?"

I waited for her to answer, but she was silent. I took it as a sign she was mulling the possibility. Perhaps she was coming around to the wisdom of my request. I stared into the firelight, mentally pleading with her, mentally begging her not to abandon me.

A scrape like metal against stone broke the silence and a powerful whoosh startled me from my thoughts. I whipped around, but the chamber was empty. The only movement was the silky white curtains draped over the balcony's arch as they billowed with a gentle breeze.

Druansha was gone.

I went to the balcony, but the terrace was empty as well. I slumped against the wall, angry and frustrated but not entirely surprised. It wasn't the first time she'd left without explanation.

I stared out to the rolling green hills, watching the twilight transform them into shades of blue and gray and purple. What should I do? What could I do?

Nothing, it seemed, but wait.

I gazed past the hills to the steeper, darker mountains along the horizon. Was she out there somewhere? From this perch, I could see only green grass below, the trees in the distance, and the dimming sky above. No people, no animals, except a bird soaring among the clouds.

As I gazed upon it, I could see that was no bird, not with that reptilian tale. Was that a horse's mane flapping in the wind? It was too far away to be sure, but when it beat its majestic wings, it flew not like a bird but rather slithered through the air like a snake.

What a curiosity!

But then, why should that surprise me in this upsidedown place? It was all so much to take in.

Or maybe it was the exhaustion catching up to me. How long had it been since I was standing with the Balmoral Fayte Guardians?

Did they know what had happened? They'd seen me dragged through the doorway between our worlds, but what must they think? Did they wonder if I was dead?

A tiny voice inside whispered, *Would they care?*

Not so long ago, I could have disappeared and no one would have given it a second thought. They might have been surprised and alarmed and worried about the danger to others, but it would pass soon enough. A new maid would be hired, the work would get reassigned, and whatever hole I had left in their society would be filled.

But not now. Marlie Carlisle, Mrs. Crossey, and my newly discovered Bellington family would hold out hope. They would want to find me, and they wouldn't give up. Surely, Lucas cared as well.

If only there was some way to let them know where I was.

But I didn't even know where I was. Not really.

I leaned against the arch. I didn't like feeling helpless, but even if I could escape this room and this palace, where would I go? I didn't know how to return to my own world. My only hope was to do what Druansha wanted and wait.

For how long? An hour? A night? A week? She had left without giving me the slightest clue. If I knew, I wouldn't have to wonder if my request for Lucas's Sliver had been a grave error, which it increasingly seemed to be. I could use the time more productively and search for it myself. Surely, it was here somewhere. Probably even in this palace.

But where, exactly? I mentally repeated the route from the Throne Room, re-examining every door, corner, and alcove for clues.

A gentle knock broke my concentration.

"Yes? Come in," I called.

Azender inched open the door. When he saw me and no one else, he entered more boldly.

"I've had the food hall prepare tea and sandwiches. Shall I bring them in?"

"Oh, yes. Is it teatime already?" I searched around for a clock but found none. "How do you keep track of the time?"

"Time? Why would you bother with the time? No one here ever does." He slipped out the door and returned with a brass cart that held a teapot, cup and saucer, and three tiered platters piled with finger sandwiches, fruit tarts, and biscuits.

I'd never seen so much food included with tea, even for Queen Victoria herself. And this was all for me? My stomach growled, reminding me it had been hours since my last meal. Embarrassed, I covered it with both hands. "I didn't realize I was so hungry. I do apologize."

"Nonsense. It's hardly necessary."

I was about to pick up a triangular sandwich filled with something that looked like a chunky carrot spread when I remembered my manners. I pulled back. "May I?"

He gave me a funny look. "You needn't ask my permission, Your Highness."

I looked behind me. Had Druansha returned? No, the room was still empty. He must be having fun at my expense. "Don't be silly. Jane is adequate. Or Miss Shackle, if you want to be fussy about it."

His white eyebrows quirked, and those dark eyes turned deadly serious. "But you are Queen's granddaughter."

"Yes, I suppose—"

"Then Your Highness it is, and Your Highness it shall be. Is the tray to your liking then, *Your Highness*?"

He was waiting for me to respond, but I couldn't even breathe, let alone speak. Somehow, I managed to nod.

He bowed and left the room, leaving me alone in that luxurious chamber with that decadent feast and those two terrifying words echoing inside me: *Your Highness.*

Those words taunted me as I sat in the silence. I wasn't a royal. I wasn't a princess. Even if that monster Krol was my father, I was just Jane, a kitchen maid. Nothing more.

Yet, here I was, being treated like Druansha's equal, like someone who deserved a royal tea service.

I deserved none of it.

Was it a trick? Queen Rhilasa already wanted me dead, or at least stuffed away in a dungeon somewhere. If she caught me flaunting a royal title and privileges, I would end up in that dungeon for sure. Was that his plan?

I stared at the platters of sandwiches and tarts. The hunger pangs that had gnawed at me only a moment ago were now replaced by a sick, sour feeling deep inside. I poured a cup of tea and dropped a sugar cube into it. As I sipped, I wandered the room, looking for something to distract me from my thoughts.

I sipped again, and the steam tickled my nose and cheeks as I breathed it in. Finding myself back at the balcony, I stared out to the horizon and the darkening sky. On one side were the hills and farther mountaintops. On the other, I could make out a darker border beyond the flat expanse. Was that the Gray Woods, where I'd stood with Krol?

I pushed away the thought. I didn't want to think about him or Queen Rhilasa. He was a monster who nearly destroyed my world, and she was the monster who made him what he was.

There was nothing I could do about either of those things, and I certainly couldn't force her to hand over Lucas's stolen Sliver.

The one thing I could do was use my time here to find that Sliver myself. It wouldn't make up for all the harm my father had done to him, but it was something.

How to do it, however, was the question I still couldn't answer. Without my Faytling and without my visions, what chance did I have? I returned my empty teacup to the tray and looked over the delicacies. Still nothing appealed.

Instead, I removed my indigo robe and laid it across the back of a chair, then went to the dressing table and picked up the hairbrush. It was larger than what I was used to, as was everything in this room, but it was reassuring to hold something so ordinary. I pulled out the hairpins that held my knot in place and brushed the long, lazy waves until they were soft and smooth.

A knock on the door startled me.

"Come in, Azender."

When the door opened, it wasn't him but a handmaiden. She had cloven hooves and goat legs, like Azender, but her fur was the tawny color of a lion's mane. She bounded in. "I've come to collect your cart, Your Highness, if you're finished."

"Yes, thank you," I said, flinching, before swinging

around to face her. "But please call me Jane."

She had the greenest eyes I'd ever seen, and that sand-colored hair was pulled up into a bun behind her deer-like ears and short curled horns. Her haunches were covered to the knee by a simple gray frock and white apron that almost brushed the floor when she dipped into a quick curtsy. "Lovely to meet you, Jane. I'm Breenagor, but everyone calls me Bree."

Her exuberance was infectious. I found myself smiling for no reason at all. "It's lovely to meet you, too, Bree. You needn't go to any trouble on my account, though. Really, I'm a maid, like you."

The creature stopped straightening and fluffing the settee's pillows and gave me a funny, crooked look. "Oh, miss, that's not true at all. I know who you are."

My cheeks flushed hot. "I suppose secrets are difficult to keep in a place like this." As a royal servant myself, I knew that better than most.

She tilted her head, and her cheerfulness faded. I noticed the gently curving horns protruding above her forehead ended in sharp points. "Secrets? It's no secret, miss. But to answer your question, yes, word travels fast within the palace."

It had certainly been true at Windsor Castle and Balmoral, whether the servants were Fayte or not. Somehow royals and nobles alike remained oblivious to the fact that the men and women who served them also had eyes, ears, and brains. That oversight, however, generally worked in the Fayte Guardians' favor.

And it gave me an idea. If the servants here were anything like the Guardians at home, perhaps it could work in my favor.

I set down the hairbrush, rose from the stool, and tried to appear more confident than I felt. "Bree," I said, "would you be willing to help me find something?"

CHAPTER FOUR

MY HEART NEARLY stopped as I waited for Bree to answer.

She shuffled to the fireplace, where she picked up the iron and poked at the logs. Finally, she said, "I suppose my answer will depend on the thing you're trying to find."

The coy reply gave me pause. Had I overstepped? Should I try to recover by requesting a washbasin or something equally benign?

But then, this might be my only chance to find the Sliver. I couldn't be timid, not now. I straightened, pushed my hair behind my shoulders, and took a deep breath. "It's something that belongs to a friend. I believe the Queen has it, and I want to retrieve it."

She set the iron back in its holder and brushed soot from her hands. "It's the Sliver, isn't it? The one you asked for in the Throne Room?"

Yes, gossip did travel fast through these corridors. I lifted my chin. "It is, actually. She took it without his permission. It was stolen from him, and my friend needs it back. His life depends on it."

"*His* life?" A single eyebrow rose on her forehead. "Your friend is a sweetheart, then?"

My cheeks flamed. I'd never called him that, at least not aloud, but I couldn't deny it. She'd know it in an instant. "Yes, you could say so, but it's complicated."

"It always is." She sighed, but there was a hint of a smile. A hint of understanding.

"I don't want to cause you trouble. I just want to know if there's a place where the Queen might keep such a thing."

"Her own chamber, I suppose."

My shoulders sank. If the Sliver was in the Queen's private chambers and if they were anything like Queen Victoria's private rooms, they would be so heavily guarded it would be impossible to sneak in, let alone sneak anything out.

Bree shifted uneasily, and her glance darted away. Nearly in a whisper she added, "Or maybe the Collection Room."

The word rattled me. *Something new for the collection.* That's what the Queen had said to Azender. "What does she keep there?"

Bree still avoided my eyes. "I don't know exactly. I've never been there myself, but everyone knows that's where she keeps her gems and baubles. She doesn't trust anyone to get near them, all those crowns and diadems and coronets." She gnawed her lip. "And other things."

"What other things?"

"It's not my place to say, but there are rumors that she keeps unusual items in there. Things that require the attention of a caretaker who lives within that room. Or maybe he's a guard."

"You aren't sure?"

She shook her head. "No one is. Nobody is allowed inside. No one's even allowed to know where the room is. Before the Queen warded the place into oblivion, the food hall would receive a daily order for a meal, with careful instructions for its delivery. A maid would take the meal and the instructions, and by the time she returned, she'd have forgotten where she'd gone and what she'd seen."

"The Queen's wards can erase memories?" I knew wards could be strong, but my mother was the only one I'd ever known who could wipe away memories.

Bree nodded. "But not long ago, some of the maids started to remember, despite the wards. When word got out, the Queen dismissed them. Every one of them who ever stepped inside. Which is lucky for me, I suppose. That's how I landed a position here."

"If you arrived after they were gone, how did you learn of the place?"

She lowered her voice to a whisper. "I know one of the maids who was sent away. She told me what she saw."

"Which was…?"

She shrugged. "She doesn't remember much. It was dark, she said. Like nowhere else in the palace. No windows, no Lumen stones, only a candle or two for light."

"Did she see anything at all?"

"None of the Queen's treasure. The wards must have blocked that. She remembers flashes of things: shelves packed with bottles and jars, cases of books and scrolls. And the caretaker."

"Do you think he's still there? If the maids aren't taking him food, he must have gone."

"No, he's still there. The food hall makes his meals, but only Azender or Troxell takes them now. They're the only ones the Queen trusts."

"Sounds like he's more of a prisoner than a guard, then." Maybe that's what the Queen had meant about adding me to her collection. Lock me away in a secret room where no one could ever find me.

"If the Queen is keeping something she doesn't want anyone to find—like the item you think she took from your sweetheart—she might be keeping it there."

"I think so too. Can you help me find it? Can you help me get past the ward?" What was I saying? If that was the place the Queen had intended to send me, it could be a trap. If I disappeared into a secret room, there would be no Reckoning or anything.

But then, Druansha had said the Queen couldn't harm me without putting herself at risk. And, if I could get in to search for Lucas's Sliver and out again without the Queen knowing I was there, it was at least worth a try.

Bree's brow wrinkled, and she shook her head.

I tried to take her refusal in stride. "Never mind. I shouldn't have asked. I'll find another way."

"It's not that I don't want to help. It's the wards. They make the room invisible to anyone who doesn't know where to look for it, and I haven't been here long enough to even have a clue."

"Oh." That was disappointing.

"If you give me a few days, though, I could try to find out more."

I went back to the dressing table and picked up the brush. I lifted it to my hair, but all I really wanted to do was hurl it across the room. "Thank you," I said, holding a smile to hide my disappointment, "but I don't know how long I'll be here. We may be leaving soon."

"Leaving? Where?"

"Druansha called it the Seilie High Court. Do you know it?"

"The Queen is taking you to the Seilies? She never goes there."

A knock rattled the door, and Azender entered.

His disregard of common courtesy annoyed me, even more so when I saw the devious glint in his eye.

"What is it?" I asked.

Bree retreated to the back of the room and busied herself by fluffing the bed's pillows and pretending not to listen.

Azender clasped his hands behind his back. "Your Highness's presence is requested at the Queen's table. Dinner will be served in an hour." He bowed, stepped back with one hoof, and pivoted before retreating through the door.

Behind me, Bree whispered, "Dinner with the Queen?" She sounded as shocked as I felt.

I lurched forward. "Azender, wait."

He turned. "Yes, Your Highness?"

I bristled at the words. "Are you sure it isn't a mistake?" Please let it be a mistake.

His expression remained unchanged. "There is no mistake. I'll be back in an hour to escort you. Be ready." As though it was an afterthought, he peered around me. "Breenagor, I shall hold you responsible."

I heard a soft shuffle behind me. "Yes, sir. I'll see to it."

"That means she must be presentable," he added.

"Yes, presentable. I understand, sir."

Then he closed the door behind himself.

I waited to hear the latch click before I wheeled around.

"I can't go to the Queen's dinner! It must be a trick. Do you think she'll try to poison me?"

Bree considered it. "I doubt it. She hasn't poisoned anyone in years, not since... oh, it doesn't matter."

"Of course it matters! I'm not going. Tell him I won't go."

"You must calm yourself, Your Highness."

I cringed. "Please don't call me that."

"Fine, but there's no need to work yourself up. It's not good for the complexion."

"Who cares about a complexion? The Queen wants me dead, and Druansha isn't here to stop her."

Another knock on the door sent icicles shooting through my veins. I stared at Bree. She stared back.

"Hello? Anyone in there?"

It wasn't Azender. It sounded like a boy.

My instinct was to shoo him away, but Bree must have divined my thoughts because she shook her head.

Perhaps she was right.

"Yes?" My voice quavered, and I reproached myself for it. Even if I felt like a scared little chicken, I could at least look brave. I squared my shoulders and braced for the worst.

"Could someone please open the door? My hands are full."

Bree rushed to get it. Standing at the threshold was a liveried young faun with raven-dark hair and eyes like black pebbles holding a rectangular box that was nearly as large as he was.

"This is for you, mistress. Compliments of the Queen."

I frowned at Bree. Another trick?

She smiled at the page. "Thank you, Challey. Set it on the table, if you would."

He nodded and deposited the package on the low table in front of the fire. Then he bowed to me. "Thank you, Your Highness." He nodded at Bree and left.

"But what is it," I called after him.

His face brightened. "A gown, of course. Mr. Azender said you're to dine with the Queen, and you'd be needing something besides..." He seemed to struggle for a word.

I glanced down at my plain linen dress. "Yes, I suppose you're right." I might even have laughed if I weren't so unnerved.

"Is there anything else I can get you?" A warm and genuine smile spread across his face and put me at a little more at ease.

A litany of replies crossed my mind: Lucas's Sliver, my Faytling, a way back home. But I kept them to myself. "No," I said, "but thank you. This is quite enough."

Enough for what, however. That was still a terrifying

question.

Bree pounced on the box. "Open it, mistress. Don't you want to open it?"

Honestly, I wasn't sure. Why would someone who wanted me dead send me a gift? Why would she invite me to dinner?

"I know what you're thinking," Bree said, "but maybe she's had a change of heart."

Was that possible? Were the gown and invitation peace offerings?

Bree planted her palms on the top of the box. "Shall I open it? You must be dying to see what's inside."

One of us certainly was, but curiosity was getting the better of me too.

Beneath her fingers, the box's surface gleamed like a freshly polished pearl. I tugged off a glove and ran my own bare fingertips across it, hoping to feel some hint of the sender's intent. If there was anything there, the wards blocked it. Disappointed, I slid the glove back on.

"Just a little peek?" Bree stared through the small space she'd formed between her thumb and forefinger.

"Fine." I lifted the box's lid and pushed aside a frothy layer of tissue paper to reveal a bodice of pale blue satin with glass beads sewn into the scooped collar and flower petal sleeves. They glistened like dew drops.

Bree's fingers flew to her lips. "Have you ever seen anything so elegant?"

I lifted the garment from the box, and the fabric slipped through my fingers like water. I held it close. The proportions felt right, and it truly was exquisite.

Bree squealed. "It looks like it'll fit. But there's only one way to know for sure."

My resolve gave way. Moments later, Bree was folding my old dress, and I was standing in front of the dressing mirror, snug in the new gown and tugging at the back laces with little success. "I may need some help with these."

Bree set the tidy bundle on the edge of the bed and relieved me of the laces. She gave them a sharp yank. "Too tight?"

The stays sewn into the front and back seams pressed into my flesh like blades. I nodded and gasped, "Too tight."

She peeked over my shoulder at my reflection as she loosened the laces.

Now I could breathe without struggle. "Much better. Thank you."

After more adjusting and fluffing of the skirt and petticoats and smoothing of the folds, she came around to the front. "You may not like to be called a princess, but you certainly look like one."

All I could do was blush.

"And the gloves? What will you do with them?" Her tone made it clear she assumed they would be coming off.

I gazed down at the ivory leather. Perhaps she was right. The gloves certainly didn't add to the gown's appeal, and with the wards, there was no need for the protection. I tugged off the left one and flexed my fingers, then removed the right one. I pressed the gloves together before setting them on the dressing table. I stared at them, then at my bare hands, and a chill passed through me. I grabbed the gloves again and slipped them back on. "I think I'll keep them."

I caught Bree's confused look in the mirror. "Of course, mistress. May I fix your hair? I'm rather good with a brush and hairpins."

I was happy to move on to another topic. "If you can manage something, I would appreciate it."

She set me at the dressing table and went to work with the hairbrush.

I watched the gleam in her eye as she pulled the bristles through my waves, and it made me wonder if she truly saw me as a princess. Even now, staring at myself, all I saw was an awkward girl playing dress up. Which would the Queen see? Would she ever see me as her granddaughter?

Bree stopped brushing. "What is it?"

"Do you think the invitation is sincere? Do you think the Queen is trying to make amends?" Even as I said the words, I could feel hope surging within me. I wanted it to be true. Perhaps she would give me back Lucas's Sliver. Perhaps everything was going to be all right after all.

"It certainly seems possible," Bree said. "Why would she go to the trouble of giving you such a beautiful gift if it was all a trick?"

I wanted to believe that far more than I cared to admit. "It's a good sign, I think."

"Of course it is." She hovered over me like a mother hen, plucking at the petal sleeves and smoothing the skirt folds. Then her smile faded. "But you should still be careful. Don't let your guard down too much. Be courteous, of course, but cautious too."

Bree's cheerful smile was replaced by something sharper. She was speaking from experience.

"What happened, Bree?"

She grinned and shrugged off the question. "Oh, twiddly beans. There I go, saying things I shouldn't. Gran always tells me I talk too much. She warned me not to let it get me into trouble here in the palace."

As she plucked at my sleeves, I watched the struggle behind her eyes.

"It's all right," I said. "You can tell me."

She flashed another weak smile. "You're very kind, Your Hi— I mean, mistress. Is there anything more I can do? Mr. Azender will be here shortly to collect you."

Already? Butterflies swarmed beneath my corseted stomach. Even if I looked ready, I didn't feel like it. Was it wise to sit in a room with the Queen without Druansha to protect me?

Bree must have seen the fear on my face. She leaned

close and whispered, "It will be all right. Just remember, she cannot harm you. Not before the Reckoning."

Not before the Reckoning. At least it was something.

I stared at the self-assured young woman looking back at me from the mirror, the one who would soon face Queen Rhilasa. "I know she can't hurt me," I said. "I just hope she knows it too."

CHAPTER FIVE

"WHAT IS TAKING so long?" It was the third time Azender questioned why I'd fallen behind as he escorted me through the labyrinth of Lumen stone corridors and shiny white staircases. Frustration dripped from his words.

"It's the slippers. There's something wrong with them." I tried to hasten my pace, but a wobble in the right heel was growing worse with every step.

"What a pity," he said in a way that wasn't at all sympathetic. "I'll be sure to mention it to the Queen, if we ever arrive."

The sarcasm wasn't necessary. I knew I was causing a delay. I should have realized these slippers would be trouble the instant I put them on and noticed the wobble. But no, I'd let Bree talk me out of wearing my own boots. Her arguments made sense, of course, but now that I was hobbling through the palace at a snail's pace, I would have traded these fine, silk slippers for my old, leather boots in a heartbeat.

"There's no need for that," I told Azender. He was probably hoping I'd fall flat on my face anyway. "Are we nearly there?"

"Nearly." More irritation.

I limped along, trying to keep my weight off the troublesome slipper, while Azender hastened his speed. He rounded a corner and disappeared. By the time I reached the corner, not only was the corridor empty, but it forked in diverging directions. Which way had he gone? I listened for his footsteps. I could make them out, barely, in the distance, but the echo against the polished stone floor made it impossible to determine which direction he'd gone.

I made a choice and proceeded as quickly as I could manage. At a corner, I paused and listened. Were those Azender's footsteps? I didn't know, but I followed them anyway. Down one corridor and then another until I was utterly lost.

I paused again to listen, but the corridor was silent. No footsteps, nothing. I called out. "Hello?" I held my breath and listened. Still nothing. I cursed the heel. I cursed the slippers. I even cursed Bree, though I knew it wasn't her fault. Azender was gone, and I had no idea where I was or how to get where I needed to be.

I closed my eyes and tried to calm my panic. Once he realized I was no longer behind him, he'd search for me. He'd be angry and I'd be late, but he would find me. I only had to wait.

I slumped onto a chair between two marble pedestals bearing bushy green ferns in an otherwise empty part of the corridor. I pulled off the offending shoe and saw the heel had slipped from its metal pin and spun out of place. I tried to push it back into alignment, but the stupid thing snapped off in my hand. I stared at the two pieces, horrified, until I heard a door unlatch farther down the hall.

Eagerly, I rose to hail whoever emerged and beg for directions to the Queen's room.

When I saw an unmistakable head of thick golden hair on a burly little man, I froze. Troxell. Same black boots, same uniform, same long, braided beard. It was him, I had no doubt.

I pulled back behind a marble pedestal. Through the lattice of fern leaves, I watched the guard pull the door closed behind him and proceed the opposite direction along the corridor.

For an agonizing moment, I debated whether to go after him. Should I ask for help and risk being dragged off to some dungeon, or stay hidden and endure the Queen's ire?

The answer was obvious.

I pulled off my remaining slipper, dropped them both beside the pedestal, and raced to reach the Master of the Guard before he disappeared from view. I was gaining on him and about to call out when I passed the room he'd left. He'd exited and pulled a door closed. I'd distinctly heard it latch. Yet the wall beside me was solid. No door, no window—nothing.

I couldn't have imagined it. Troxell had absolutely emerged from a door somewhere along this wall.

I moved closer to examine it and brushed my gloved palms over the wall. I didn't even care about Troxell anymore, not if this was the warded room. Lucas's Sliver could be here, if only I could find the door.

My fingers slid over the gently glowing Lumen stones. Nothing about this wall looked different from the others, and it felt solid beneath my gloves.

But maybe…

I tugged off a glove and touched the wall with bare fingertips. The surface was almost cold to the touch and as smooth as glass. Then, a spark. A flash of red-orange light appeared above my head. It burned bright for an instant then split apart, forming two fiery lines that traveled in opposite directions, each for the length of a man's arm, then dropped straight down to the floor.

The outline of a door.

When I touched the center of it, the door swung inward, revealing a room on the other side.

This had to be the warded room, and just as Bree had said, it was different from any other room I'd seen so far. Inky darkness gathered in the corners behind the flicker of a single candle's flame where it sat on a rough, wooden table. Yet even in that dim light, I could make out overstuffed cabinets and shelves with long rows of books and scrolls on one side of the room and more cabinets and shelves bearing glass bottles and clay jars on the other. From that opening, the pungent smell of sulfur and something sour flowed out, reminding me of the apothecary shops back home.

I peered down the corridor, but Troxell was no longer in view. If I hurried, I could probably still catch him.

But I no longer cared about him or the Queen. Curiosity nudged me inside the forbidden room, a temptation that made my bare toes curl and sent goosebumps crawling over my arms.

Carefully, I stepped into the room and saw a low-burning fire burned in a modest hearth. Alongside it were more shelves laden with glass vials arranged in crooked rows. On another wall stood a cabinet with dozens of tiny drawers behind a worktable covered in open jars and bottles, a stone bowl and pestle, and a small, unlit brazier with a fist-sized cauldron perched above it.

Above the cauldron hung one of the vials filled with white and silvery gray ribbons suspended in a shimmering liquid, where they slid and twisted around each other.

"Are you still here, Troxell? I told you the elixir is not ready, but I assure you it will be done in time."

The tremulous voice startled me. In the shadows across the room, I saw a figure moving toward me. When he stepped into the light, I could see it was a man, not a dwarf or a faun or even a fae, but an old man hunched and shrunken with age. His white beard fell to his waist, and one hand gripped the handle of a cane. When he lifted his face to the candlelight, his eyes were milky white.

"I'm so sorry," I blurted. "I'm lost. Please excuse me." I stumbled back toward the open door.

He shuffled forward, sweeping his gnarled wood cane to clear his path. "Who are you? Who's there?" Anger sharpened his voice.

I wanted to tell him I meant no harm, but I bit my tongue. A blind man couldn't identify me if I said nothing. I retreated into the corridor as quickly and quietly as I could and pushed the door closed. The moment it met the wall, the outline flashed bright again then disappeared, once again leaving the wall a solid, unbroken surface.

I stood there for a long moment, trying to hold onto the image of that room yet feeling it slip away.

"There you are!" Azender stormed toward me. His eyes burned with rage, and his nostrils flared. "What are you doing here? What have you done?"

I blinked hard. Why was I here? I glanced around. I had been trying to find him in this maze of corridors, then my heel broke. Yes, I was trying to fix my heel. But my feet were bare. Where were the slippers?

He stamped one hoof so hard upon the stone floor it rattled the walls. "Answer me!"

"I was trying to find you," I cried. "I stopped to mend my slipper." I had been sitting on the chair halfway down the corridor. How had I gotten here? Why was I holding one of my gloves?

Something felt wrong. Something was missing, but what?

An animalistic growl churned deep within him as he fixed me with that angry glare. That sinister sound was surely meant to frighten me, but I held my ground. I didn't fear him. If he could harm me, I was sure he would have by now. He was only a servant to the Queen, nothing more and certainly no better than me.

We stayed that way—him staring at me, me staring back—until he spun around and proceeded down the corridor. "Follow me," he said over his shoulder. "And stay close."

He didn't speak again until he placed his hands on the knobs of a pair of wide, silver doors. "Don't forget yourself, human. Princess Druansha is not here to protect you."

"Is that a threat?" I wanted to be confident, but I was sure my trembling voice betrayed me.

"Merely advice," he said as he pulled open the doors and led me into a stark chamber where a crystalline dining table and two high-backed chairs were arranged beside a fire that raged in the hearth.

Azender stood at attention with his chest puffed out. "Your Majesty, the guest has arrived."

"Thank you. She may sit."

The Queen's voice rose from the chair facing away from the door. I couldn't see her at all.

Azender approached the table and snapped his fingers at me, cuing me to follow.

I stopped beside the unoccupied chair and smiled at the Queen, who despite her towering size, still seemed dwarfed by the extreme height of the white velvet chair. The firelight sparkled in her sapphire eyes and made her high-collared bodice shimmer as though the fabric itself were in motion.

I would have said something in greeting, but there was no smile upon her lips or friendliness at all. My hopes for a change of heart or the return of Lucas's Sliver melted against the intensity of her stare. If that wasn't why she'd called me here, then what was the purpose? A chill passed through me despite the fire's warmth.

Her stare persisted through the silence.

Was she trying to read my thoughts?

I emptied my mind. Druansha had said her mother's

43

ability was uncertain, and I didn't want to risk it. Behind my weak smile, I focused on the hope that she'd see it was never my intention to kill my father or harm him in any way. He'd merely left me no choice. Then I focused on the chair beside me. Was I to pull it out myself or wait? I couldn't recall the protocol for guests back at Queen Victoria's castles.

Luckily, Azender pulled it out and waited for me to sit before tucking it back in.

"Thank you," I whispered and wondered if that was the proper thing to say.

It didn't seem to matter. The Queen's attention moved to a gelatinous green mound in the center of her plate. She poked it twice before setting her spoon down and leaning back. "I see you received my gifts."

I glanced down at the gown, and my hands instinctively touched my middle, where the stays pressed into my flesh. "Yes, Your Majesty," I murmured as Azender took my napkin and placed it on my lap. "And I thank you for it. It was an unexpected surprise."

"I detest human clothing. The smell sickens me. And what of the slippers? I hope they weren't too much trouble."

Her lips twitched into a wicked smile, and I knew in that instant she already knew the truth. Was she daring me to complain?

"They're splendid, thank you." I forced enthusiasm into the words and pulled my naked toes away from the skirt's hem.

One of her eyebrows hiked upward, and she poked again at the jiggling thing on her plate.

The table in front of me remained bare. No plates, no utensils, not even a goblet in sight. The rumble in my stomach reminded me it had been quite some time since my last meal, and I regretted not eating anything from the tea cart when I'd had the chance.

I glanced around, eager for my dinner as well as some reassurance I wasn't alone with this woman. Back home, footmen usually delivered the food to the Queen's table and stood by to cater to requests. There was no one standing by here, even Azender had disappeared. The Queen and I were utterly alone.

I shifted in my chair and laced together my fingers in my lap. I reminded myself to smile.

The Queen scooped a spoonful of the green stuff on her plate, then set it down again. She leaned back and folded her arms. "You must know this day has not turned out as I'd planned." She sipped from her silver goblet without taking her eyes off of me.

A knot formed in my throat. Since we both knew she'd intended to imprison me before Druansha stopped her, I wasn't sure what she expected me to say.

"I haven't upset you, have I?" Her thin, razor-sharp eyebrows pinched together, making a distinct wrinkle over her nose along her otherwise flawless forehead.

I pulled back my shoulders and returned her stare. "Of course not." A weak chuckle was all I could manage. "To be honest, it hasn't turned out as I'd expected, either."

She ran a pointed fingernail along the base of her goblet, and my mouth went dry. Why wasn't there someone who could bring me something to drink?

"Tell me," she said, her gaze still locked on the pewter, "were you as surprised as I was that my daughter rushed to your rescue?"

This is my grandmother, I reminded myself. She was family, though it hardly seemed possible.

"I suppose I was," I said, measuring my words with care. "But she's always been a very good friend to me. More than a friend, really, although it was only recently that I learned of our blood connection."

"Indeed." She winced as if that reminder caused her pain.

Whatever hope I'd harbored that I could evoke some familial compassion or appeal to her reason died in that instant.

Again, her fingernails tapped the goblet's base, a hard, demanding click like the ticking of a clock. Like my time was running out.

"If you would indulge a mother's curiosity," she said, "when exactly did you become acquainted with my daughter?"

A harmless question on the surface, but her eyes told another story. Had Druansha broken a rule coming to my aid? Had she breached a trust?

"It was so long ago, I hardly remember. I'm grateful she's allowing me to use her chamber. It's such a beautiful room."

"It certainly is," the Queen murmured. "I've often wondered what keeps her too occupied to use it herself. I can only assume it has something to do with her strange fixation on your kind."

"You're referring to humans?" I shifted again. She wasn't even trying to disguise her disgust.

She glanced away, to the flames licking at the logs in the hearth. When she looked back at me, her cheek twitched. She touched the silver diadem resting upon her white-blond hair, as though to remind me of her significance.

Or, rather, the lack of mine.

"No, I do not mean humans. I mean the Fayte Guardians. That lot has taken so much from my daughter and turned her from her own kind. What have they offered in return? Nothing but centuries of grief. It will be a happy day when she's rid of them."

Attacking humankind was one thing, but attacking Fayte Guardians struck a much harsher cord. My simmering rage was reaching its boiling point. "You shouldn't speak of them that way. They've done nothing to you." It was no way to speak to a Queen, but I didn't care. What good were manners when one was dealing with a monster?

Malice flashed in her eyes. "They've done more than you know. But no matter. You see, I may not be able to kill you... yet... but no one said anything about killing them."

CHAPTER SIX

"OH, YOU SHOULD see your face!" The Queen laughed a long and grating laugh. "That would be something, wouldn't it? Killing Druansha's little playthings. Oh, I've considered it many times, but it would make her so disagreeable. Perhaps one of these days…"

She was only saying these things to upset me, I knew that, but it was still so difficult to keep my anger under control. Luckily, a liveried faun finally showed up with a tray. He approached the Queen and whispered into her ear.

"No, there's no mistake," she said, still looking amused.

The attendant shuffled to my side of the table with his eyes averted and set the tray in front of me. My stomach rumbled so loudly I was sure the Queen could hear it, and my cheeks grew hot with shame. Still, it felt like an eternity for him to remove the silver cloche.

When he finally did, I already had one hand on the smooth silver handle of my fork and the other on my knife, eager to tuck into whatever was on that plate.

At least I was until I saw what was there: a mound of spiny thistles floating in a milky liquid, along with something that might have been shards of tree bark and crumbled brown leaves. The putrid stench forced me back in my chair.

Across the table, Queen Rhilasa smirked after sipping from her goblet. "What's the matter? Not hungry?"

Whatever appetite I'd had was long gone now. "I can't eat this."

"Pity," she said and made a show of scooping a spoonful of green aspic and depositing it in her mouth. "Thistles are quite delicious this time of year. Firm spines, tender centers. You really should give them a try."

I poked one of the spiny things with my fork and imagined the prick of those pointy ends on my tongue and scraping along my throat. Was she serious or was this some new cruelty? I speared one of the little things and lifted it to my lips, but the thought of putting it in my mouth made me gag. I returned it to the plate.

The Queen chuckled.

"Why did you ask me here?" My anger and frustration were getting the better of me. "I hope it wasn't to threaten the Fayte Guardians. You'll never succeed."

The amusement drained away, leaving a deadly serious sneer. "Won't I?" Then it was gone, replaced by another saccharine smile. "Or perhaps I'm just having a bit of fun with you."

My anger doubled. "Why bother?" I focused on clouding my thoughts, so she wouldn't know how frightened I was. "Why waste your time?"

That hateful smirk returned. "For one thing, I wanted to get a better look at you without my daughter hovering about."

I hung my head. It had been stupid to come. How could I have thought there would be any reconciliation with this monster? I should have known better.

"You fear you are in danger," she continued, "but I assure you that isn't the case, not yet anyway. The Reckoning has been called. There is no changing that. And yet, I still have questions."

"What kind of questions?"

She folded her arms. "I don't know how my son was able to keep you a secret. He was never good at keeping secrets."

"He didn't know about me, not until recently."

"Is that so? How interesting." Only she didn't look like she thought it was interesting. She looked like she wanted to pluck out my eyeballs with those claws of hers.

"And your mother. Don't you fear you'll end up like her?"

She was taunting me. She must know my mother's fate was a mystery to me. "I don't know what you're trying to accomplish, but you're wasting your time. I will not betray the Fayte Guardians, if that's what you think. Ever."

Rhilasa's head dropped back, and hateful laughter again filled the chamber. When she looked back at me, the shadows made her sapphire eyes look black as night. "You should be afraid," she said. "You and every one of your Fayte Guardian friends should be very afraid."

This was a mistake. This dinner was no olive branch, it was a warning shot. She'd made no mention of my demand for Lucas's Sliver, and if I asked for it now, I was sure she'd laugh in my face. Fine. Let her play her games. But if she wanted someone to pay for her loss, I wouldn't allow her to drag the Fayte Guardians into it. "I am responsible for Krol's death. Me alone. The Fayte Guardians had nothing to do with it."

"Hardly nothing," she spat. "They have turned my daughter against me."

"They didn't do that. They don't know anything about you. I didn't either."

At first, she looked surprised, then she nodded. "I should have guessed. That is how she keeps their love to herself. She has erased the rest of us."

Was she jealous? Angry? Was she both? I truly didn't

know.

Apparently, I wouldn't find out, either. She pushed back from the table and rose.

"I have tired of this," she said, smoothing the flawless length of her shimmering gown. "Your human smell has ruined my appetite. A guard will escort you back to my daughter's room." She touched her napkin to the corners of her mouth, dropped it on her chair, then made her way to an elaborate panel beside the hearth.

When she placed her palm upon the panel, it sprang back, revealing a chamber on the other side. She glanced back at me. "The carriages will be ready at daybreak. You should be as well." The door slammed shut behind her.

I was still fuming when the Queen's guard delivered me to Druansha's chamber, but my anger only fueled my resolve. If the Queen had no intention of turning over Lucas's Sliver, she was leaving me no choice. I would find it myself.

How to do it, though. That was the question. How could I find a room so heavily warded that no one knew where it was? There had to be some indication, but would I know it if I saw it? Would I feel that part of him calling to me if I was close?

As the guard led me through the labyrinth of palace corridors, I scrutinized every wall and every door we passed. I searched every corner, every alcove, every turn.

When we reached Druansha's chamber door, I knew I had only one option left.

The dwarf opened the door and shoved me through it.

"Your Highness, you're back!" Bree cried when I stumbled in. She set the chemise she had been folding on the bed and hurried toward me.

"Please don't call me that," I muttered.

"Right. I mean, mistress. You've returned so early. I trust the dinner went well."

I ignored her and forced a smile for the grimacing

guard. "Is there something else I can do for you? I can't very well prepare for bed with you standing here."

His face pinched so hard his bushy, brown eyebrows plunged down to his bushy brown mustache, making it look like a fuzzy rat sitting on his nose. "The Queen says I'm to keep an eye on you."

I threw up my hands. "Why? I'm going to go to bed."

When he grimaced again, Bree stepped forward. "D'gherin, you needn't trouble yourself. I'll see to her."

"That's not what the Queen said."

She moved closer to him and dipped her head to the side coyly. "I can see why the other guards admire you."

He frowned. "They do? I mean, you can?"

"Of course, silly. But that's just like you. So strong, yet still so humble."

His pink lower lip protruded beneath his mustache. "Right, I am humble, aren't I?"

She giggled and batted her hand at him. "D'gherin, you are so funny."

His chest heaved, and it took a moment for me to realize he was laughing.

She bobbed her head back and forth playfully then said, "Do you think the Queen would mind if you waited outside the door? We'll be right inside here. My mistress said she'll be turning in for the night, so we can give her a little privacy, don't you think?"

His stocky shoulders slumped as he considered it, and his eyebrows rose and fell as he worked through the logic. At last, he said, "No point watching her sleep. But if you need anything, Miss Bree, if she gives you any trouble, I will be right out here. If you holler, I'll break down this door, if I have to."

"Aren't you the sweetest thing?" she said and shooed him into the corridor.

"There. That's better," she whispered when the lock latched behind her. "Now tell me, what happened with the

Queen?"

She coaxed me to the far side of the room, where the nighttime breeze would carry our words out to the balcony and far from D'gherin's ears.

"It didn't go well, did it?" She was staring at me.

I reached behind my back and groped for the bodice laces. The sooner I got out of this gown the better. It only reminded me what a disaster the night had been and how much I'd failed. "I was stupid to think she was trying to make peace between us," I whispered. "I think her only intention was to insult me. It certainly wasn't to return my friend's Sliver."

I yanked harder on the stubborn laces. I didn't care if they ripped or if I tore the gown. I'd happily rip it to shreds if I thought it would make me feel any better.

"Here, let me help." Bree relieved me of the task. "What happened to your slippers?"

I gnawed my lip. What did happen to my slippers? I'd replayed the whole walk to the Queen's dining room and still couldn't remember. They had wobbled and pinched my toes, and I remembered losing Azender and sitting down to fix the heel. Then I remembered walking with him again in my bare feet. I had absolutely no idea where I'd lost the slippers. "It's a long story," I said and hoped she'd leave it at that.

Luckily for me, she was more curious about my encounter with the Queen.

"I'm sorry the dinner wasn't what you'd hoped. What did she serve? I'd wager she had the food hall prepare something special."

The memory of that rancid slop turned my stomach all over again. "Special doesn't begin to describe it. It wasn't even food. It was awful. Dried up spiny thistles drenched in white goo. Dried tree leaves and bark. It was horrible."

"Thistles? She served you thistles?" Only she didn't sound appalled. She sounded amused.

I whipped around. "Why is that funny?"

She sucked in her cheeks. "It's not funny. Thistles in milk pudding is definitely an acquired taste. Did you eat anything at all?"

"No."

"You, poor thing. You must be starving. I could send down to the food hall—"

"Don't bother."

"You must eat something."

"There isn't time."

"Why not?" She finished unlacing me and handed me the night chemise she had left folded on the bed.

I waved it away and went to the corner chest, where she'd folded my clothes. I took my dress off the top and slipped it over my head. Then I pulled the pins from my hair and let it fall over my shoulders.

"You're going to sleep in that?"

I set the pins on the dressing table and wove my hair into a loose braid. "I'm not going to sleep. I'm going to look for the Collection Room."

"You can't do that," she stammered. "If they catch you, they might throw you in there, and no one will ever hear from you again."

I spun around. "Good. It will save me the trouble of having to find it myself."

Bree shook her head. Only slightly at first, but then with vigor. "No. It's too dangerous."

"But the Queen can't hurt me, remember? What's the worst she could do?"

"I don't know, but that's what scares me. And that's what should scare you too."

"I don't care. I have to do something. I can't leave without that Sliver."

She huffed and paced. She wanted to argue, but there was no argument.

"I appreciate what you're trying to do," I said, "but the

Queen left me no choice."

Bree stopped pacing and folded her arms. "What if there was another way?"

CHAPTER SEVEN

"YOU WANT ME to go to the food hall? How could that help?" Though, I had to admit, the prospect of finding something more appetizing than thistles was tempting.

Bree touched her finger to her lips and glanced at the door. We had to assume D'gherin was still on the other side. "There's someone I think you should meet," she whispered. "Someone who may be able to help."

"To find the Collection Room?"

Her head wobbled. Not quite a yes and not quite a no, but something in between.

"You said the maids who could remember that place are gone."

"It isn't a maid."

Not a maid, but someone who knew about the hidden room. Fine. It was a better plan than searching on my own. But there was still a problem. "How will we get past him?" I jutted my thumb toward the door and D'gherin.

"Don't worry about him. I know another way out. He'll never even know we're gone."

I lowered my voice till it was barely a whisper. "A secret passage?" Queen Victoria's castles certainly had their fair share of them.

"No, silly. But there's a maid's room connected to this one. I noticed it while you were with the Queen. Look." She led me to the wall beside the dressing table. In most places, the rows of smooth stones overlapped one another, but here they aligned. They fit together so tightly, it wasn't noticeable unless you looked closely. Now that I did, I could see it plainly.

When Bree pressed one of the stones, the door sprang back. I poked my head through the opening and saw a small room with a bare cot and a simple chest of drawers.

"I'm sure this was a room for Princess Druansha's handmaiden when she was here, but there's no need for it now. Doesn't look like anyone has used it in ages."

I had to agree. "But how does this help us?"

"The room doesn't, but that does." She pointed to the far wall, where a narrow door stood in the shadows. "There's an empty sitting room on the other side that opens to another corridor. We can get to the food hall that way without D'gherin ever seeing us leave. What do you think?"

"I think you're brilliant."

She beamed and handed me my boots. "We can go whenever you're ready."

As I tugged on my boots, my stomach reminded me again that I hadn't eaten in a good long while. "While we're there, do you think I could get something to eat? Maybe something that isn't thistles or bark?"

She grinned. "I'm sure we can find something."

Once my boots were buckled and my hair was pinned back up in a knot, we slipped into the maid's room and shut the door behind us, latching it quietly.

Moments later, we were padding through another empty corridor. Over her shoulder, she whispered, "Stick close, mistress. There's no telling who might be creeping about."

I did as she said, but it hardly seemed necessary. There

wasn't a soul in sight. "Where are the footmen and the pages? I haven't even seen a chamber maid." An army of servants populated the upper floors in Queen Victoria's castles, even when she wasn't in residence.

"It's usually the guards at this hour, and be glad they've made themselves scarce. They tend to be a grumpy bunch."

Grumpy didn't begin to describe the Dwarven Guards I'd encountered so far. They were cruel, plain and simple.

As we pressed on, I noticed the Lumen stones were dim in the vacant corridors until we entered. Then slowly the light brightened.

"How do they do that? How do they know when someone is near?"

Bree touched her lips and mulled the question, then shook her head. "They just do it. Don't your Lumen stones do the same?"

"We don't have Lumen stones. Just plain old regular stones."

"Oh, pity. They are quite useful."

They were, of course. They also made me miss my Faytling. I touched the place on my chest where the crystal usually rested and wondered what the Queen had done with it. Would I ever get it back?

As we rounded another corner, I recognized the chair where I'd tried to fix my missing slippers. I stopped and stared at it. There was something else I remembered about that spot, something...

The harder I reached for the thought, the farther it drifted. Then it was gone.

Bree had continued on, not realizing I'd stopped. When she finally did, she was several lengths ahead of me. She hurried back. "Are you all right?"

I blinked hard and tried to shake the uneasy feeling. "I don't know. Maybe I'm lightheaded from not eating. Are we nearly there?"

"Almost."

She led me down another passageway, then a flight of stairs where I was met with the savory scent of simmering onions and herbs. We had to be close, and my stomach rumbled again in anticipation. I inhaled another deep breath. "Whatever that is smells delicious."

Bree lifted her nose and sniffed. "Roots and onion stew, if I had to guess. Smells like something my Gran makes."

"Was she a cook?"

"A kitchen maid, well, before..." She sighed.

"I'm sorry." I could see the memory pained her. "I didn't mean to pry."

Bree's head snapped back. "It's not that. I just miss her. She was trying to teach me to make this stew before I came to work here, but I never could get it right. I'm more of a baker. I always have been. She liked to warn me, 'Breenagor, you cannot live on breads and cakes.' And I'd always say, 'Of course not. You forgot pie.'"

Her laughter made her eyes crinkle and her shoulders shake, and seeing her joy made me laugh too.

We were still giggling when we rounded the next corner, and the food hall opened before us. It was no larger than Windsor Castle's kitchen but with higher ceilings, taller windows, and an intricate network of metal flues built over the fire pits scattered throughout the room. Alongside each was a worktable, and around the perimeter were cabinets and open shelves that held pots, pans, and bowls of every imaginable size, along with baskets of fruits and vegetables, sacks of dried goods, and bundles of herbs and other ingredients.

The place was nearly empty, but there was still one cook, a faun with a chestnut mane shot through with streaks of gray. She stirred the contents of a massive black pot as it bubbled over a fire smoldering inside a brick ring.

Bree walked up to the pot, peeked in, and shook her

head. "Gran would say too many roots, not enough herbs."

The cook planted a fist on her ample haunches and glared at her critic. "Would she now? And what else would Old Grinella have to say?"

I braced for another harsh volley, but Bree's frown gave way to a wide, eager smile. "She'd say she misses you, I'm sure. It's good to see you, Aubrok. I've come by a few times, but I always seem to miss you."

"The company's better in the later hours," she said, casting a quick but meaningful glance around the empty kitchen. "I'm happy to see you, though, Miss Bree. And how is Grinella these days?"

"Staying out of trouble, mostly, but she still misses her friends here. That hasn't changed."

Aubrok's lips pulled in, and she shook her head. "It wasn't fair what happened. Not fair at all. You tell her, if she needs anything, just let me know. And not just me. Any one of us would do anything for your grandmother, you know that. You, too, Miss Bree."

Bree swallowed hard. "Thank you. Actually, I was hoping I could ask you for a favor. That's why I'm here. Why we're here." She gestured to me. "This is Jane."

Aubrok straightened. "The human?"

Bree faltered a bit but rallied again. "So, you've already heard?"

"I've heard some talk, yes." She paused and glanced around before continuing in a lower tone. "I heard she killed Prince Krolaidh."

My cheeks colored. I didn't like being discussed as though I were invisible.

Aubrok watched me but spoke to Bree. "She must be stronger than she looks because she doesn't look like much."

"She is his daughter, you know," Bree whispered back.

The older faun stopped stirring. "That can't be."

I cleared my throat, then did it again until they both looked at me. "What Bree says is true. I am his daughter, and I only defended myself. He was trying to do worse to me, and it was the only way to stop him."

The older faun smirked then reached for a bowl of what looked like salt on the nearby table and sprinkled some into the pot. "You won't find any here who will mourn his loss. He was a difficult child who became an even more troublesome adult. I can only imagine the cruelty he must have inflicted on your mother. That poor, sweet creature. It's more than anyone should have to bear." She *tsk*-ed and shook her head.

Her words hit me like hammers. "You knew about my mother?"

Aubrok's eyebrows pulled together, and she stared into the pot, ignoring me.

"If you know something, please tell me. She was taken from me when I was very young, and I would appreciate anything you can tell me."

Bree moved closer to her friend and touched her arm gently. "Do you know something? It's her mother, Aubrok. She deserves to know."

The older faun glanced up reluctantly. "You don't know what happened to her?"

"I've seen visions of her with my father," I said, "and I know she loved him and that he loved her, at least for a time. I've seen small moments, but never the final moments, though I've tried."

Aubrok's brow furrowed. "You have visions? A Reader's visions?" She shook her head, dubious.

"I've never been called that, a Reader, but I do have visions. Does that matter?"

"If you're a Reader, you shouldn't be here," she said. "Readers make trouble, always making trouble. I have nothing to tell you." She turned her back and stirred with greater deliberation.

Bree stepped around to face her again. "That's not why we're here. You've got it wrong."

I held back to let Bree make her appeal. If this creature knew something about my mother, I wanted to know what it was. But I also wanted to find Lucas's Sliver while I had the chance.

The handmaiden leaned closer to her friend and whispered so low I almost couldn't hear her. "Gran told me about the Collection Room. She told me she's been there, and I think you have too."

Aubrok pulled back and shook her head, fear plain on her face. "Don't say another word about that place. Forget you ever heard of it."

"You do know it, don't you?" I whispered, inching closer, curiosity urging me on. "Just tell me how to find it, and I'll leave. I need to find a Sliver the Queen took from a friend. Please, you must help me."

Aubrok pulled her wooden spoon from the pot and stormed away, leaving Bree and me to stare after her. She crossed the room to the furthest corner, to shelves filled with red and green vegetables.

Bree went after her, and I followed close behind. When we caught up to Aubrok, I thought the old faun would dart away again, but she only pretended to be busy picking through the red vegetables, pulling the biggest and ripest specimens from the pack.

"Please, if you know something," Bree urged gently, "just tell us. Jane only wants to help a friend. You've worked in this palace longer than anyone; you know it better than anyone. You can help her."

Aubrok continued her task. "It's quite impossible," the older faun said rather calmly. "You know my memory isn't as good as it used to be."

Bree stared at her, stunned into silence.

I stepped forward. "Please, Aubrok, please tell me how to find that room."

"Gran told me it's enchanted," Bree whispered. "That it can only be seen when the door is open. When it's closed, it disappears like it was never there and all memories of it fade. If that's true, how did you find it?"

Aubrok examined a ruby red vegetable and set it alongside two others she'd already selected. "Your grandmother doesn't know everything. I see she's still wasting time on idle gossip and silly stories."

She turned to me and tilted her head to the side. "I'm sorry, but I cannot help you. Now let's forget all this nonsense, shall we?" Aubrok placed her vegetable into a pouch she'd made with her apron. "If you like, I'll fix you both a nice bowl of stew. Or, maybe you'd like a slice of meadowberry pie?"

She sashayed away, as though the matter had been settled.

Nothing was settled. I didn't want soup. I didn't want pie. I wanted to find that room.

Bree rubbed the furry spot between her tiny horns. "I'm sorry. This was a mistake. I shouldn't have brought you here. I really thought she'd help. I was so sure. Can you forgive me?"

I smiled as best I could. "Of course. I appreciate you trying to help."

She brightened. "Aubrok's meadowberry pie is the best in the Brightlands. You really should try a slice."

I touched my stomach. I wasn't hungry anymore. Even the thought of food made bile rise in the back of my throat. "I'm not feeling well. I think I'll go back to the room and get some sleep."

"I'll go with you," she said.

I held out my hand. "No, I'll be fine. You should stay and enjoy the pie. I know the way back. The day's just catching up to me. All I want to do is crawl into bed and fall asleep."

Her lips twisted with doubt. "You're not going to go

looking for the room, are you?"

"Of course not. I was just angry earlier. I know it would be foolish. I'm going to wait for Druansha. She'll know how to help."

"Wait for Druansha, yes, that's a much better plan. She knows how to deal with her mother. When I'm done here, I'll check in on you, though. To be sure you're all right."

"That's very kind of you. But don't be surprised if I'm already asleep."

CHAPTER EIGHT

I HAD NO intention of waiting for Druansha, and I had no intention of returning to her chamber. I was going to find that hidden room, with or without Aubrok's help. I owed Lucas that much.

When I saw a ginger faun in a maid's apron walking by, an idea struck me. I hailed her. "Hello! I'm looking for a guard. Do you know where I might find one?"

"Are you the human? Oh dear." With eyes cast down, she bobbed a curtsy and hurried away. I watched to see if she glanced back, but she never did, and when she turned a corner and disappeared, I scolded myself for not going after her.

I set off to find a guard myself and was halfway up the stairs when I heard her behind me.

"There she is. The human."

When I turned back, she was directing a guard my direction.

"Excellent! You found one," I exclaimed.

My attempt at humor didn't go over well with her or the guard, but it didn't matter because she hadn't brought back just any guard. This was Troxell himself.

"What have we here?" His eyes narrowed on me, and

his fingers tightened around the dagger sheathed at his side.

There was no going back now. I straightened and tried to smile. "Hello, Troxell. I was wondering if you might escort me to the Collection Room."

"The Collection Room?" The maid covered her mouth with both hands.

Troxell tipped his head toward her. "You best be on your way."

She nodded vigorously and retreated.

When we were alone, Troxell approached me. "What are you up to, half-breed? What game are you playing?" His hand was still on his dagger.

"It's no game." I threw up my hands to show him I wasn't hiding anything. "You might not believe this, but I truly want to go to the Collection Room."

He sneered. "You do, do you? And why is that?"

Why was he questioning me? I strode toward him with my hands still splayed out in front of me, so he wouldn't interpret my approach as an attack. "I'm curious about the place."

"Curious, huh? We'll see about that. You can stop right there, put your hands on your head, and turn around."

I did as he said, and a moment later I felt the sharp point of his dagger in my back.

"That isn't necessary. I'll go willingly."

"Just walk."

He led me up the staircase, along a corridor, up a second staircase then down another. By the sixth corridor, I realized he was running me in circles to confuse me.

We went on that way for what felt like an hour, and I was so exhausted and so turned around, every corridor looked the same.

"Stop here," he demanded.

Was this a passageway we'd been down already? It was all starting to feel fuzzy. "May I sit for a moment?" While I waited for an answer, I leaned against the bare wall and closed my eyes, feeling the exhaustion creep over me.

The dagger jabbed me in the side. "Wake up. We're here."

When I opened my eyes, I was no longer staring at a blank Lumen stone wall. There was now a door carved into it, opening inward. "Is that what I think it is?"

"You wanted the Collection Room, you got the Collection Room."

My heart raced, but there was something else too. I moved closer and touched the stone door. I remembered this place, but how?

"Get inside." Troxell pushed me.

When I stepped over the threshold, I recognized the bookshelves and the cabinets. I recalled the rows of jars and bottles. In the corner, the smoldering fire burned, just as I knew it would be. Shadows danced against the walls and gathered in the corners, making the room as foreboding as any dungeon.

Had I had a vision of this place?

Troxell pushed the door closed behind us. "Old man!"

A familiar shuffling and a gray-bearded man appeared from the shadows, steadied by a wooden cane. "Troxell, I have already told the Queen, the elixir needs time."

"I'm not here for that," the dwarf barked. "I've brought you something. An addition for the Queen's menagerie."

I knew before he turned toward the dim, amber light that the old man's eyes would be solid white. Had I seen him before? Had I been in this room, or was it a vision I'd forgotten?

"It's you," the old man said. He swept the space in front of him with the end of his cane as he moved closer. "You've returned?"

The old man knew me?

"Returned?" Troxell huffed. "What do you mean

returned?"

The old man straightened. A strange look came over him. "It's good you've returned, Troxell. I was having difficulty with that troublesome drawer again. Do you think you could pull it free for me?"

"Again? I told you last time to use the candle wax around the edges, so you wouldn't have this problem." He groused but still went to the cabinet and wrapped his thick fingers around the drawer pull. Before he could yank the sticky drawer free, the old man lifted his cane high over his head and brought the end down square on the back of Troxell's skull.

For a long moment, the dwarf didn't move. Then he slumped to the ground, completely unconscious.

I didn't speak or make a sound. I only stared in silence as the old man pulled his cane back to his side and thumbed through a row of glass jars on the cabinet beside him. He plucked one from the pack, removed the stopper, and bent down to the dwarf. After he lifted Troxell's head, the old man poured a drop onto the dwarf's tongue.

"That should do it," he said and rose. "If you would be so kind as to take him out into the corridor and close the door."

I stared at Troxell's lifeless body and nudged him with the toe of my boot. He didn't stir. "He won't move."

"He's not as heavy as he looks. Dragging should work just fine."

"You want me to drag him?" I was not going to drag the Master of the Guard into the corridor.

"Once he's gone, we may discuss why you're here."

Lucas's Sliver. But how did he know? I grabbed one of Troxell's hands and pulled. The old man was right. The dwarf moved rather easily. It took only a few moments to get him to the door. I opened it, and after carefully checking the corridor, I pulled him out and propped him against the wall. I slipped back inside and shut the door again.

"What will happen when he wakes up?" I envisioned a beet red face and a stabby dagger aimed at my midsection.

"He won't remember how he got there. I expect he'll assume it is a side effect of the potion he takes for ward immunity. It can be rather unpredictable." He settled onto a stool at the worktable and felt around the brazier and the vessel with the bubbling liquid suspended over the embers.

"You don't seem surprised to see me."

"You were here before. Do you not remember?"

"I've never been here. I've been searching for this place."

"You have forgotten. Pity."

"What do you mean?" I inched forward, wary.

"Did she do it? Is that why you're here?"

"She? Are you referring to the Queen?"

He stared at me with those blank white eyes. His trembling hand, weak and pale in the firelight, touched his brows and brushed over his bald and wrinkled head. "The Queen? No, dear girl. Did Madeleine not summon you?"

That name paralyzed me. "Madeleine? Who is Madeleine?"

His fingers froze upon his forehead then dropped down and found the hook of the cane leaning against the table beside him. He worked himself into a standing position. "I have no wish to play games. Who are you? Tell me your name."

"I'm Jane. Jane Shackle."

His thin, colorless lips pursed. "I know that name. The daughter. You are Madeleine's daughter?"

I went cold. "Madeleine Ross is my mother. Do you know her? Have you seen her?"

I was frantic now, but I didn't care.

He touched his chin with those thin, crooked fingers. "Madeleine has spoken of you. But Shackle is not your true name. That is from the time in the village, when she pretended to be the widow to keep you both safe. Shackle. Such an odd name for a woman seeking her freedom, don't you think? Or, perhaps even then she knew she might never truly be free. It did serve its purpose, however. A false name for a false widow. So, you've kept it?"

My name was false? Yes, I suppose it had to be. "It's the only name I've ever known."

"You sound like her, you know," he said quietly. "At least before…"

"Before what?"

He shook his head. "It was foolish to come. You were safer in your world."

"It wasn't my doing. Queen Rhilasa brought me here." If he didn't know that, perhaps he didn't know the rest of it, either. "I killed her son."

The old man touched his wrinkled forehead, and he sighed, a long, agonizing respiration. "Then it's true. The heir is dead."

"I didn't know he was her heir. He told me he was my father." Had the old man known that? I watched his face, searching for an answer. "Since I'm here, however, I want to get back what the Queen has stolen."

He settled both hands on his cane and steadied himself. "Yes, of course."

I still didn't know what he meant, but a tingling sensation passed through me. Was it the Sliver making itself known? Carefully, I removed a single glove and brushed my fingertips over the table beside me, searching for a clue. Instead, a powerful pain took hold of me. Not my pain, but another's. And anguish. Fear. Were they his feelings? Did they come from Lucas's Sliver? I concentrated harder.

"You are a Reader."

I retracted my arm, though I'd been close to something. "Why do you say that?"

"You're Reading the table, are you not?"

He was blind. How could he possibly know? "I was searching, yes."

"Your mother was an excellent Reader. She may still be, in her own way. Did you know that about her?"

"No." The day Mrs. Crossey told me about the Fayte Guardians and that she knew my secrets, she told me my ability was passed down from my mother. I'd seen that Madeleine was a Scryer in my visions, but that was all. I'd never sensed that she could see the memories of others. "You keep mentioning her, but you haven't told me how you know her."

Sadness crept over his face. "It's a pity you know so little."

I wanted to scream at him, *Then tell me!* Instead, I said, "You're right. It is a pity she left when I was so young."

"She mentioned that. It is her greatest regret."

"She said that?"

"Many times."

"Then she is still alive? Do you know where she is?"

He settled onto his stool again. "Where she is? Where does she go? I wish I knew. You see, I miss her too."

"When was the last time you saw her?" It was all I could do to keep my voice even. I wanted to scream at him and pound my fist on his wretched table. I wanted an answer, and he was talking in circles.

"Your mother is strong. She has outlasted so many others."

"Other what? Who?"

His trembling fingers rose to his lips. "I've said too much." He rose again and shuffled toward the shadows at the back of the room. Before I'd seen only darkness, but now that my eyes were more used to the shadows, I could see it wasn't a wall but a wide-open archway leading into another room.

"Don't leave." I followed after him. I was too tired of

71

secrets to let him get away.

When I entered the dark room, I could no longer see him. "Mr. ..." I called out before I realized I didn't know his name. "Please, don't leave."

I heard something scrape then a moan.

"Are you all right?"

Another moan. Another scrape across the floor. Had he fallen? Was he hurt?

I returned to the worktable to grab the candle. When I brought it back to search for him, I could see dozens of crates and cabinets pushed against the wall. "Hello? Are you still here? Can you hear me?"

A soft whimper. Another moan. I followed the sound to a large crate. The candle's flicker reflected on metal bars that covered an opening.

I stared more closely. This wasn't a crate. It was a cage. I glanced around. They were all cages.

I bent down to peer inside, and the flicker caught two shiny eyes staring back at me. The creature crouched in the corner, but I wasn't afraid. The bars were thick and sturdy, though the rancid smell of old straw and mildew sent my hand over my nose.

Inside the crate, something moved. As my eyes adjusted to the darkness, I noticed it was the creature's hand, with grimy creases and ragged fingernails.

And it was unmistakably human.

In my shock, the candle slipped, but I caught it before it dropped. I inched closer to the bars. Inside I could see a wild shroud of long, dark hair. Deep within that nest of tangled strands, I saw a face I'd seen in my dreams and visions.

The creature was my mother.

CHAPTER NINE

I STARED INTO the woman's eyes. "Madeleine?"

Her head lolled, and she moaned again. Through the shroud of unkempt hair, she stared past me, a flat, steady gaze devoid of recognition. She didn't know me. Yet, how could she in this state?

"Madeleine," I whispered again. "It's Jane; it's your daughter."

Her eyelids fluttered, but the dazed expression remained. Her lips twitched. Was she trying to speak?

"It's me, Mother. Can you understand me?"

The woman shifted her head, and I could see both eyes now. Her gaze locked on me.

"Jane?" A hoarse, dry whisper. She lifted a hand, and her fingers gripped the metal bar in front of me.

I crouched closer and lifted my hand to hers, gently brushing her fingers with my own. My body shook with a powerful jolt. The dim light surrounding me grew dark then exploded into a blindingly bright light.

When I could see again, I was no longer in the Collection Room beside a cage. I was on a hillside, in a thick wood. Behind me, I could hear a burbling stream. I turned, searching for it.

What I saw instead was a woman standing a few paces away, her linen gown and wavy, dark hair waving in the breeze. I moved closer to see her face, but I already knew those deep-blue eyes and rosy, upturned lips. This was the woman I'd seen in my visions. The woman who broke my heart.

"Madeleine?" I whispered.

She threw her arms open, inviting me to rush in. I did and gladly. I didn't care that I didn't know where I was or if this was a trick. I embraced her without hesitation.

Let the visions come, but instead of a vision, I felt only the soft press of her hair against my cheek and the warmth of her arms around me. I buried my face deep in the hollow of her neck and breathed in the lavender scent that surrounded her.

How long had I waited for my mother's embrace? All the friends and family I'd found were dear treasures to me, but this was my mother.

"It's all right," she murmured in my ear. "You are safe here. We both are."

Safe from what? And where were we? We'd been in the Collection Room, that dungeon-like place inside the Brightlands Palace, but now we stood beside a glen of the tallest trees, each with trails of iridescent light coursing through them.

Was this a dream?

She pulled away but kept hold of my shoulders. "I know you have questions."

The clouds above streaked with violet, raspberry, and blue as the sun hung low behind the hills. The trees, those astonishing trees, winked and glimmered against the darkening sky.

Was it my imagination, or did they resemble just a little those strange trees beyond the Windsor Castle wall?

"Yes, they are similar," she said, knowingly. "But this is not that place."

No, this was not the English countryside. Here the colors of the sky and land swayed and swirled like wet watercolors on a canvas. Every tree and flower and blade of grass glowed with an inner fire.

"This is my place. My Other Place."

Behind me, a breeze rustled the branches, and somewhere nearby birds chirped their songs. All around, colors merged and separated, as though we were standing inside a painting as it sprang to life. "How is it possible?"

"Don't be frightened," she said. "I can come here to get away…"

Her voice trailed off.

For a moment, I saw her again as I'd seen her before, locked in a cage like an animal.

She squeezed my hand, and that terrible image faded. Again, I saw her in the white dress in front of me.

"What happened to you?" I asked.

"I think you already know." She dropped her gaze. "It wasn't always so bad. I was a guest at first. I could move about. There were even visitors I once called friends. But no longer, not since the Queen learned of it."

How could Rhilasa be so cruel? "Why does she treat you this way?"

My mother watched me and waited, giving me time to accept the conclusion on my own. Yes, she was right. I knew.

"The Slivering?" Of course it was the Slivering. I'd known it the moment I saw my mother. Perhaps I'd always known it. That's all the Queen had ever wanted from my mother, or from any human. It's what my father had sought, at least at first.

"Is that why the Queen brought you here?" my mother asked. "Has she Slivered you?"

"No, not yet." Had that been her intent? *Add her to the collection,* that's what she'd said to Azender. Or had she intended something even worse?

My mother didn't look surprised, only confused.

I swallowed hard. "I killed Krolaidh, you should know that."

Her shoulders sank.

"I had to," I rushed to add, guilt piling atop every other emotion. "He would have killed me, and I thought he'd already killed you. He meant to Sliver Queen Victoria and take her place. He wanted to rule the British Empire himself."

She looked up and squeezed my hands. "You cannot stay here. You must leave."

"Come with me," I begged. "We can leave together."

"That's impossible." A world of sadness lived in those words. "I'm almost gone. But not you. You are strong. That strength shines so brightly within you. Leave now, before she steals it. She'll stash you away and take that wonderful light for herself."

"She can't," I said. "She may want to, but I've invoked the Reckoning. That protects me, for now."

My mother's eyes quirked. "Yes, the Reckoning. I saw it. Rhilasa must convince the Seilie High Court, but she could win them to her side."

"You saw that in my thoughts?"

"Does that surprise you?"

It shouldn't have, not if she was a Reader as well. Still, I bristled.

"I won't, if it makes you uncomfortable. But we've been apart for so long. I want to see all that I've missed."

I pushed aside the fear of opening myself and let my mind go blank. Even as I did, I sensed her memories opening to me as well. Images swirled within me like a tornado. Some I recognized, like my mother with my aunt Lavinia. I saw them sitting together in the Bellington cottage, where I'd spent so much time. Then, my mother was sitting with Krol beside the stream on the Windsor Castle grounds.

At the periphery of those images, I sensed my memories flowing to her. The days I'd spent in the Windsor Castle kitchen with Mrs. Crossey, the journey to Balmoral Castle with Marlie and Lucas, learning to phantom walk with Aunt Lavinia. We stayed that way for so long, all those memories bleeding one into the other.

As we stood in that imagined place where the sky glowed its vibrant hues and the images washed over me like a waterfall, I could hardly focus. I was lost in the tangle of our memories, holding onto each one, examining it, before reaching for another.

"I took something from you long ago," Madeleine said. "I want to return it."

Her words broke the spell I was under. All the memories surrounding me drifted away. When it was just the two of us again in her watercolor world, standing beside her gentle stream, she tightened her grip on my hands. "When I took your memories from you, I was trying to protect you. I thought you wouldn't miss me or feel any sadness if you couldn't remember. It was never meant to be permanent, and now I see how much pain that caused. I am so sorry, my little one. I never wanted to hurt you. I never wanted to leave you."

"I know, Mama." I had never uttered that word before, yet it felt so easy, so familiar. It felt like I'd been saying it all my life.

Tears welled in my mother's eyes, and she touched her lips. She swallowed hard then said, "Are you ready?"

My mother pulled away from me in the dream world, severing the mingling of our minds. When I came back to myself, I was still in the dingy, dark room sitting in the dim candlelight that licked at the tears flowing down my mother's cheeks. I knew her then as I hadn't before. I remembered our years together, all the laughter and the pain. I remembered our cottage by the sea and meals by firelight. I remembered… everything.

I stared into her eyes, her real eyes, as they focused on me.

"You cannot stay here." When my words cracked, I realized I was crying too.

She shook her head and opened her mouth, but no sound issued. She swallowed hard and tried again. "Go."

She only mouthed the word, but I sensed the urgency.

I heard a noise from the other room.

"Your Majesty, is that you?"

The old man. Were we playing that game again?

"Is the Sliver prepared?"

The Queen! I hadn't heard the door. Had she been here long? I huddled low beside my mother's cage, praying Rhilasa stayed in the front room.

"Your Majesty, as I told Troxell, the distillation requires more time."

"I don't have time."

My mother mouthed the word again: "Go." She reached a finger through the metal bars and touched me. This time, I wasn't plunged into her alternate world. Instead, it shot a warning through me like a shout in my ear. *Go, before it's too late.*

But how? I'd be seen.

"Perhaps there is something," the old man said, and I heard their footsteps coming closer.

I blew out the candle as they entered the back room.

"What was that?" the Queen asked.

"What, Your Majesty?" the old man said.

"Woldryd, is someone else here?" Before she finished her question, the turquoise light of her crystal brightened the room.

Did she sense my presence? I sank into the shadows against the wall.

"Only the specimens," he said. "I haven't yet done the rounds."

How many prisoners were here? But there was no time

to check. I had to get out.

If the Queen discovered me, I'd end up in a cage of my own. "I'll be back," I whispered and crawled to the next pocket of shadows.

"Show me what you've collected from my beauty," the Queen demanded. "I want to see the quality."

I heard their footsteps growing closer. I sucked in my breath and hunched down into the space between two crates.

"It's still excellent. Quite surprising after all this time." They passed by without slowing and continued on.

I peeked around the corner and couldn't see either of them, so I made my escape. When I reached the doorway and found it closed, I paused. Should I hide and wait?

"Alert me as soon as it's ready," the Queen said.

I had to go now. I opened the door slowly and crawled through the opening, staying as low to the ground as possible to remain out of sight.

I was pushing it closed when I heard the Queen.

"Why is the door open? I'm sure I closed it."

"Which door, Your Majesty?"

I didn't wait to hear the rest. I stood up, hiked the sides of my skirts, and ran.

CHAPTER TEN

I RACED THROUGH the corridors, jumping at every odd sound, every strange creak, and whipping around every few moments to be sure I wasn't being followed. All the while, I repeated to myself, "Madeleine is in the Collection Room, Madeleine is in the Collection Room, my mother is in the Collection Room." I couldn't—wouldn't—let the wards steal my memories again.

When I finally pushed into Druansha's chamber, I slammed the door behind me and collapsed against it.

"Madeleine is in the Collection Room," I said aloud, clutching at the memory.

"Where have you been?"

I shrieked at Bree's wail. "Don't do that! You nearly scared me to death."

"I could say the same," she countered without apology. "I thought the guards had locked you up, at least until Mr. Azender came looking for you."

Madeleine is in the Collection Room.

"I figured he'd know if they had you, so then I didn't know what had happened."

"What did you tell him?" *Madeleine is in the Collection Room.*

"I didn't want to tell him I didn't know, so I told him you were sleeping." She motioned to the bed, where someone was curled up beneath the covers.

I lowered my voice. "Who is that?"

Bree stormed over and threw back the quits, revealing a line of carefully arranged pillows. "I told him it was you, and it was a good thing he believed me. I'd already be tossed out on my tail if he hadn't. Where have you been?"

"I found the Collection Room." *Madeleine is in the Collection Room.* I decided against telling her about surrendering myself to Troxell or that I'd somehow discovered the room before the dinner with the Queen and forgotten it. "You must help me remember. I can't let the wards make me forget. Madeleine is there."

"Who's Madeleine?"

"My mother. The Queen locked her in a cage. It's horrible. I have to get her out."

Bree paced, trying to absorb the news I was still trying to process myself. "You didn't tell me you were looking for your mother. You told me you were searching for your sweetheart's Sliver?"

The Sliver. I'd forgotten to look for it. But there had been all those jars along the shelves. It must be there. "When I get back, I'll find the Sliver and free my mother."

Mother. I still couldn't believe it. I dropped into a chair. *Madeleine was in the Collection Room.* I wanted to scream the words. I wanted to hug Bree and dance around the room.

She frowned, still confused. "Why did you leave her there?"

"The Queen walked in."

Bree's hands flew to her mouth. "She caught you?"

"I got out before she could. The old man helped me. She may already be gone, but I'll wait a bit before going back, just to be sure." Mentally, I retraced my steps. I knew the way. I could make it there in a few minutes. How would I get my mother out, though? The old man had helped me with Troxell and to leave, but would he help me rescue my mother?

"You can't go back," Bree said, her lips pursed tight.

"Of course I can. She's locked up in that room like an animal. I'm not asking you to go with me. I won't put you at risk, but I am going."

"Mistress, there's no time. Mr. Azender will be here any moment to collect you. The last time he left, he said he'd be back within the hour. It's nearly that now."

"He's coming now? In the middle of the night?"

"Mistress?"

"Why can't he wait till morning?"

"Mistress, it is morning."

"No," I muttered. I darted for the balcony. It was late, yes, but hardly morning. I grabbed the heavy drapes that had been pulled over the silky sheers and pushed them aside. A pale gray light spread over the hillside. In the distance, the golden glow of daybreak.

How could that be? I'd only been in the Collection Room an hour, two at the most.

At least it had seemed so. How long had we shared the vision?

"He will be here any moment, but it's fine," Bree said as she hurried to the dressing table and grabbed a brush and comb and dropped them in a case that sat open in front of the mirror. "I've packed some things for you. I don't know how long you'll be gone, but it should be enough to get you through a few days."

"Bree. I can't leave."

The door flew open and Azender stormed in. "I demand you—" He stopped at the sight of me. "You're awake." His creased forehead smoothed as his anger ebbed. "How good to see you up and about, Your Highness." He coughed into his fist as he tried to regain his composure. His gaze slid from the top of my head down to my toes and back up again. "It's a shame you couldn't find something suitable to wear, but no matter. We must make do. Come with me."

"No."

The word hung in the air between us.

He turned back, his eyebrows plunged in a scowl. "Pardon?"

"I can't leave. Not yet."

"Why is that?" He rocked back on his hooves and laced his fingers together as if to add, *This should be good.*

At the dressing table, I caught a glimpse of my disheveled self in the mirror. "I certainly can't go looking like this. I need time to freshen up. Tell the Queen I'll be down presently."

The old faun smoothed the rise and curl of his gray pompadour and cleared his throat. "Her Majesty has ordered that I escort you to the carriages now." Impatience edged his words.

I didn't care. I wouldn't abandon my mother. Instead, I settled onto the dressing table's stool and did my best impersonation of the noble ladies who attended Queen Victoria. "You can plainly see I'm not ready. I'm sure Her Majesty will understand. You may tell her I will be down *presently.*"

His cheeks reddened. "But, Your—"

"You heard me, Azender." I feared his wrath, but I feared losing my mother even more. Through the mirror, I held his gaze, daring him to press the issue.

I thought we'd reached an impasse, but then he bowed and retreated without another word.

When he was gone, Bree giggled. "Your Highness, I've never seen anyone stand up to him."

I stared at my reflection. A brave, confident face stared back from the mirror, but inside I was crumbling to pieces. "Bree, what am I going to do?"

She came up behind me and dipped her head. "They have given you no choice. You must go."

"But what about my mother? And Lucas? I cannot abandon them."

"I know, mistress. I'm sorry."

My fingers went to the empty space on my chest where my Faytling should be. "I wish the Fayte Guardians were here. They'd know what to do."

"Who, mistress?"

"Back home, they're servants and protectors for our Queen. My mother used to be one, and now I'm one too. If only I could speak to Mrs. Crossey or Mrs. Bellington. They'd know how to save my mother and get Lucas's Sliver back. They wouldn't give up."

"They sound like my grandmother." She paused and glanced away. "Can you keep a secret?"

"Of course. You're already keeping mine."

"I didn't tell you everything my grandmother told me more about the Collection Room. She told me she saw things she could never forget, things that haunt her still. I thought she was trying to scare me to keep me from coming to the palace, but now I think she was telling the truth. If we can speak to her, she might be able to help."

"How? If she's not here, what could she do?"

"She has friends, special friends far more powerful than the Queen.

"I appreciate what you're trying to do, but I won't sit by and hope someone else saves my mother or finds Lucas's Sliver. I can't risk it.

Except the door was rattling. In the distance, I could hear the march of a dozen Dwarven Guards growing closer. They were coming for me.

My time had run out.

CHAPTER ELEVEN

THE CARRIAGE RUMBLED along a dirt road that meandered through grassy fields and low sloping hills that glowed with a golden sheen beneath the gathering sunshine. From my window, I stared out at the hazy peaks and ridges along the horizon and wondered what existed out there in that dreamy landscape.

But then, this whole place felt like a dream. The sun was still low in the morning sky, but what did that mean in a place like this? All my life, the span of a day and a night was fixed. Moment to moment, hour by hour, a day's length changed only in reassuring and predictable ways.

This, however, was not my world, and nothing here was reassuring, much less predictable.

Just one sun, yes. But one moon? I thought back. The night sky had been a cloudy one. I recalled stars, but were they the same ones I could see from the Windsor Slope? Was this the same sun that warmed the cheeks of Marlie, Mrs. Crossey, and the Bellingtons? Did it shine on Lucas Starwyck?

"You're worried, aren't you?" Bree watched me from the opposite bench.

"A little." I bit my lip and glanced at the dwarf.

The grim little man sneered back, though much of his expression remained hidden beneath the mass of ash blond hair that covered the lower parts of his face and most of his Dwarven Guard uniform.

"All right," I conceded. "A lot." I gave her a long look that I hoped she knew meant *I'm afraid I made a mistake.*

When Bree had told me, in a rushed and hushed whisper back in Druansha's chamber, that she knew how to get her grandmother's help, I'd relented. But convincing Azender that Bree should join me nearly ruined the plan before we even left the palace. In a fit of desperation, I'd grabbed my stomach and doubled over.

Bree knew exactly what I was doing and played along. "You see," she told the old faun. "She's not feeling well. You must let me tend to her."

He'd scowled at us for a full minute before relenting. "I will assign a guard to your carriage so there's no funny business."

The chaperon wasn't ideal, but it was a comfort having Bree with me. The guard's presence made it a challenge to learn exactly how she intended to get her grandmother's help, however. When I couldn't stand another silent moment, I turned to the guard. "Will we be making any stops along the way?"

He slid a surly look my direction. "We'll stop if the Queen wishes to stop. Not before."

The coach swayed and settled. Bree glanced out the window. "She must wish it now, then."

The guard grunted something under his breath and leaned out the door. "Driver, what's this about?"

The hollers of coachmen ahead of us drowned out the reply. I peered out to see two liveried fauns circling a cart piled with baggage in front of us.

"Try the red case there," one yelled. "That one, under the brown trunk."

"That's it," the other replied. "Bring it around."

It required both attendants, each grasping a side handle, to muscle it from the stack and lug it toward the Queen's coach.

Bree nudged my knee. "Mistress, you're looking a bit pale. Are you feeling well?"

I was still watching the fauns, who had brought the case back and were trying to retrieve a different red bag. "Fine. Just a bit tired." Considering I had only napped after missing an entire night's sleep, I thought I was doing rather well.

Bree's lips tightened. She looked at the carriage's open door, where our guard was now chatting with one of the guards marching alongside the caravan. She leaned close and whispered, "You don't look well. I think you need some fresh air."

When she gave me a long, knowing look, I finally caught her meaning.

"Yes, I think I am feeling a bit lightheaded," I said. "Maybe some fresh air would help."

She brightened and scooted toward the carriage door. "Guard?"

The little man pulled away from his colleague to glare at her. "What do you think you're doing? Sit down. Those are the orders."

"But the Princess isn't feeling well. I fear…" She gave me another meaningful look.

I covered my mouth with one hand and my stomach with the other.

"I'm afraid she's about to be sick, right here."

He stared at me in horror. "Don't you dare make a mess. I won't clean it up. Do you hear me?" He pulled back from the door. "Fine. Get out."

Bree stepped out first and held the door for me. "Just a little air. That's all she needs, then she'll be good as new."

I kept my hand on my lips and hurried out of the coach.

"Make it fast," he said, keeping his distance from me just in case.

I waited until we were several strides away before I whispered, "Where are we going?"

Bree glanced back at the guard then giggled. "I'm going to introduce you to my favorite Quew."

"Your what?"

She gave me funny look then pointed at the pair of bovines covered in long ginger hair pulling our coach.

"Oh, the hairy cows. Back home, they don't usually pull carriages. Don't you have horses?"

"What are horses?"

"Never mind."

We passed the cart where another four faun coachmen had joined the first two to pull down crates and trunks, trying to get to something buried deep at the bottom.

She kept walking past the Queen's carriage, which was three times the size of ours. She didn't stop, though, until we came the Quew that led the five-Quew team pulling the Queen's coach. It was much larger than the others, and its long hair was the color of pure white snow with turquoise and silver ribbons braided through it.

Bree bobbed a curtsy to it then turned to me. "Mistress, allow me to introduce my friend, Mandryl."

The animal reared back its massive head, and I could see a glint of black eye and a pointed ivory horn peeking through that shaggy white mane.

"Hello, Mandryl. I'm pleased to make your acquaintance."

The animal chuffed and shook its head. Its gaze slid to Bree. "She's the one? The cause of all this fuss?"

The surprise of hearing that clear baritone voice coming from that strange animal nearly knocked me over.

"It's not her fault," Bree said. "She didn't want to come."

The animal swung its head toward me again.

"Yes, exactly," was all I could say. My limbs were trembling like I was already on trial.

"Which is why—"

A ruckus from the Queen's carriage stopped Bree.

"You, get away from there!" It was Azender. He hopped down from the open door and waved his arms, warning us away from the beast.

"What are you doing traipsing about?" He craned his head around. "Where is your guard? Guards!"

Bree whispered, "We should get back before there's trouble."

Weren't we already in trouble? Still, I nodded and followed her lead when she curtsied again to Mandryl.

We were just beyond the Queen's coach and nearly back to our own when Bree stopped and pulled a shiny red fruit from her pocket. "I forgot to give this to Mandryl. You go on. I'll be just a moment."

Before I could argue, she was racing back to the front of the line.

Azender's pompadoured head poked out of the coach's open door again. "Didn't I tell you to get away from there? Guards!"

"It's only a treat," Bree yelled at him. She held it out to Mandryl, and when he accepted it with his wide, fleshy lips, she leaned in close to his ear and gave his head a hearty rub before galloping back to me.

"I'm warning you," Azender shouted as she passed. "Next time you step out of line, I'm turning you over to the guards."

"It won't happen again, sir," she said, but even from a distance, I could see the devious glint in her eye.

"What are you up to?" I demanded when she caught up to me.

"Oh, nothing. Nothing at all."

Of course, I didn't believe her for a second.

When we reached our coach, our chaperon was still

standing at the door with the other guard, but now there was a third one as well, dressing him down.

"They tricked me, captain," our guard wailed back. "They said they were just getting a bit of air. They didn't say nothin' about messin' with the Queen's Quews."

"You shouldn't have let them out of your sight, D'rig," the burlier one said. "At all!"

"Yes, sir. Understood, sir. Won't happen again."

"See that it doesn't." He puffed out his chest and marched away.

When D'rig turned, he sneered. "You two, get inside before I throw you in." He gestured at the door.

"We didn't mean any harm," Bree muttered as she waited for me to climb in. She followed behind me.

"Quiet!" He entered after us and slammed the door so hard it shook the carriage. He folded his arms over his beard and stared into the empty cushion in front of him.

Bree and I settled into our places without a word and remained that way as the caravan lurched forward. I stared out the window and watched one green pasture give way to another.

At some point, I fell asleep because I was awakened by the mutters of our guard as he peered out his window. Whatever he was seeing had him so agitated he was leaning out the door and yelling at the driver. "Why are we headed into the village? There's a faster road alongside the river. What's the meaning of this?"

His yells awakened Bree too. She stretched out of her slump and yawned. "What's happening?"

"It appears we're headed for a village," I said as the guard glared at me.

She glanced out the window. "We've made excellent time, then."

"This is the Seilie High Court?" I gazed out again, eager to see more, but there were only a scattering of huts ahead.

"Seilie Court isn't a place. Any nitwit knows that," the

guard scoffed. "And this isn't Seilie lands, either."

"No need to be rude." Bree shot back. "This is Spire Point. The last Brightlands village before the Seilie border."

I sank back against the cushion and watched the huts approach. There were only a few along the road, with pastures and cropland surrounding them.

As we traveled, other buildings appeared. Dwellings, mostly, with porches and windows, but also shops and other businesses, all with signs hanging over their doors. At least I assumed they were signs. The markings on them appeared to be writing, like the ancient runes and scribblings I'd seen in Headmistress Trindle's history books.

The guard dropped back against his cushion with a thud. "Seems we're catering to the whims of beasts now. Next thing you know, the Queen's Quews will be wanting to ride in their own carriage."

I caught Bree's eye. "Did I miss something?"

The dwarf folded his arms in a huff. "Driver says a Quew demands refreshment. Doesn't care that the Seilies await our arrival, and apparently the Queen don't, either." Then he swallowed and checked himself. "What I mean is, Her Majesty deserves better consideration."

"Of course, she does," Bree offered, sympathetically. She watched the buildings pass. "Any idea where we'll be stopping, I suppose?"

"The tavern," D'rig said.

Bree brightened.

"Why, what's—ow!" I barked.

"Did you say something, mistress?" Bree gave me an innocent look like she hadn't kicked my shin. "I'm so sorry, did I bump you? Oh, twiddly beans. A thousand apologies. I was just trying to adjust..." Her excuse trailed off when D'rig's bored gaze drifted back to his own window.

A stern side eye made my displeasure known, but I was too curious about what was happening to remain angry. I watched as she stared out the window. Was she looking for something? Or someone?

The outer farms had been constructed of little more than burlap, mud, and sticks, but the buildings we passed now were an odd mix of shacks and shanties. Some were short and wide, others narrow and tall, and each one was painted in once-brilliant colors that had aged and worn to dusky hues. If one stood in the middle of the village and twirled, I imagined it might feel like one was falling into a kaleidoscope.

When the coach came to a stop, the guard threw open the door and peered out. Over his shoulder, I could see the front of a broad two-story building of tangerine walls, exposed brown timber beams, and a pair of swinging black doors. Skirting the outer wall was a railed veranda with a sign too dingy to read hanging crooked over the door.

The commotion of the caravan had brought out a handful of ragged fauns and dwarfs to gape at the carriages and carts. Some must have realized it was the Queen's entourage because they doffed their caps and bent to one knee. "Your Majesty," a few muttered in sloppy unison when the Queen emerged.

"Inform the proprietor of our arrival," she instructed Azender then glanced at the crowd assembling around us.

I whispered to Bree, "Why are they staring at her that way?"

She waited for our guard to open the door and clamber out.

"Some have never seen her before, only heard rumors and stories," she said. "She rarely visits the villages. You needn't worry, though. The people here are harmless. Mostly, anyway. They only look rough."

Rough was putting it mildly. I dropped my voice to a whisper. "Is this your doing?"

A coy smile played upon her lips. "Just follow my lead."

At the moment, it seemed that meant doing nothing. She sat and stared out the window at nothing in particular. I took another look at the tight cluster of buildings lining the road beyond the inn. They were all built chockablock, one skewed and topping another, or leaning together like drunken neighbors, and every one was in some state of disrepair. "Why is it named Spire Point? I see no spires."

Bree's face darkened. "There used to be a Crystal Spire. Before it was taken from us, it stood right there in the center of the village." She pointed to a small park behind the tavern.

In the middle was a garden with a raised alabaster pool that reminded me of the divining pools.

"You should have seen it," Bree said. "It was so lovely, especially in the morning when it shimmered and glowed with the sun's first light."

"What happened to it?"

She rubbed her palm over her face and glanced at the dwarf through the window. He wasn't paying attention to us, but he was still within earshot.

She lowered her voice. "The Queen removed it after the King died. It was to be a monument at his burial site."

"So, you can still visit it?" As if that were any consolation.

Her expression clouded. "Perhaps someday. The memorial hasn't been built, and no one can say where the Spire is."

"Oh." The subject was clearly a sore one.

"Some don't believe the Queen ever intends to build the monument."

"Then why take it?"

Bree shook her head. "That Spire was the heart of our village. The Old Ones spoke to our sages through it. It kept the ways of the old magic alive and kept our memories strong. She didn't like that."

A crystal with curious power. I touched the place where my Faytling should be. "The Queen took a crystal from me as well. It's not as grand as yours, but it's special to me. Every Fayte Guardian has one. They become part of us."

"Then you understand," she said. "I hope you get your crystal back."

"I hope we both do."

Beside the inn stood a stable of ginger-colored Quews and a row of tented pavilions, mostly vendors selling fruits, vegetables, and freshly baked bread that filled the air with a mouth-watering scent. I inhaled deeply. "Oh, that smells good."

Bree sniffed. "Not bad, but we don't have time for that."

She eyed the crowd and the Dwarven Guards taking positions around the carriages and carts. She was up to something, but what?

Our guard opened the door. "May as well get comfortable. We're going to be here awhile. I'm going to get a pint. Don't move."

He slammed the door and marched off toward a group of guards huddled on the veranda, but Bree was quick. She thrust out her hand and caught the door before it closed.

When he didn't hear the door rattle, D'rig whipped back. "Don't test me, girl."

She flashed innocent eyes. "It's just that Her Highness requires the necessaries."

"The what?"

She gave him a long, woeful look. He rolled his eyes at me. "Is it urgent?"

I nodded.

"You best be quick about it," he muttered. "You're supposed to stay put."

"Of course. We'll be quick as can be," Bree said.

"Believe me, Her Highness is as eager to get to the Seilie Castle as anyone."

He stepped aside, giving us room to exit the coach. What was she up to? Did she need the necessaries? I doubted it. She had a plan.

"This way, mistress."

I followed her to the door.

She swung it open and held it for me. The stench of old ale and mildew nearly stopped me cold.

"No time to dally." The smell didn't faze her as she darted across the room, navigating a dozen trestle tables filled with villagers, some deep in conversation over tankards of frothy drinks. I stared at the commotion on the other side. The Queen and her entourage were there, getting the royal treatment from what must have been the tavern's proprietress.

"The sisters can make a lovely roast nip hash with peas and morels, Your Majesty," said a simpering faun as she adjusted the starched collar of an elegant if faded blue frock.

The Queen ignored her, so Azender stepped forward. He touched the proprietress's elbow and leaned in. "It's a most kind offer, madame, but the sisters needn't go to the trouble. The Queen has all she requires. But if there is a private room, perhaps. Something a little apart from the…" he gazed out over the crowded main room.

Many in the room, I noticed, watched them in return. No one, as far as I could tell, was paying any attention to Bree or me, so no one stopped us as we threaded our way through the crowd.

Along the back wall, at a doorway covered by a burgundy curtain, Bree stopped and glanced back over her shoulder. "Ready?"

"For what?"

Still, she pushed through the curtain and left me to follow.

On the other side was a kitchen, dominated by a large hearth with a roaring fire that was doing a tidy job of heating several kettles, all suspended by a network of iron hooks. The contents of those kettles filled the place with the savory smells of simmering onions and celery, probably carrots and potatoes, rosemary, sage, and thyme. At the very center of the room was a long table where three raven-black fauns in aprons were kneading mounds of dough.

"Good afternoon, ladies," Bree declared cheerfully. "Don't mind us. We're only passing through."

"Is that so, Breenagor?" muttered the smallest of the three, who was wiping her flour-dusted hands on her daisy-print apron. The cool reception might have worried me, but the twinkle in her eye that followed and the hint of a smile made it clear the cook held no ill will.

"What kind of greeting is that for your favorite apprentice?" Bree touched her chest and pretended to look insulted.

"An apprentice who ran off to work in the palace?" the one at the farthest end of the table said before flipping her mound and rolling her fists into it.

"Never mind her. We all know well and good what you're doing there. But you should tell your Gran to stop in once in a while," said the last. She was no taller than Bree, but her belly was twice as round. "She hasn't come by in an age."

"Of course she hasn't," complained the one in the daisy apron. "You kept badgering her for her berry tart recipe the last time she was here. It's no wonder she's stayed away. She's avoiding you, no doubt."

The little one dipped her chin. "Yes, well, it's only a recipe. She doesn't have to be so stingy with it. But, fine, you tell her I won't mention it again. Probably."

Bree waved. "I'll tell her, of course." Then she nodded and smiled and hurried past them to another narrow door.

She grabbed the handle but stopped and turned back. "If it's no trouble, I'd be eternally grateful if you wouldn't mention that you saw me, should anyone inquire."

The cooks chortled.

"Same old Breenagor," I heard one say as we headed into a narrow lane behind the building.

"So, we aren't going to the necessaries, then?" I asked as I tried to keep pace with her.

"We can if you need to," she said. "But certainly not here."

CHAPTER TWELVE

WE WERE WELL along the deserted lane when Bree finally slowed down. I fell in step beside her. "Are you sure your grandmother can help?"

She took a moment to mull her answer. "If anyone can, she can."

It wasn't a yes, but dubious help was still better than no help at all. I knew I should be grateful that Bree was at least trying. "How did you put Mandryl up to this, anyway?"

That devious look returned. "He knows Gran is the finest baker in the village. I told him I'd bring something back for him if I could sneak in a visit."

"You bribed him?"

"It's only a food bribe. It hardly counts. But yes."

"What if they discover we're gone?"

Bree waved off the concern. "D'rig thinks we're in the tavern, and we'll be back before they're ready to leave. Mandryl will make sure of it."

As we continued down the alley, the buildings became so dense and tall, only a ribbon of blue sky remained visible. The few inhabitants we saw paid no attention to us, just tossed their trash into the trench or grabbed a crate from the stacks piled against the back doors and hurried out of sight.

Most were fauns, but there were lanky fae and stubby dwarfs as well. They all seemed to be going about their ordinary business, and not a single one looked our way. No one said hello, no one even smiled. When an old and crippled fae hurried back through his door when he saw us approach, I had to know why. "What's wrong with everybody?"

Bree frowned. "What do you mean?"

"They run away like they're afraid of us."

"Don't take it personally. People just keep to themselves. They have to these days."

"Why? What happened?"

She shrugged. "The Queen has eyes and ears everywhere."

"Spies?"

"Or worse."

"What could be worse?"

"No one knows for sure, but some say that since she took the Spire, there's no limit to what she can do. It might be rumors to scare people, but it's enough to make them want the Spire back."

I would have discounted her fears, but hadn't Druansha been surprised by the blue lightning Rhilasa had wielded in the Throne Room? Did that power come from the Spire too?

"Do you think you'll ever get your Spire back?"

She sighed. "I hope so."

Two fauns wearing wide wicker hats and dingy work shirts with sleeves rolled to the elbow emerged from a back door and proceeded toward us, keeping their heads together in whispered conversation.

Bree smiled when they approached. "Hello, gentle friends. Nice day, isn't it?"

They scowled at her and kept moving.

Bree only shook her head and made a sharp turn between two buildings onto an even narrower and darker passage.

I wondered where we were going. The alley was choked with crates and rubbish, and the buildings pressed against each other. Every one leaned at some odd angle, and a few seemed on the verge of collapsing altogether. I was about to ask if it was safe to proceed when Bree's hand shot out to stop me. She peered around, then knocked on a faded green door beneath a tattered black awning.

"Who's there?" a shaky voice demanded after a long pause. "I don't want any trouble."

Bree leaned close to the wood and whispered, "Gran, it's me. It's Bree."

When the door pulled open, I saw an older, rounder version of Bree standing before us. Two wide gray eyes beneath a silvery crown of hair that was pulled up into a bun at the top of her head. Protruding just in front of her faunish ears were two curled and pointed horns.

She reached out and yanked Bree inside. "Come in, hurry up. The street's no place for you. Oh!" The old faun pulled up a pair of gold-rimmed spectacles that were hanging from a chain around her neck and squinted through them. "Who are you?"

Bree turned to me, embarrassed. "Mistress, this is my grandmother, Grinella Obble. Gran, this is Princess Jane."

"The human girl?" The elder faun moved in so close she had to bend her neck to see my face. Her nostrils flared with each warm breath.

"Yes, ma'am. I am human." I looked at Bree for reassurance.

She waved her grandmother away. "Gran, give her some space. She won't hurt you."

The old faun snapped around. "How do you know? She's *human*." She pulled off the spectacles and let them fall to her bosom.

"She's not here by choice. The Queen forced her."

Grinella pulled back, wary. "Why would she do that? The Queen doesn't care for humans, you know that. We all know that."

Bree shot me an apologetic look. But I didn't know what to say, either. I resorted to the only thing I could say. "The Queen brought me here because I killed her son, ma'am. She wants revenge."

The old faun's hands fluttered to her mouth. "You *killed* the heir?"

Bree stepped between us. "She had good reason. Didn't you?" She turned to me, urging me to agree.

"He would have killed me," I stammered. "It was self-defense."

Grinella shook her head, dubious. "They said nothing of that. Why wouldn't they tell me that? They know the truth. The Old Ones always know the truth. Oh! What was I saying? Never mind, never mind." The older faun squinted and shook her head then wandered away. "Come in, and settle yourselves. Tell me, have you found it yet? Do you know where it is?"

Bree's glance dropped to her feet. "Not yet, Gran. I'm still looking. We're traveling with the Queen's caravan to Seilie High Court. They stopped at the tavern. I saw the sisters there. They said you haven't visited in a while. They'd like to see you."

"The Queen is taking you to see the Seilies? Sounds serious."

"They've called a Reckoning to decide what should happen with the Princess."

Grinella's eyes narrowed as she took my measure. "So, that's the reason for the Reckoning? Very interesting."

Bree grimaced. "You already knew about it? But how?"

"How did I know? Hm, yes, how did I know?" Grinella fidgeted. "Don't just stand there, Breenagor. Where are your manners? Please, offer the human a seat. Have you eaten? I have ginger cake fresh from the oven. Maybe with a dab of sweet powder, just as you like it?"

Bree shook her head as she led me to a small table set in the center of a simple, but cozy room warmed by a corner fireplace. She touched her stomach. "Of course we'll have some ginger cake. No one makes it like you, Gran."

The compliment made the old faun beam. "I'll be back in a jiffy."

We settled in as Bree's grandmother disappeared behind a curtained doorway. On the other side, cupboard doors opened and shut, and plates and utensils clattered.

Bree turned back toward the curtain. "Who were you speaking of just now, Gran? Who knows the truth?"

"The truth about what, dear?" Grinella called back.

"I don't know. That's what I'm asking."

Grinella poked her head back through the curtain. "How about a spot of tea with the cake? The kettle is already on the fire."

Bree looked at me. I nodded. "That would be lovely," she called back.

The older faun disappeared again, and we could hear more cupboards opening and closing.

"She always does this," Bree muttered to me. More loudly, she tried again with her grandmother. "Were you referring to the Old Ones? Because that's actually why we're here."

There was silence on the other side of the drape. No answer, no movement, nothing.

I leaned close and whispered, "Who are the Old Ones? Does she mean the Seilie High Court?"

Bree shook her head. "The Old Ones aren't Seilie. They're much older. They make the worlds. They made this world when our kind fled your world."

"You fled? I didn't know. Why?"

"It was a long time ago. Before I was born. Even

before she was born." She jutted a thumb toward the other room, where the clatter had resumed. "The Old Ones knew it wouldn't be safe after the humans arrived. Not for us or the fae or the dwarfs or anyone. So, they dreamed of this world and gave it to us."

I wanted to know more, but Grinella pushed through the curtain again, carrying a tray with a teapot, three cups, and three small plates, each bearing a thick square of a tawny-colored cake covered in what looked like white powdered sugar. She set the tray down then pulled two smooth wooden forks from her apron pocket. "Here you are," she said. "Don't be shy."

At the sight of that spongy square and the sweet smell of ginger and treacle, every other thought left my head. I grabbed the fork and dug in. I closed my eyes and savored the delicious treat.

When I opened them again, Bree and Grinella were both staring at me. "What?" I touched my lips. Were they covered in crumbs? Was powder smeared on my chin?

Bree glanced down. "I think you were moaning. We thought something was wrong."

"Quite the opposite, actually. But..." I paused, suddenly shy.

Grinella stared at me, worried.

I lifted my empty plate. "Is there any more?"

The old faun's concern gave way to a proud smile that made her eyes glisten. She rose from her chair and took my plate. "Of course there is, dear. Stay right there. I won't be a moment."

She disappeared into the other room, and Bree leaned over. "There's nothing she likes better than people who appreciate her food. She'll love you forever now."

When she returned and set the plate in front of me again, there was a fresh square of cake, even larger than the first. I tucked in.

Grinella settled back in her chair and sipped her tea.

"Gran, I was just telling my mistress about the Old Ones." Bree watched her grandmother closely.

The old faun glanced away, avoiding her granddaughter's gaze. "Oh? And why is that, dear?"

Bree set her teacup down and placed both hands on the table. "I was hoping to ask a favor of you."

Her grandmother almost choked on her tea. She set the cup and saucer down carefully on the table. "A favor? What sort of favor?"

Now it was Bree's turn to look uncomfortable. Her eyebrows rose and fell and pulled together as her lips pulled from one side to the other. Finally, she said, "Something happened…" But then her lips twitched again, and I knew she was struggling.

I swallowed my mouthful of cake and turned to Grinella. "Ma'am, I found the Queen's Collection Room."

Grinella's eyebrows shot up. "In the palace?"

I nodded.

"And you escaped?"

I nodded again.

Her eyes flashed a mixture of concern and resignation, then finally sorrow. "But the wards? How did you break them?"

I'd wondered that myself. Why had I forgotten the first time, but not the second? The only difference was my mother. Was it because she'd pulled me into her vision? Or when she returned my memories? "I don't know. I went there to find a Sliver the Queen took from my friend, but I found—" A stone formed in my throat. I couldn't speak or even breathe.

Grinella's expression softened. She leaned forward. "What did you find, dear?"

I looked at Bree, and she nodded gently, urging me to be honest. "I found my mother, ma'am. The Queen is holding her captive there." The image of Madeleine behind those bars came back to me, and the guilt that I hadn't freed her when I had the chance. All that anger and shame swept over me again.

Grinella watched me, her expression inscrutable. Then her chin dropped to her chest. Was she angry? Disappointed? Would she throw me out?

I rose and went to the door. "This was wrong. I shouldn't have come here. I shouldn't—"

"I remember your mother," she said in a voice so small and sad it seemed to come from someplace far away. "That dark-haired woman in the cage. Such a beauty, and such a fighter. She's still alive?"

"Yes," I said. "Barely, but she's alive. I think the Queen is draining her."

"The Slivers!" Her fingers touched her lips as if the word were a curse. "She's still doing it? But it's been so long. That poor woman would be…" She rose, shaking her head. "Rhilasa swore she was done with that." Then she turned to me. "My dear, I am so sorry. It must have been a terrible thing for you to see."

Emotion welled within me. I gripped my skirts till my fingers went white, but I managed to swallow the knot in my throat.

Still, Bree came to my aid. "Her mother is still aware. She communicates."

Her grandmother frowned. "Is that true?"

"When she touched me, she pulled me into a dream. She spoke to me there, and we shared memories." I didn't tell her of the memories she returned to me or how close I'd come to being discovered by the Queen. All I could say was, "I couldn't free my mother before I left, but Bree thought you might know a way to do it."

Grinella sat back down and stared at my hands on the table. "That's why you wear those gloves, isn't it? You're a Reader. Just like her."

I nodded. "Is there anything you can do to help me save her?"

She touched her lips and then her forehead, but finally, she said, "There may be something." She rose slowly and went to a tall cabinet with two doors that opened wide to reveal dozens of drawers of varying sizes. She pulled one and lifted out a tiny, wooden box.

When she opened it, revealing the contents, Bree slammed both palms on the table. "You still have that? But the Queen demanded them all."

"I've kept it hidden well enough." Grinella brought the box back to the table and set it in front of herself.

Inside, I could see a shiny lavender-pink stone that looked like my crystal without its golden filigree jacket.

"Is that a Faytling?" I asked.

"It's a piece of the Crystal Spire," Bree said. "Some, like Gran, use them to connect with the Old Ones, but the Queen demanded they all be turned over when she took the Spire." She turned back to her grandmother. "She knew you had this. What did you give the guards when they came for it?"

When Grinella lifted the stone from its case, a light sparked within it, making it glow like a Faytling. "A bit of pink glass. They didn't know the difference."

"Does it still work?" Bree asked.

"Of course, it still works, silly girl." Grinella covered the glowing stone with her other hand and closed her eyes. She remained that way for a long moment, then opened her eyes again.

I stared in amazement because her eyes were no longer the color of strong tea. They burned with the same brightness as the stone.

"It is good to feel you again, Old Ones."

I knew she wasn't speaking to Bree or me, so I followed Bree's lead and remained silent as Grinella nodded and made small noises of assent and understanding. When she spoke again, she closed her eyes. "Of course, I understand. I will tell her."

106

When she opened her eyes, they were brown again.

"I'm sorry to say the Old Ones have no knowledge of your mother or any Slivers. The Queen blocks them from the Collection Room. They have been curious, however. They have worried about her secrets."

I didn't know who or what the Old Ones were, but disappointment hit me hard just the same. It truly had been a mistake to leave without my mother and the Sliver. I'd had one chance to save them both, and I'd squandered it. "Then, there's nothing more to do," I whispered, as much to myself as to her. "I have truly failed."

"No, dear girl, not failed," Grinella said. "The Old Ones cannot help, but I can sense from the stone your mother has her own plan. Did she share this with you?"

I wiped away the tears that were welling in the corners of my eyes. "What plan?"

"She will reveal it when you return. She can wait. She has already waited all this time."

It wasn't the answer I wanted. "But what if the Queen prevails at the Reckoning? If she wins, I doubt she'll allow me to return. She promised me a horrible end."

Grinella exchanged a tense look with Bree.

"I cannot foresee the Reckoning's outcome, but I can tell you the High Court would never allow the Queen to take your life while you are in their keeping. Life, in any form, is too precious to them. If she prevails, she will have to return you to the Brightlands. It is the only place she can do as she pleases. So, there is every reason to believe you will return, for better or worse. I know, however, that was not the answer you had wished for." Her sorrow appeared genuine.

"It isn't. But it is a comfort to know I might have another chance, however difficult it may be."

Bree took her last bite of ginger cake. "Gran, can you think of anything that might help? Once she gets back to the palace?"

The old faun placed the stone back in its box and poured herself another cup of tea. "I can be no help to you there. I know so little of those things, but the Seilies will not abide it if they discover the Queen is again Slivering. They would have banished her after the Shadow Rite."

"What's the Shadow Rite?"

Neither Bree nor Grinella answered my question. They were both staring at the door, listening hard at the voices we could hear in the distance.

"That's the Queen's guards," Bree said with panic in her eyes. "Do you think they're looking for us?"

Grinella rushed to the door and held her ear to the wood. "It's definitely guards." She waved us both toward the back room. "You must go. Keep to the alley. If someone stops you, tell them you went to the orchard. Here." She grabbed two shiny red apples from a basket on the sideboard and shoved them at Bree.

The shouting grew closer. I recognized the gruff cadence of the Dwarven Guards.

"Any sign?" one barked. "Check the building there."

Someone pounded on Grinella's door so hard it strained the metal hinges.

"Go!" Grinella mouthed to us and made shooing movements with her hands.

Bree kissed her grandmother on the cheek and ran toward the back room. She paused in the kitchen long enough to grab a hearty slice of the ginger cake and dropped it in a pouch she made with her apron.

"For Mandryl," she said before heading for a back door. She inched it open and peeked out. "It's clear," she whispered over her shoulder. "C'mon."

We set off down another narrow path, searching among the stacks of discarded crates and piles of rubbish for signs of the guards. When we came upon a silver-bearded faun in a chair with a potato in one hand and a paring knife in the other, he fixed us with a pebble-black gaze.

I froze when he said, "Breenagor, is that you? What are you up to, girl?"

Bree only smiled. "Just visiting Gran, Mr. Thorndroggle. Nothing special."

He made a *tsk* sound. "Better hurry on, then. Steer clear of the square, unless you're looking for trouble."

"Yes, sir. Thank you, sir." She bobbed a quick curtsy and hurried on. I did the same and ran after her.

CHAPTER THIRTEEN

"THEY'RE HERE! THE half-breed is here!" The Dwarven Guard's voice cracked as he hollered to the others standing at the tavern door before he rushed toward me, spear hoisted and aimed at my chest.

"You silly thing, what are you screaming about?" Bree was practically laughing at him, which might have put me at ease if I could see anything funny about the blood lust in this little man's eyes. "My mistress was hungry. She didn't care for anything inside, and there's an orchard just down the lane. The apples are in season. Delicious." She took one from her apron's pocket and bit into it, making an exaggerated face as she savored it.

My heart still raced, yet I remained silent for fear a tremble in my voice would give us away. When she tossed me the second apple, I bit into it eagerly.

"We've been searching for you. D'rig said you'd run off. The Queen is furious."

Bree laughed again. "We told him where we were going. If he'd been paying attention instead of tossing back tankards of ale, you'd know where we were. Honestly, what good would it do to run, anyway? Look around.

Where could we go? Besides, my mistress has no reason to run. The sooner we get to the Seilie High Court, the sooner she'll be cleared." She gave me a look.

"Right. Exactly," I said, though I wasn't sure if that's what I supposed to say or not. She nodded, so it must have been good enough. "So, you see, this really isn't necessary." I stepped to the side of the spear tip.

The dwarf's thick, black eyebrows pulled together as he puzzled out whether to believe us. When another guard joined him, he tightened his grip on the spear and aimed it at me again.

"Stay where you are," his partner demanded and turned his spear on us as well.

Instead of being intimidated, Bree waved them off and walked past them. When she looked back and saw me gaping, she waved for me to join her. "Mistress, we don't have time for their nonsense. We must get back to the carriage."

I smiled at the diminutive men as I moved around them, though it probably looked as forced as it felt. "Are you sure you know what you're doing?" I whispered when I caught up to Bree.

She paused when the door shut behind us and a half a dozen heads turned our direction. "Not really, but if we act guilty, they'll know we're guilty. If we don't, they may give us the benefit of the doubt."

It wasn't the soundest of strategies, but I followed her lead anyway and tried to smile like I meant it. I took another bite of the apple.

As we neared the Queen's carriage, Bree darted up to Mandryl and rubbed the furry side of his head. She slipped him the cake so quickly I saw only the churn of his jaw and what looked like a smattering of powdered sugar near his lips.

"Thank you," she whispered before joining me again.

When we reached our own carriage, it was empty. No

D'rig. No driver. Bree pulled open the door, and I stepped inside. Once she was in and the door was closed, the disappointment settled over me. We'd come so far, and for nothing. I dropped my face into my hands and choked back tears.

"Mistress, what is it?"

"I never should have left the palace. I know what your grandmother said, but I could have taken one more moment to free my mother."

She sighed. "I know you believe that, but you couldn't have saved her that way. Where would you have taken her? There's nowhere to go in this world where the Queen couldn't find you. My grandmother was right. You will need the High Court's help, whether you want it or not."

I leaned my head against the cushion. "What I need is Druansha. Why hasn't she returned?"

Bree stared down at her hooves and the hem of her dress. "I'm sure her heart will break when she learns what you've discovered, but she never would have left you if she didn't believe you could take care of yourself. You are stronger than you think you are, mistress. I know you want to help your mother and your friend, and I believe you will. Princess Druansha believes in you. But you must believe it as well."

Her words were touching, but deep down, I knew the truth. I had failed.

~ ~ ~

I awakened to Bree shaking my knee.

"We're here," she whispered.

Here? I was back in the Balmoral kitchen, fretting over a spoiled stew and trying to salvage it with handfuls of dried herbs that were inexplicably stuffed in my apron pockets. But as the dream faded away, I remembered where I was.

Not Balmoral and not a kitchen but someplace I could never find on a map.

I straightened and rubbed the warm place on my cheek where I'd worked myself into a crevice between the cushion and the carriage wall.

Beyond the carriage window, the sky was dark except for a line of golden lanterns suspended from posts along a tree-lined lane. Beside us, D'rig sat upright and alert, though he ignored us as the carriage came to a stop.

Bree and I sat, waiting for instructions. Outside, two guards in unison announced the Queen's arrival in deep, gruff voices, but D'rig's wide and shaggy noggin filled the carriage window on his side, blocking us from seeing anything that was happening.

"Is all well?" Bree asked, her voice edged with irritation.

"Dreadful reception," he muttered, "Inexcusable. Only guards to greet the Brightlands Queen? Abominable."

"It is rather late," Bree offered.

"Terrible excuse. Oh, there. Finally, a proper official. About time."

I craned to see around D'rig's head, but it was impossible.

"Is it a Seilie Minister?" Bree asked. "I've never seen one before."

The guard scowled at her. "Don't be daft. It's not a Minister, of course. But someone of rank, surely."

"Did the Queen bow?" Bree pressed.

"She's getting out of the carriage now," he said. "No, he's bowing. Now the official is leading her inside. Oh, there goes Mr. Azender along with her." The guard pulled back from the window and fell back against the cushion.

When our carriage approached the arched porte-cochere to be received by a team of footmen and maids, the guard barreled out before us and darted away without even looking back.

"Which of you is the prisoner?" a young, liveried footman asked as he stood at the door to help us out.

"Prisoner? If you mean my mistress, this is Princess Jane," Bree said with Azender-caliber pomp.

The lanky fae with the teardrop ears twisted his lips into a disapproving sneer as he extended his hand toward the door. "Of course. If you would kindly direct yourself to the door there, you will find an escort to your rooms."

My limbs tingled after being stationary for so long, but it was the sight of the castle before us that stopped me cold—if it could even be called a castle. From a distance, it had appeared to be a stone tower with the typical turrets and terraces built against a sheer cliff wall. But now that I was closer, I could see its many colonnades, windows, and buttresses were part of the cliff, with a cascade of vines and leaves and pretty white blooms hugging its smoothly curved contours.

The blooms gave off an enchanting white light that brightened when they were fully opened and dimmed as the petals closed, and they were brightest at the richly carved door.

As I neared, I could see the intricate design was not as it first appeared. The door wasn't carved wood, but hundreds, maybe thousands of slender vines and roots tightly woven together. As we approached, they slithered apart to create an opening we could walk through.

"Welcome to Seilie High Castle, Your Highness. If you will follow me."

The tiny squeak of a female voice sounded friendly enough, but even as I scanned the vestibule, I could not see the speaker.

"Over here, by the staircase, Your Highness."

The staircase that dominated the far end of the room was as much a natural wonder as the door, comprised as it was of deep green vines, some as thick as tree trunks and others as slender as twigs, all interwoven to form the steps and railing that ascended to an upper floor that was almost entirely obscured by thick and leafy branches. More white blooms along the walls and the ceiling filled the space with soft light, but I still saw no one. I leaned toward Bree. "Can you see her?"

Bree squinted as her gaze roamed the place, then she brightened. "There." She pointed at a flower resting upon the staircase's first baluster, its white petals stretched open in full bloom.

Something hovered above the pistils. A hummingbird? When I moved closer, I could see it was a tiny human figure with pale-blue skin and deeper blue wings that fluttered like a butterfly.

"It is not polite to point, now is it?" The tiny creature tipped her nose up like Headmistress Trindle used to when she was peeved.

Bree pulled her hand behind her back.

Both of us straightened and tried not to appear surprised by our greeter.

"Please pardon me," I said. "I've never met a Seilie before."

"A Seilie, oh goodness no. I'm a Sprite. And while we're clearing things up, might I ask what's happened to your ears, dear?"

My hands flew to the sides of my head. Even through the leather gloves, I could feel they were just as they should be. "My ears are fine, thank you."

Bree whispered, "She must think you're fae."

"You're not fae?" The little flying lady fluttered closer. She adjusted the pair of tiny spectacles that sat upon her tiny nose. "But they said you're the daughter of the Brightlands heir. The daughter from… oh, not fae, not entirely."

Then, in an instant, there not just one fluttering creature, but a whole swarm of them. I tried to stand patiently amid the fluttering of so many shimmering wings and so many little voices whispering, "It's her," "This is the one," "Isn't she odd?" and "Brave, they say, very brave."

"What is this?"

Druansha's voice rose above the others and instantly dispersed the cloud of wings. The relief of finally seeing her again, and so casually descending the stairs, nearly brought me to tears.

Now that the sprites were gone, I noticed Bree hunched down on the floor with her arms wrapped over her head. I tapped her shoulder. "What happened? Are you hurt?"

She peeked up through her arms. "You can't be too careful with sprites. They're a vicious breed. Did you see their teeth? Sharp as razors. I knew a faun who was nearly flayed alive by a swarm of those monsters."

"Let's not judge them too harshly," Druansha said as she reached the final steps. Her fingers glided along the vine that formed the banister rail, and it undulated beneath her touch. "They were only curious. I'm sure they meant no harm. Isn't that so, Iris?"

The bespectacled sprite who had greeted us was fluttering near my ear. "Of course, Your Highness. We were just getting acquainted with our guests."

As Druansha approached, white flowers bloomed along the vines that formed the wall beside us and cast their light. "Is Jane's accommodation prepared?"

"Yes, Your Highness." Iris flew closer to the Brightlands Princess. "The chamber adjacent to your own, just as you requested."

"Good. Then I'll take them up myself, if that's all right with you."

The way the Sprite demurred, I knew she had no real choice but was pleased to be asked. "Very good, Your Highness. I'll check with the coachmen about the baggage."

"Thank you, Iris." Druansha turned to me. "Now tell me, are you well? You were expected hours ago. Was there trouble?"

Bree and I exchanged glanced.

"Well?" Druansha said.

"We stopped for the Quews to refresh themselves in the village." I hoped the answer was acceptable.

Druansha frowned. "The Quews?"

Bree stepped forward. "It was Mandryl, Your Highness. He was thirsty. But it was only a short visit, I mean, stop."

"I see." Druansha touched the corner of her mouth. "Spire Point. Isn't that your home village?"

Bree looked like she'd forgotten how to breathe. "It is, ma'am."

Druansha let Bree squirm through the silence. Then she turned back to me. "Perhaps we should retire to your room."

As she headed up the stairway, Bree shot me a look that seemed to ask, *Should I be worried?*

I held up my hands and hiked my shoulders. The truth was, I was worried. There was so much I needed to tell Druansha, but how could I when the whole place seemed to be... *alive*.

"Are the walls moving?" I asked when we reached the top step. Parts seemed to be made of rock, while others looked like tree roots, trunks, and branches. Even the air seemed alive, as fresh and fragrant as a springtime meadow. As we moved along the corridor, the space ahead seemed to widen at our approach and brighten with new blooms.

"They do have a tendency to move," she said, almost chuckling. "The Seilies have a deep appreciation for life, and that life, in all its varied forms, appreciates and serves them in return."

"So, they built their castle from living things?" Another

white bud opened ahead, casting light in a shadowy spot.

"No one built the castle. It's more like a gift. When the Seilies made this land their home, all the trees and vines and green things that lived here worked together to create these spaces. The Seilies have always lived in unison with the natural world. It is their way."

I nodded as though I understood, which I didn't. It was becoming a familiar feeling, however. The Brightlands Palace, Spire Point Village, now this. All these strange new places. I was still musing about it when another bloom opened, and Iris appeared.

"I was just wondering, Your Highness, would you care for some refreshment to be brought to your rooms?"

Druansha turned to me. "You must be famished after the journey. Would you like something?"

I'd been too harried to consider it, but now that I did, there was a gnawing in my stomach. "If it's no trouble."

Iris's wings fluttered. "No trouble at all."

Before I could say thank-you, the petals closed around her, and the bloom pulled back between two vines. I turned to remark on the marvel of it but Druansha was standing in an opening in the wall that hadn't been there a moment ago.

When we stepped over the threshold, the flowers along the wall illuminated to reveal a chamber that looked more like a cozy meadow than a room. A canopy of tree branches and leaves made up the ceiling, and what appeared to be a bed and table were formed from the same vines and tree roots that formed the walls.

Druansha looked around and frowned.

"Bree, you packed a bag for Jane, didn't you?"

"I did, Your Highness. Everything I thought she could need."

"Could you check downstairs? It should have been sent up by now."

"Of course, Your Highness." Bree curtsied before

leaving the room.

Druansha waited until the wall closed the opening behind her. "Now," she said, turning her attention fully to me, "will you please explain what happened in the village?"

An overwhelming rush of emotion washed over me. There was so much to tell her. About the village and everything that happened before. "It was my fault. Bree was trying to help me. She asked Mandryl to stop so she could take me to see her grandmother."

Druansha touched her forehead. "And why would she do that?"

"She was trying to help me figure out how to rescue my mother. I found her in the Collection Room. I think Lucas's Sliver is there too."

Druansha lifted both hands and stopped me. "Your mother? In the Brightlands?"

"She is! She's in a prisoner in the Collection Room. I saw her, and she gave me back my memories. I remember everything."

Druansha stared at me like my face was a puzzle that made no sense. "Madeleine is alive." It wasn't a question, just a statement of utter disbelief.

When I nodded, she went to the edge of the bed that was covered in a quilt formed of yellow flower petals and sat. "When? No, how…?" She shook her head then started again. "Please tell me everything."

CHAPTER FOURTEEN

THE CONVERSATION WAS a long one, and I had only gotten as far as fleeing from the Collection Room and leaving my mother in that horrible cage when Druansha and I were interrupted by a knocking on the other side of the wall.

"Tea and treats, Your Highness."

I recognized Iris's sweetly high-pitched voice.

Druansha grimaced but quickly recovered herself. "Yes, of course. Please, come in."

The vines and roots slid apart to create an opening in the center of the door, allowing Iris to enter. She flew to a spot where other vines had pulled apart along the wall to reveal a tall, open cabinet holding a teapot with teacups and platters of small sandwiches, biscuits, and colorful fruit.

She zipped quickly around the food and tea, then turned back to us. "The preparers have put together what we've been assured is a proper afternoon tea. Your handmaiden suggested the fare, so I hope it is to your liking."

Druansha examined the feast. "It looks wonderful. You

have outdone yourself, Iris."

The sprite beamed in a way that made me smile too.

"Please," Druansha said, "give our regards to whoever is responsible."

Iris darted across the room with a quick aerial flip before stopping in front of Druansha. "Euphonia will be so pleased to hear it." She slipped through a small gap between two vines in the wall that closed securely behind her.

Druansha's smile disappeared.

"Your mother is in the Brightlands Palace? You are absolutely sure?"

"Yes, absolutely. She's greatly diminished, but when she touched me, she was strong enough to carry me to a dream world. There, she appeared just as I remembered her in my own visions."

Druansha went to the cabinet and poured two cups of tea.

Her silence unnerved me. "Did you know she was there?"

It was a question I'd considered and dismissed at least a hundred times during the long carriage ride. Druansha had kept so many secrets from me over the years. Would it be so surprising if she'd kept this from me as well?

She met my gaze and held it before answering. "I did not. I was told and I believed your mother had perished trying to cross between our worlds." Her glance broke away and locked on the tray in her hands. "But I should have known it was a lie. I should have *known* it."

My fear that she'd betrayed me vanished. I believed her.

"But she is alive, and you've found her," she said, finally releasing the tray and lifting both cups. "We must thank the stars for that."

"Can you free her?" It was my last hope.

During the long hours in the carriage staring at the

scenery and feeling the wound deepen as the miles pulled me farther from where I needed to be, where my heart was telling me I should be, despite Bree's consoling words, I told myself Druansha could do what I'd failed to do. She'd save my mother and Lucas just as she'd saved me so many times.

When Druansha's expression darkened, I turned away.

"I've never sensed your mother in that palace," she said, sadly. "My mother's wards must have prevented it, and she is even stronger now. Even if I thought there was some way I could tear through those walls to get to Madeleine, I wouldn't dare leave you alone in this place now. Not with her here. How can I trust my mother to abide by the rules of the Reckoning if she's been hiding this crime from me all this time?"

Her refusal sucked the air from my lungs. How could she do this?

"Truly? You won't help me?" My voice broke.

She didn't answer. Instead, she went to another wall and touched it, making the vines move apart to reveal a terrace that overlooked a dense woodland. Above the treetops, the moon was a slender crescent surrounded by stars so bright I could see the silhouette of the mountains along the horizon.

As I watched her gaze out to that horizon, my despair became desperation. "If you won't go, I will." I stormed to the door. "I don't care about the Reckoning, and I don't care if the Queen comes after me. I will not sit by while my mother suffers." I touched the door and waited for the vines to pull apart so I could leave.

"Wait."

Her voice was calm.

The opening stood before me, but I couldn't step through it. I wanted to get back to the Brightlands and my mother, but something held me still.

"I can't stop you from leaving," she said, "but there is

something you should see first."

~ ~ ~

Druansha gazed up at the night sky and all its tiny sparks of starlight. A gentle breeze lifted her long, pale hair and billowed her silky gown. "I'd hoped we would have more time."

Time for what? Her refusal to help my mother left me no choice. "I have to go."

I expected more argument, but instead she stepped onto the balcony and disappeared behind the wall.

What was she trying to do? Distract me? I wasn't going to follow her, I wasn't—

A powerful thud stopped my thought, and a scrape, like a knife's blade dragging over rock. Then something huffed.

Something was out there with her.

I bolted to the balcony, but by the time I got there, she was gone.

What stood facing me instead was a shimmering, blue beast that fixed me with a burning golden stare.

"It's all right," the beast said in a voice that didn't seem to belong to a beast at all. It sounded like Druansha, if her lyrical voice had been trapped within that towering animal of midnight-blue scales with a flowing, pearlescent mane that swayed in the nighttime breeze.

"Come closer," she said. "You are in no danger."

The more she spoke, the more like Druansha she seemed. Not just the voice, but the movement of her head, with its protruding snout breathing steamy gusts from its nostrils and small, leathery wings folded against her serpentine neck, where a lavender crystal hung upon a leather belt.

Was that Druansha's crystal?

I crept closer, and the animal's eyes half closed. When I held up my hand, it nudged its snout against the ivory leather of my gloves, warming my palm with her breath. As we stood there, the winged beast released a deep mewling sound that reminded me of a kitten's purr, if that kitten were the size of a carriage.

"What are you?" I whispered, more to myself than the creature, but it regarded me with understanding.

"I am the same as you have ever known me. I am still Druansha."

That was nonsense. It wasn't possible. But yet, there was a time not so long ago I would have said that about the Fayte Guardians and the Brightlands and this whole baffling world. I was struggling to understand, but how was the only word I managed to utter.

The blue-black beast extended the giant wings upon her back then folded them again. She closed her eyes and shook her head.

Had my confusion amused her?

"I would have explained it all to you first, but there isn't time. We must hurry before it's too late."

Too late for what? But the question eluded me. I was still struggling to understand that this dragon beast could be Druansha.

"If you've ever ridden a horse, you should have no trouble."

The closest I'd ever come to riding a horse was sitting in a carriage. She must have sensed my trepidation because she lowered her snout and said, "Will you trust me?"

Despite her massive size, there was still a tenderness in her eye and a softness in her manner. That more than anything reminded me of the Druansha I knew. I nodded.

"Step closer. Yes, there. Now hold my belt and keep a strong grip. That's important."

I did as she said, finding a foothold between her haunch and the base of a wing and wrapping my fingers around the leather belt before closing my eyes.

"Do not let go, and do not peek. Not yet."

In an instant, I felt a disorienting sense of falling then rising and the *whoosh* of chilling wind against my face. I tightened my grip on the belt and pressed myself against her hide.

Were we going through another portal? I'd lost consciousness when the Queen pulled me into this world, and I had no memory of how it felt. More cold air gusted around me and swirled through my hair, tugging strands free from the knot atop my head.

When the worst of it had passed, I yelled out, "Is it almost over?"

"No," the dragon rumbled back, "but you may open your eyes."

I peeked through the flowing mane that shimmered blue and purple and green as I hunched against the soft contours of her back.

After several more minutes, she leaned her head back. "We're nearly there."

I pushed myself up to see we were soaring above a blanket of thick clouds. It was as if the world were made of downy pillows, and starlight glistened upon her body. I nestled against her, still holding fast to the belt that wrapped around her like a dragon-size necklace.

"Are you comfortable?"

"Yes," I called back, despite being overcome by the wonder of it all. We were flying! How was it even possible?

As my courage returned, I leaned to better see the wispy clouds below, yet my cold fingers were losing sensation. I released one hand to open and close my fist to increase the blood flow, but I slipped from my perch.

Instantly, I was tumbling over the dragon's haunches, groping for something, anything to hold, but it was already too late. I was plummeting through the sky.

The dragon released an eerie, guttural roar then banked around and dove, her wings folded back, giving her arrow-like speed.

I comprehended little of it. I felt only the biting wind whipping through my hair and freezing my cheeks. My skirts and petticoats flapped up and against my face, but I had no care for modesty. My only thought was this: This was the end. I'd survived Krol's attacks and Queen Rhilasa's attempt on my life only to end as a bloody smear across the landscape. I would never see Mrs. Crossey or Marlie or the Bellingtons. I would never know a true kiss from Lucas Starwyck, and I would never be able to return what my father had stolen from him.

Worst of all, I would never have another moment with my mother.

I clenched my eyes, but I could still feel the whoosh of the dragon's hulking form diving past me. When I looked again, I saw her curl up beneath me, and she caught me neatly on her back. Spotting the leather belt, I grabbed it with both hands and held on with every ounce of strength I could muster.

"It's all right," she cooed. "You're safe."

With a racing heart, I pressed myself against her back, taking refuge in the long strands of her mane and thankful for her bulk.

"Were you frightened?" she asked after flying in silence.

"Of course I was," I wailed. "I thought it was all over."

"Hm, unfortunate," she mused.

Her lack of compassion stunned me. "Did you want me to fall?"

"No, absolutely not," she said quickly. "But now we know."

"Know what?" Now that my fear had subsided, only anger and confusion were left.

"We know that ability is not within you. Fear such as that would have sparked a change as a survival instinct, if nothing else."

Her words were clear, yet I still struggled to understand

them. "Did you think I could change into something like you? Like a dragon?"

"Or a dragonfly, or any number of winged creatures." Her broad shoulders shrugged gently. "So, yes, I did wonder."

Such a thought had never occurred to me. My visions had always marked me as different from everyone around me, even other Fayte Guardians. But to change into another form?

"You probably should try to be more careful," she added, "but I can put your mind at ease. You were never in any real danger."

"An easy thing for you to say. You have wings."

"I do." She flapped them twice for emphasis. "And you can be sure I would have used them to ensure your safety."

"Hm."

"Are you angry with me?"

"No," I said.

"You are, but that's good. It means you're no longer afraid. Now, if you'd just slide up a bit. I'm going to need to move my legs."

I pulled myself into the soft hair growing along her neck. From there, I could see beyond her girth as we descended through the clouds and approached a dense forest sloped along a hillside that glimmered in the starlight. We sliced through the air until Druansha's great head pulled back, then her front legs reared up and we descended.

But the leafy canopy extended as far as I could see. As I scanned the landscape, she banked gently and circled back around. Where did she intend to land?

That's when I saw it. A clearing directly below that hadn't been there a moment before. Even as I stared, the circle widened.

I blinked hard, sure the shadows were playing tricks on me. Still, the clearing was definitely growing. Was it

Druansha's doing? Krol had manipulated tree roots, perhaps she could as well. "Are those trees moving?"

She chortled softly. "Don't sound so surprised. You'll understand soon enough."

I was growing accustomed to her vague replies, so I simply held tight as she descended and came to a gentle stop in the center of the clearing. I kept hold as her neck swung around and her spine twisted and stretched as she lowered herself to a prone position, making me sway and lurch where I sat.

I stared at the ground surrounding us. There was no grass or low shrubs, only freshly turned soil.

"Could you step away?" she asked. "I'll need space to shift back."

I found a footing in the crux above her knee. From there it was a short hop to the ground.

Once she was free of me, she rose and circled around herself, like a cat settling in for a nap. But instead of reposing, sparks of lavender light flew off her and grew into flashing tendrils that lengthened until they encompassed her entirely.

When the brightness faded, Druansha stood once again in her womanly form, dressed as she had been on the castle terrace.

She smoothed her feathery gown and approached me. "Are you well?"

My legs still wobbled from the flight and my head still swam with the thrill of it all, but I nodded. "Just surprised, I suppose. I had no idea you… your…uh…"

"A dragonfly is not my only form," she said. "I have many."

Of course, it made sense. I smoothed my skirts and sleeves to ensure everything was in its proper place. If she could turn herself into a dragonfly, why not a dragon? Why not any creature? "You're right. It was silly of me to be surprised."

"Not silly. I know it takes some getting used to. If you want to know the truth, sometimes I forget humans cannot change their shape. How distressing it must be to be stuck in a single form." She pushed back a stray, pale strand the breeze had blown across her cheek. "I suppose this adventure has taught us both something."

"Do you mean because I didn't change?"

"I do."

Why did it feel as though I'd failed her? "Is that why you brought me here? Was it a test?"

"Partially. I wanted to know before you met the Seilie Ministers. They will question you, and it will be better if you respond truthfully."

"Do you think I would lie?" I reeled at the insult, but deep down, I knew she had reason to believe I might. I'd lied so many times in my past. I had been a thief who stole memories to fill the empty holes in my past. I had been a liar who bent truths when it suited me.

When Druansha was trapped in her dragonfly form for years in my world and was my only true friend, she witnessed all my foibles and faults. She knew me better than anyone.

"Not lie," she said, gently. "But you don't yet know everything about yourself. That's also why I brought you here, to the Old Ones' Grove."

"The Old Ones?" Grinella Obble had asked them to help my mother, but they said they could not. Perhaps I could persuade them myself. Yet, if they were here, they must have hidden themselves deeper in the forest. As far as I could see, there were nothing but trees.

Majestic trees, to be sure. Trees unlike any I'd ever seen.

I'd grown used to the glimmers that pulsed through the living things in this world, but here the brightness of those glimmers made them a wonder to behold. Light traveling through tree trunks and out to the tips of every branch and shimmered through a kaleidoscope of colors. As I watched, the brightness passed from one tree to the next, as if they were taking turns.

Druansha watched too.

"Do they always do that?" The pulsing lights were still jumping from one tree to another, but now the circle was closing around us. Their roots undulated in the ground like octopus arms, manipulating their movement across the surface.

Druansha only smiled. "They're curious about you."

"They?"

"The trees."

Was she mocking me? I wasn't sure but this was no figment of my imagination. The circle was definitely shrinking. "Why?"

"Don't be frightened."

"Are they friendly?"

Druansha considered that for a moment. "More like family."

"That doesn't make sense."

She cocked her head to the side and sighed. "Perhaps not yet, but in time."

By now the trees had formed a tight circle around us. When I looked up, their canopies had nearly merged and all but eclipsed the sky.

"Greetings, Old Ones," Druansha said to the dozen or so oaks encircling us.

These were the Old Ones?

I waited for a response, but there was only a simultaneous brightening of that glimmer coursing through them.

"Yes, this is Jane," she said, an answer it seemed to a question I hadn't heard. "I thought it was time you met her for yourselves."

I leaned close to her and whispered, "Are they speaking to you?"

"They are. They can speak to you as well. Remove your gloves and place one hand on the ground and the other in mine."

I removed my gloves and did as she said. Squatting to the ground, I placed my left palm flat against the soft earth. When she took my right hand in hers, I marveled at how small my fingers were compared to hers. My hand disappeared entirely when her fingers wrapped around mine.

She paid no attention to my size at all. Instead, she lifted her face to the night sky with her eyes closed. Before I could ask what I should do, she started to grow. Not just taller, but her arms and fingers stretched and thickened, and the soft weave of her dress hardened and darkened around her, becoming a solid cloak of bark. It took only a moment for her humanly features to disappear into a replica of the towering oak trees around us.

Only one subtle difference set her apart: the light coursing through her trunk, branches, and leaves was not silver as theirs was but remained her characteristically soft violet hue.

I was so stunned by her transformation, I didn't realize I was changing too. When I looked down, my dress had become a shell of hard brown bark, and slender green sprigs pushed out of my chest and back, and in seconds grew into broad branches that sprouted smaller branches and lush green leaves. I tried to wiggle my toes, but instead felt only a tangle of roots plunging deep beneath the soft soil. My fingers tingled at the touch of the breeze caressing my new green leaves. "How did you do this?" The question issued from me somehow, though I didn't know how.

"I didn't do it," Druansha said. "You did this yourself. It seems you have an ability to change after all."

CHAPTER FIFTEEN

HOW STRANGE THIS was. Every part of me felt like a tree, but I was also me, with my same thoughts and understanding. "Did you know?"

"I only hoped," Druansha said, her leaves swaying in the breeze. "I was disappointed when the fall didn't change you, so I didn't expect it to happen, yet here you are. No one imagined it was possible, certainly not my brother or my mother. No one fully knows what you are capable of doing."

"If you had doubts, why did you bring me here?"

"Even if you didn't transform, it was important for you to see this place and to meet the Old Ones. But since you have transformed, there is something else you should know as well."

I waited for her to say more, but instead of speaking, I felt something tingling along my roots.

Be aware.

That message rang through me, but it wasn't like the inner voice I heard from Krol. It didn't even come to my awareness as words but rather as pure meaning. I also knew it didn't come from Druansha, or at least from her alone, but from the whole circle of trees around me. They were all speaking, a symphony of voices entwined together.

Feel everything.

I didn't understand at first, but slowly it became clear. My sense of being a single tree fell away. My branches and leaves touched Druansha's and then others. My roots tangled and mingled with them as well, and theirs were already tangled and mingled with others. Through this network that seemed to have no limit, we were linked. We were all connected into one larger, greater whole. As that feeling and that understanding settled over me, nothing felt the same. Not even time.

My perception of moments smeared into a blur. The past overlapped with the present, and they both seeped into the future. The boundaries between them grew hazy or were lost entirely. Slowly, my awareness grew beyond the Old Ones' Grove to the larger world around us, and even beyond that.

Did it extend to my own human world? Before the question had fully formed in my thoughts, I could see Mrs. Crossey and Marlie Carlisle. I could see them with Lucas. Oh, Lucas. I ached to be with him again and to feel his strong fingers holding mine.

But he looked different. I focused on the image and tried to bring it into focus, but he wasn't still. He wasn't even in one place. It was as if I were watching him do five, ten, dozens of things all at the same time, and each of them overlapped the other. Some were distinct, others only hazy shadows, and they all laid one upon the other.

They are moments of the past and present, future and possibility. Here, time is not one thing or another. It is not so rigid or bound. It is all.

It was the Old Ones' voices, and I understood.

It was comforting to be surrounded this way and peaceful in a way I'd never known and barely understood. I'd never felt so at ease and free from my own worries.

Every small fear or concern melted away, leaving only a sense of being part of something greater, like a drop of water in an endless sea. I could feel myself slipping away, but I wasn't losing anything, only becoming something so much more.

Then slowly my mind pulled away from the union. I could feel my limbs shrinking and returning to human form. I resisted and grasped at the expansive feeling even as this new way of knowing receded.

Then I was back in the clearing and back to myself, an ordinary young woman with ordinary limbs.

Druansha stood beside me in her womanly form, watching me.

"Is this a dream?" I whispered when I found my voice.

"Not a dream," she said.

"I want to go back." But it was more than that. It wasn't a desire but a compulsion that tugged at every part of me. Every nerve ached to return to whatever I had been.

"You will return, one day. But you must focus on this moment now. I thought you should experience it, however, the fullness of that knowing and being, the ties that bind the fae to the Old Ones. Each of us is made of earth and light and air, and we come to think that is all we are. Now you have seen there is so much more."

Yes, that was the feeling. A sense of becoming more than oneself, something so much gloriously more. "Like a candle's flame falling into the sun."

"Yes, something like that. I wanted you to feel it, even for this short moment. It is your birthright. The Old Ones' Grove is the cradle of our kind. Your fae blood remembers, and now the Old Ones know you."

I thought of the images of all the possibilities superimposed one atop the other. "This is how you know, isn't it? It's the source of your prophecies."

A light twinkled in her eye. "Yes, in a manner of

speaking. I have used that Sight. What I cannot see, the trees tell me. They know much more than I."

During the union, I'd sensed I had only brushed the surface of their knowledge. I also knew she was holding something back. I'd felt that from the Old Ones too, and I realized I already knew the answer. "Your mother doesn't approve of you coming here. She doesn't like to see you use your gifts to benefit humans."

Her glance drifted away. The subject of her mother wasn't a welcome one.

"My mother has never forgotten or forgiven the loss of our homeland. Humans took that from us, and nothing can ever redeem them in her eyes."

"You returned because you were curious." I was beginning to understand even as I said the words. I could see the images in my mind of an ancient ceremony and an ancient people. "You revealed yourself to the ancient druids and helped them."

"I was curious about them, and I learned those humans were not what my mother said they were. There were even those I grew to admire."

Boudica's image blossomed in my mind, and I didn't know whether it had come from my own thoughts or Druansha's or somewhere else entirely.

Druansha's pale cheeks glowed pink. "Yes, I suppose I admired her most of all. She was not at all what my mother had taught me about humans. Boudica was fierce and intelligent and so incredibly loyal to her people and her family, and also to her land. When the invaders threatened to take it from her, she was so determined, so devoted to her purpose. Not for herself, but for others. She saw herself as a guardian only. When she appealed through the druids for my help, I was moved by that purity."

"Is that why you gave her the Fayte Blood?"

"To help her, yes, but also to help the fae. Boudica pledged to protect the land for her people, but I hoped an alliance between us might also make it safe one day for fae kind and others who fled, so we might return one day. That's what my mother never understood. That was always my hope for the Fayte Legacy. I still hope for it. The Fayte Guardians all share the fae blood, but they also share Boudica's blood. You are all her descendants, and in a smaller way, mine too."

How wonderful it would be if her vision could become reality. But if she truly wanted that future, why was our communication so limited? "Why must there be Scryers and Converging Ceremonies? Are they truly necessary?"

"Yes, unfortunately. The barrier between our worlds is thinnest during a New Moon, and while I can communicate with any Fayte Guardian, even ordinary humans with more effort, the Scryers are the most perceptive among you. Over time, it made the interaction easier and kept disagreements to a minimum."

"Disagreements?"

"Faced with the same facts, not everyone arrives at the same interpretation. While I can foresee peril, what I see most often are possibilities not certainties. The closer the event is, the fewer options there might be, but there are always other possibilities."

I thought again of those spectral, overlapping images I'd just seen. "Just now I saw images of the people back home, but they were like ghosts layered over each other. Sometimes they were walking, sometimes sitting. There were so many of them, I didn't know which to focus on."

"That's how it can be. Past, present, future, and possibility always mingle. With practice, you can learn to see the patterns and discern them, but it's never precise or exact."

"What about the Reckoning? Can you see what will happen there?" I immediately regretted the question. How could I worry about myself when Druansha had been focused on far larger issues?

I sensed a sadness within her that deepened my regret. "I'm sorry, but I cannot tell you that."

"No, I'm sorry. I should not have asked."

"I cannot say because I truly don't know. Only the Seilie Ministers hold the strands of fae time. Only they can see the outcomes. That's one of the reasons why Rhilasa despises them."

"Oh. I didn't know."

"My mother fears what she cannot control, and she grows to hate what she fears. When it comes to the Seilies, she has good reason. They are an intractable people, and they have never trusted her."

"Because of the Shadow Rite?"

She cut me a sharp look. "What do you know of that?"

"Nothing, really. Bree's grandmother mentioned that it put your mother and the Seilie High Court at odds."

She sighed. "That is putting it mildly."

I could see the subject agitated her. "We needn't speak of it," I offered gently.

She straightened and swallowed hard. "You have a right to know. When my father discovered my mother in the Gray Woods, she was near death, and he took pity on her. He brought her back to the palace, and the healers all said there was nothing to be done. But my mother whispered to my father of a practice among her people, a way of separating a part of one soul to merge with another. She called it the Shadow Rite. Our healers refused to perform it, but my father begged. Somehow, he had already fallen under her spell that very first day."

"So, a healer Slivered your father for your mother? Was that her first?" Even as I said the words, I knew I shouldn't.

Druansha only shrugged with a sadness that made me want to weep. "It may have been. Or maybe not. After it was done, she returned to full health, and my father rejoiced. It is said they were wed before the next moon."

The story reminded me of the old children's tale of the sleeping princess awakened with her charming prince's kiss. In this case, the charming prince gave far more than a kiss, but I imagined Rhilasa awaking with stars in her eyes just the same. "Were they happy?"

"Perhaps," she said. "For a time. My father only saw the best in her. He made excuses for her. Out of love, I suppose. He clung so desperately to what he wanted her to be that he couldn't see what she truly was. When there were whispers about her need for more Slivers, he refused to believe them. Some accused the Queen of stealing Slivers from him while he slept, but there was never any proof of it. At least none I've found."

"Do you think it's possible?"

"Yes. In a way, I even hope for it, because if it wasn't that, it was probably something far more heinous, and I don't want to believe that, even of Rhilasa."

"I can't imagine what that must have been like for you, living through that."

She sighed. "I suppose that's why I come here, to find solace with the Old Ones. They have always offered comfort, and it was here that I first heard Boudica's call and found my purpose. Looking back, I can see it was also a distraction, and perhaps even selfish. Perhaps I should have done more for my brother. He was so angry with me for leaving him alone with our mother, but she always seemed different with him. I thought he was safe with her because he reminded her of herself. I reminded her of my father, and that, as you can imagine, was a crime by itself. Whatever she may say, she has never wanted me in the palace."

We sat in silence for a long time, watching the stars twinkle in the inky black sky, each of us with our own thoughts, until Druansha let me know it was time to go back.

"I don't want to go," I said. I wasn't trying to be

obstinate, but I feared the Seilie High Court. Here there was only solace.

"You must," she said. "For now, at least. Rhilasa won't rest until we see this through. She will never stop hunting you if we run now."

I tried to envision what awaited me, but I didn't even know where to start. "What will it be like, the Reckoning?"

"I've been told you will be questioned. Each side will be given time to explain her part and declare her truth. The Seilie Ministers will listen, and then they will decide whose cause is just."

Fear stabbed at me again. "Do you know what will happen to me if they side with her? Your mother said it would be terrible."

Druansha didn't lift her gaze. "I imagine it could be. You are tied to us by blood, but, like Rhilasa, the Seilies have never shown any love for humans." I watched despair cloud her eyes. Perhaps it had been a mistake to refuse Rhilasa's offer of a quick death after all.

"To think," I said, "yesterday I was saying goodbye to Balmoral Castle and preparing to return to Windsor. My biggest concern was whether rain would delay my journey by one day or two. I certainly wasn't expecting to be spirited away to"—I opened my arms—"this."

As we stood in the clearing, the dark sky lightened a shade to the east. Day was breaking, and at that moment I wished with every fiber in my body that I could push back the sun. I wanted the night to go on. I never wanted this moment to end.

"We must return," Druansha said, with sadness in her words.

I wanted to be back in my own world with my friends and my family and the kitchen, where my only concern was persuading Lucas to join me at Windsor.

But those wishes were like dreams that flickered away at first light. I might never see Lucas or anyone I loved ever again. I had to accept that. I took a deep breath and turned to Druansha. "You're right. We should go."

"Are you all right?"

I nodded, but in my heart I knew I was lying again. I wasn't all right, and I feared I never would be again.

CHAPTER SIXTEEN

THE SEILIE GUARDS were more cordial than their counterparts in the Brightlands, but they were just as single-minded when it came to carrying out their duties.

It verged on ridiculous to think someone believed I required fourteen of those lofty creatures, all garbed in white and emerald livery with crimson-hilted blades sheathed on both hips, to escort me to the Reckoning. But if that's what they deemed necessary, so be it. I was certainly in no position to argue as they marched me, six on one side of me, six on the other, with one in front and another behind, from my room to someplace deeper in the castle.

At least I wasn't alone. Furtive glances over my shoulder assured me Druansha and Bree remained close by.

To keep my mind off my nerves, I tried to focus on my surroundings. It had been dark when we'd arrived at the castle, but now in the morning sunshine, I could see the castle, which was carved into the steep cliff, had a twin structure on the opposite side of a steep ravine. A bridge of interwoven tree roots and leafy vines linked the two sides, and it was across this bridge that the guards led me now.

On the other side, we ascended a staircase carved into the stone till we reached the very top of the hill and entered what appeared to be a cathedral formed of milky white crystals that jutted from the earth to form the sides of an open-air sanctuary that glowed under the morning rays.

We entered between two towering pillars and moved down the aisle between long wooden benches that were already filled to capacity with hundreds of onlookers, mostly fauns, dwarfs, and fae, with some sprites flying above them, making the place buzz with the hum of whispered chatter.

In front of us, two white banners bore the sigil of seven golden crowns bound together by a red rose and green vines. They hung at either end of a raised dais, where I assumed the seven Seilie Ministers would observe the proceedings.

"The center chair sits higher than the others," I mused aloud. "Why is that?"

"The Ministers rule equally," the guard beside me replied without breaking his marble-like expression, "but for proceedings such as this, they choose one to serve as the High Court's Voice. That one speaks on behalf of all." He directed me to a single seat set in front of the benches on the right side of the aisle, and ushered Druansha and Bree to the bench behind it.

Across the aisle, Queen Rhilasa was already seated with her attendants, including Azender. She watched my entrance with a dismissive smirk.

I swallowed my fear and refused to give her the satisfaction of seeing me squirm. I could at least deny her that.

Now that we were close, I could also see the lectern at the dais's base. Behind it stood an amphibious creature no taller than Bree who wore a black vestment with a white and emerald stole. He flipped through the pages of a massive book while holding a monocle to one bulbous eye.

My nerves were starting to get the better of me. With Druansha and Bree behind me, I felt alone. Exposed. It wasn't fair, I told myself. Was I a prisoner? Was I already presumed guilty?

You are guilty.

The inner voice was my own, but I resented it none the less. So I sat, fidgeting with the folds of my skirts and gazing around at the crowded benches as my guards retreated to positions along the perimeter.

The room quieted, and when I glanced up to see why, I saw seven robed figures garbed in crimson vestments trimmed in gold approach the dais in single file. Each wore a slender golden band over long raven hair that was as glossy and straight as Rhilasa's pale tresses yet with the same porcelain complexion. It was impossible to distinguish whether they were male or female, or perhaps both or neither. Who knew if those designations held any meaning for their kind at all?

Once they were seated, the amphibian removed his monocle and cleared his throat. "Who invokes the Reckoning at this gathering of the Seilie High Court?" His voice bellowed more robustly than his diminutive size would suggest possible.

Druansha cleared her throat behind me. When I glanced back, she gestured anxiously for me to stand.

Immediately, I rose. "I do, your honor."

Muffled snickers filled the room.

"Arbiter will do," he corrected.

"Yes, sorry," I stammered, a red-hot flush taking over my cheeks. "I do, Arbiter. I invoke the Reckoning."

Derisive murmurs stirred from Rhilasa's section, but I did my best to ignore them. I kept my eyes on the gentlemanly amphibian as he flipped a page of the great book before him and clapped his hands swiftly to quiet the chatter. "The Accused shall remain standing during the Recitation."

When he looked at me, I glanced back at Druansha and Bree. Druansha nodded, reassuring me and urging me to follow his command.

I squared myself to the Arbiter and the row of inscrutable Seilie Ministers watching me and pretended not to hear the derisive remarks coming from the Queen's section.

The amphibian lifted his monocle to his eye again and squinted at me. "You are the Accused?"

Chuckles erupted along the Queen's rows. I clasped my hands behind my back and willed myself to remain calm. "I am, Arbiter."

"Please state your name for the record."

Again, I glanced back at Druansha. Again, she nodded.

"My name is Jane Shackle."

The Arbiter nodded. "Jane Shackle, you are hereby accused of the malicious killing of Krolaidh, first son and heir of the Brightlands, who was also your own father."

Gasps erupted in the hall, but the Ministers remained unmoved. My heart thudded in my chest, though I forced myself to appear unaffected.

"In addition," the amphibian continued, "you are accused of showing no remorse or contrition for the act, and let it be noted that the Accused tried to escape before facing this tribunal, and Queen Rhilasa's forces were forced to recapture—"

"I did not try to escape!"

The amphibian raised a hand and scowled at me. "Silence!"

Behind me, I heard a dozen or more footsteps, all in unison. When I glanced back, Seilie guards had advanced on me with their palms wrapped around their crimson hilts.

Druansha shot up. "Ministers, I assure you force is not necessary. Jane is merely a stranger here and unaware of our ways. She will not make the error again."

From the dais, the one sitting in the seat of the High Court's Voice lifted a polished black stone and hit it twice upon a small block in front of him. It must have been a signal to the guards, for they pivoted and returned to their places.

"Arbiter," the Court Voice said calmly in a deep, resonant tenor.

The amphibian bowed to the dais. "Minister?"

The High Court's Voice looked to the peers on one side then the other. Though nothing was spoken and their expressions remained unchanged, some understanding must have passed between them. To the Arbiter, the High Court's Voice said, "The Court shall dispense with the formalities, so we may hear the accusation from the aggrieved party directly."

Queen Rhilasa, who had scooted forward in her seat and grimaced at the interruption, now steepled her fingers in front of herself and smiled. "A splendid idea."

The Arbiter wheeled around and pointed a webbed finger at her. "Silence!"

If the reproach was intended to intimidate her as it had me, it seemed to have the opposite effect. She beamed with self-satisfaction. Azender whispered into her ear.

The High Court's Voice noted their interaction with a frown.

The Arbiter bowed again to the dais. "It shall be so," then he turned back to Queen Rhilasa. "The Accuser may now address the Court."

I sat as she rose and stepped forward. She brushed a fingertip across her brow, smoothing her long, pale hair alongside the sharp lines of her face.

"It is with the greatest regret that I bring this grievance to the High Court's attention. It was not my wish to waste your valuable time on this personal tragedy, but as you know, the matter was taken out of my hands. It was my intention to handle it in my own way, which I was well within my rights to do—"

"If you'll pardon the interruption, Your Majesty," the Arbiter said, "but do please limit your testimony to the accusation you are bringing before the High Court. The Ministers, as you know, will decide what is and is not within your lawful rights."

The Queen shifted, obviously dismayed by the correction. "The human killed my beloved son, and she must be punished. The rightful punishment for a death is death, as it has always been and how it rightfully should be."

"Yes, we understand that is your view," the Arbiter responded. "Could you tell us how you came to the opinion that the Accused intended to kill Krolaidh?"

A flurry of new murmurs erupted in the chamber. The Queen straightened and seemed to take offense at the question.

"It is not my opinion, Arbiter. The human admits it. Ask her yourself!"

"We shall when you yield your time. Do you yield?"

The Queen cast a haughty glance around the room, daring anyone to meet it. Those I could see turned away, including myself.

"I yield." The words dripped with venom.

"Very good," the Arbiter replied. "The Accused shall rise."

I stood and looked for Druansha's reassurance again. She wasn't smiling, but she wasn't frowning, either. A knot in my chest tightened.

"Do you admit to taking the heir's life?" he asked me plainly.

The murmurs behind me halted again.

"I do not deny killing Krolaidh," I said.

Gasps erupted and new chatter followed.

"But I was only defending myself," I added forcefully.

I glanced around at the faces aimed my direction. When I searched for guidance from Druansha, she urged me to continue. I steeled my nerves and turned back to the Seilie Ministers.

"Why were you defending yourself?" the Arbiter asked.

"He was trying to kill me. He'd already killed many others, and for no apparent reason at all. They were helping him. He did it out of sheer..." The word that came to mind was evil, but I couldn't say it. After everything he'd done to me and to my mother, after all the pain and destruction he'd caused, he was still my father.

"Out of sheer what?" the Arbiter pressed.

"Sheer anger. He was incredibly angry because I prevented him from Slivering my Queen."

The murmurs started up again, and all around, eyes shot to Queen Rhilasa.

"I speak of Queen Victoria of the British Empire," I added before anyone could misconstrue my meaning. "Krolaidh meant to give her Sliver to his mother and possess the body for himself, intending to take her power as an act of revenge on his sister."

"He told you this?" The question came not from the Arbiter but from the High Court's Voice himself. The sharp line of those slender black eyebrows pulled low with disbelief.

"He did, Minister. He most certainly did."

The High Court's Voice said nothing, but the other Ministers bent their heads together and whispered.

"The human lies!"

Queen Rhilasa's outburst stunned us all. In an instant, she was on her feet and glaring at me. Pure hatred flashed in her eyes.

I straightened and lifted my chin. "It is not a lie. He hated me and my world, and he took pleasure in the havoc he caused. I don't regret ending him, and I would do it again if he forced me to it."

The High Court's Voice sat back and considered me for a moment, then leaned forward again. "You feel no remorse, then?"

I glanced back and saw that Bree's eyes were wide with fear. Druansha's pained expression worried me even more. What could I say? I had vowed to speak the truth, and this was my truth: "No, Minister, I have no remorse."

Again, gasps filled the space.

The Arbiter shook his head. "You profess no remorse, and you sought to escape before the Queen could bring you to these proceedings?"

"No, I never tried to escape."

"She's lying again," Queen Rhilasa declared. "You can ask my guards. You can ask any one of them."

The mood in the High Court was turning. Whatever support I had was slipping.

"It's not true," I countered. "There's proof."

"What proof?" Rhilasa sneered.

I whipped around and held Bree's gaze. *Tell them!*

She rose to her feet and straightened herself to her full height. "She's right. We weren't running away. We were always going to return. It's all a misunderstanding."

The Queen laughed, a harsh, mirthless laugh. "Oh, of course. Well, if a handmaiden says it's a misunderstanding, it certainly must be."

The Arbiter pounded his lectern again. "Silence! There will be silence."

"May I have the High Court's attention?"

The new voice was so quiet, I wasn't sure of its origin until Bree exclaimed, "Gran!"

And there she was, standing among the crowd seated behind us. Her crown of gray hair and horns were covered with an ivory lace shawl.

"The Gallery must remain silent!" The Arbiter

pounded his lectern again and tugged at his collar.

Undeterred, the old faun called out more loudly, "The Accused and my granddaughter left the Queen's caravan to visit me yesterday, and they always intended to return. But you do not need to take my word for it. There is proof, if you will allow me to explain."

The din around us died down. She'd piqued the crowd's interest, and mine as well.

"The Arbiter told you to be silent, Grinella Obble of Spire Point," Queen Rhilasa sneered. "Yes, I know who you are."

A chill passed through me at the threat in those words.

The High Court's voice said, "Arbiter, please approach the dais."

The amphibian adjusted his black cloak before walking back and gazing up at the seven Seilie Ministers.

Quiet words were exchanged, or rather, the High Court's Voice spoke and the Arbiter nodded. Finally, the amphibian stepped back and said, "Of course. Exactly as you say, Ministers."

Back at his lectern, he addressed the crowd. "Will the witness step forward?"

Grinella smiled with satisfaction as she shuffled past her seated neighbors, made her way to the aisle, then approached the Arbiter.

"If you will, state your full name and relationship to the proceedings."

Behind me, I could hear Bree wobbling on the edge of her seat. I heard her whisper, "I hope she knows what she's doing."

The old faun, however, looked calm and confident.

"She appears quite capable," I whispered back, though I don't know if that gave Bree any comfort at all.

Standing at the end of the aisle, Bree's grandmother wrapped her fingers around the wooden rail as though she were on a ship approaching treacherous seas.

"My name is Grinella Obble, and I live in Spire Point Village at the edge of the Brightlands. Young Jane—forgive me, the Accused—visited my home yesterday with my granddaughter, who works in the palace. At the end of the visit, they returned to the Queen's caravan, as was always their intention."

"Very good, Madame Obble," the Arbiter said. "But you mentioned there was some proof of what you say."

"Yes, the proof." She glanced down as if bracing herself. "During their visit, I learned of the human's most unusual talent."

The Arbiter leaned forward and focused intently on the old faun. "Could you elaborate please?"

"Yes, of course. What I discovered, and what can provide irrefutable proof of the truth, is the fact that the Accused is a Reader."

CHAPTER SEVENTEEN

WITH NARROWED EYES, the High Court's Voice shot a furious look at Queen Rhilasa. "Did you know she was a Reader?"

The Queen stared back at him. "It's impossible. She's a human."

The Seilie Minister glared at her for a long moment. Then, he—assuming he was a he, which still was not a certainty—turned to the Arbiter. "Bring the Accused forward." The immortal fae rose from the dais and made his way down to our level.

The Arbiter, in a panic, waved me forward.

I froze, then turned to Druansha.

She nodded, though I could see she was nervous too. Slowly, reluctantly, I made my way to the amphibian.

When the High Court's Voice approached, I could see how impossibly tall he was, taller than Druansha, and I couldn't help but stare at what a remarkable creature he was.

"That a half-fae, such as you, has the gift is quite remarkable," he said when I approached him. "How did you come by it?"

His words mesmerized me. I had to force myself to remain focused on what he said and to form a reply. "My mother was a Reader, sir."

"Was? No longer?"

I winced. "Yes, she still is, I suppose. It's difficult to say. I've only recently found her." I wanted to condemn Queen Rhilasa right there for that crime but feared it might undermine my cause.

The immortal fae's gaze found Druansha, and something unspoken passed between them.

"You are a Fayte Guardian, then?" he said. "That is what Druansha's people are called in your world, are they not?"

"Yes, we are Fayte Guardians." How odd it felt to count myself among them so easily. Though I'd only discovered them recently, I suppose I had been destined to be one since birth.

His gaze dropped to my gloves. "Do you wear those to hide your gift?"

I lifted my hands and turned them front to back, considering the ivory leather from both sides. "It has not always been a gift. Until recently, it was a terrible nuisance, if you want to know the truth."

The answer seemed to surprise him. "But not now?"

"No, Minister, not always. Shall I remove my gloves?"

"If you wouldn't mind. It will make the next part easier."

I wanted to know what the next part would be, but I was too frightened to ask. Sticking the gloves in my waistband, I held out my bare hands, palms down.

His long, smooth fingers wound around mine, sending a cool shiver shooting to my elbows and my shoulders then all the way down to my toes. When I saw wisps of emerald light flow out of his fingertips and envelop my hands, I tensed. The memory of Krol's crimson tendrils when the tree root attacked me on the Windsor Castle slope was still fresh, yet somehow my alarm dissipated almost as quickly. It was the Seilie's doing, I knew, as I watched his light twist and turn around my limbs.

Close your eyes.

It was his deep, commanding voice inside my mind, and it calmed me.

I tried to resist, but even as I strained to keep my eyes open, I could feel them closing and a darkness taking hold. I fell into a swirling that was far more powerful than the onset of a vision. At first, I feared I'd lose my balance, but his fingers tightened around mine and steadied me. I leaned into his touch and the warmth of that mystical light.

When the disorientation subsided, I was standing near the fountain in Windsor's East Terrace. It was nighttime, just as it had been when Lucas had embraced me there, but it wasn't Lucas standing with me now. It was the Seilie Minister, and he still had me in his grasp.

Is this place special to you?

His lips hadn't moved, but it was his voice again within my mind.

I know this place. I thought the words and tried to suppress the memory, embarrassed by the intimacy of Lucas's tender lips coming so close to my own.

I tried to push the image away.

There is no judgment.

He was there, in my mind. He already knew.

I want you to experience a place that gives you solace before you return to that moment when Krolaidh perished.

He must have felt me tense because he made a gentle *tsk* sound.

I don't want to go back there.

Only for a moment. Show me what you have told us, that his intent was to harm you and others. It will make this proceeding much easier. Yes, I thought that would appeal to you.

He was right. I wished for this all to be finished. I wanted to return to my mother.

Your mother? We will return to that. First, show me Krolaidh.

How can I take you there? I've never done this.

I sensed his relief. He hadn't been sure I'd agree.

You need only think of the moment. Remember it as fully as you are able. See the surroundings, recall what you can.

I cleared my mind of everything else and tried to choose a single moment. But which one? Which would show him at his most threatening?

The moment in the Balmoral Fayte's Sanctum came to mind. When I rushed in to find him attacking Druansha, her gown ripped and blood smeared along her arm. I recalled the mist all around us and the awful fear that nearly paralyzed me.

You were there but not there? Incorporeal? How can that be?

The Fayte Guardians call it phantom walking. One's inner self separates from the physical body.

I recalled all the hours spent in Mrs. Bellington's cottage practicing. I'd feared I wouldn't manage the separation long enough to save Queen Victoria…

Come back to the moment.

His words broke my distraction. I returned my thoughts to that moment with Krol, how he had threatened Druansha and me and how he had nearly killed us both. When Druansha had left and taken Krol's Faytling ring, stranding him in the human realm, I showed the Seilie how the mist had cleared and we exploited Krol's vulnerability.

Mmm, yes, I see. His anger made him reckless.

When Krol finally collapsed, I tried to suppress the relief it gave me. I focused on rushing out before my own body was buried in the rubble.

That vision faded, and I was again standing with the Seilie at the Windsor fountain, hearing the water splash and feeling the frigid night air tingle my cheeks. It was a welcome balm for my frayed nerves.

I know that was not easy. We may stay here, if you like, until you are ready to return to the Reckoning.

I closed my eyes and wished it were Lucas standing with me. Wishing he was not so far away. Yet there was still so much to do before I could return. I had to release my mother, and I had to find his Sliver. I didn't want to return without it.

Rhilasa took a human Sliver?

The Seilie's question jarred me. I'd lost myself in thoughts of Lucas.

Yes, Minister.

Were there others? How many?

Slivers? I don't know. Lucas. My mother. Possibly more.

His manner changed. Anger flowed from him like waves crashing against the shore. It frightened me.

Druansha might know better. Perhaps she could answer the question better than I.

There is a better way. Open your eyes when you are ready to return.

He released my hands, and the strands of emerald light receded with him.

I wanted to stay at the Windsor fountain, to remain immersed in that memory, but I was only prolonging the inevitable. I opened my eyes.

The return to the Reckoning was more disorienting than leaving it. The Arbiter stood in front of me, Druansha beside me. Above, the other Seilie Ministers stared down, their gazes heavy as stones, but not upon me. They were watching the High Court's Voice, who had moved to Queen Rhilasa's side of the chamber.

Once my disorientation subsided, I could hear his words.

"I have viewed the events from the Accused's perspective. Would you allow me to view them from yours, Queen Rhilasa?"

She sat with straightened back upon her bench, watching him as though she were considering his request.

Azender, who stood behind her, leaned into her ear and whispered. The Queen's gaze narrowed as her minion prattled on until she lifted a finger to quiet him. Then she stood to face the Seilie.

"That should not be necessary. I was not present, as you are aware. What view could I offer?"

"Your own. I would like to see anything that might offer some insight into your son's reasons for going to the human world. Something that might reveal his state of mind, which might aid your cause."

A sly smiled crept across her face. "My cause? Yes. I would be happy to share that with you." With a flourish of her wrist, she presented her hand to the immortal fae.

I watched for a stirring in his expression. I watched as riveted as everyone else in the chamber as he took her hand, just as he had taken mine, and the glowing emerald strands stretched from him and wound around her limb.

A struggle played out on the smooth surface of his face, but he said nothing. I could only imagine the silent communication transpiring between them.

We all watched as the Queen winced and tried to pull her hands away. The High Court's Voice held firm. When she realized he was holding her against her will, her eyes flew open in sheer terror.

"Let me go!" she roared, sending her attendants flying to their feet. That flurry of action caused a similar reaction among the Seilie guards who stood at the entrance and along the walls.

"What's happening?' I whispered to Druansha. But by then, her mother had wrenched herself free and pulled away from the Seilie Minister. Her attendants, eager to defend her, formed a protective circle around her.

"Release her," the High Court's Voice commanded, and when they did not, he made a flourishing gesture that sent a host of guards to do it.

Before they could breach the circle that had formed

around her, a cloud of sparkling turquoise smoke surrounded her, enveloping her completely in a flash of lights and glowing tendrils, all swirling at furious speed around her.

I might have thought it part of the proceedings if Druansha hadn't tried to push through the crowd in a frenzy.

The High Court's Voice motioned his guards more forcefully. "Grab her! Do not allow her to escape!"

That word sent the full chamber into disarray. More of Rhilasa's attendants rushed from their seats to block the guards who were heading toward the Queen, pushing them aside.

"You promised justice for my son," the Queen bellowed from within that cyclone of swirling light. "This is not justice. You have no care for the Prince of the Brightlands."

The High Court's Voice glared and yelled back, "You have lied to us, Rhilasa. For years, you have lied. You prey on innocent lives to feed your wicked appetite. When Kravol made you his bride, you vowed right here before this Court never to Sliver in the Brightlands. You swore it."

Everyone stopped, even the Brightlanders. They all waited for her response.

"I have kept my promise. I have never Slivered a Brightlander. I have only taken from humans."

"That is a lie," he shouted. "Fae blood flows through the humans you harvested. You took from Druansha's people."

For a long moment, Queen Rhilasa stood with a smoldering expression. Then she sneered. "You have no proof of it, and you never will. But mark my words, the half-breed must be punished for her crime. If you will not do it, you leave me no choice." At that, she held out both arms, as if commanding the swirling turquoise light to engulf her completely.

When the Seilie guards finally broke through the circle to grab her, they were swatting only at sparks and smoke. Their hands came back empty. When the smoke parted, we could see—we all could see—there was nothing there.

Queen Rhilasa was gone.

The Seilie High Court hall erupted in a roar of chaos and confusion. Guards shouted for the Queen to reveal herself. Queen Rhilasa's people screamed back at the guards, accusing them of spiriting her away, although we could all plainly see they hadn't.

I went to where Druansha stood apart from the crowd, observing the commotion with a keen eye.

"Where did she go?" I asked.

"I wish I knew."

The High Court's Voice returned to the dais to confer with the others before retaking his seat. He raised his arms. "Hear me!" he shouted, his voice rising above the chamber's din.

The demand quieted a few, but not all, so he repeated himself even more loudly. That stopped everyone.

His gaze brushed over the pandemonium. "The Brightlands Queen shall not make a mockery of the High Court. Not only has she failed to live up to the promises she made to us in the past, but she has shown no remorse for that deception. She may elude us for now, but the High Court will not rest until she is brought to justice."

The rows of stoic Seilie Ministers nodded in measured agreement as the guards put the Queen's people into chains.

"What will happen to us?" I whispered to Druansha.

She scanned the chamber and shook her head. "I truly don't know."

The Arbiter, who had joined us, glanced up, his expression fraught. "This is most unusual. Most unusual, indeed!"

The High Court's Voice struck his black stone three times for silence. When the noise died down, he motioned to the Arbiter to return to his lectern. When the amphibian did so, the Seilie cleared his throat. "We declare that with the absence of an Accuser, the High Court shall consider the claim against the Accused abandoned and the matter closed."

Bree and a good number of onlookers in the gallery applauded wildly.

"And," he continued, once the uproar had died down, "I believe this can be returned to its rightful owner." He lifted his hand with a flourish, and something gold glinted in his palm. My Faytling!

With another graceful turn of his wrist it was gone, and I felt it, descending from its leather cord around my neck. I clutched it with both hands, feeling the rush of its familiar weight upon my chest.

"Thank you!" I cried.

Druansha stepped forward. "If the proceedings are concluded, Minister, may Jane return to her own world?"

"No!" I lurched to stop her. "I cannot go yet. You know that."

Druansha pulled away.

"My mother," I begged. "I cannot leave without her or Lucas's Sliver."

She shook her head. "Leave that to me. This place is not safe for you."

I stood firm. "I won't leave. I'm going back to the palace, with or without your help."

Druansha was pleading now. "My mother has surely barricaded herself there. If you try to approach, she will attack. You will have no defense."

"Minister? If I may have a word." Azender waved a hand, which made his chains rattle behind the line of Seilie guards. "I may have something to offer this discussion."

The High Court's Voice stared down at him.

"Approach." His tone held a warning.

Two guards walked Azender forward, and more roughly than was necessary.

"Thank you, Minister," Azender said, as obsequious as ever. He bowed to Druansha before addressing her. "Your Highness, if I may, I know of ways to enter the palace that are not, shall we say, *known* to many. There is a particular passageway that leads to the, uh, chamber to which I believe the young Princess wishes to visit."

Druansha regarded him coolly. "And why would you tell me this? Why would you offer to help us at all?"

He threw up his hands, or tried to, since they were still chained. "She'll leave me here to rot. I don't want to waste away in a Seilie dungeon. When she left, she betrayed me too."

Druansha looked back at me. Her eyes seemed to ask the question, *What do you think?*

So much had happened. So much had gone wrong. The question weighed heavily on me as I stared at the ground. At my feet. At my hands.

I turned to Azender. "There is a way you can prove what you say. Are you willing?"

"What do you mean?" he demanded.

Druansha's smile told me she knew exactly what I intended to do.

"Allow me to Read you, and I will know if you mean to deceive us."

"Read me?" He tried to step back, but the guards blocked him. "Is that necessary? I've given my word."

Druansha scoffed. "Do you think your word counts for anything?"

Even as he stood there, I could see he was trying to formulate a new plan, some new scheme, but then his shoulders sank. He knew he was out of options. "Fine, then. Read me, if you must."

CHAPTER EIGHTEEN

THE FLIGHT BACK to the Brightlands upon Druansha's dragon back was easier than the ride to the Old Ones' Grove. I knew how to keep a grip on her long mane and lean deep into the curve of her neck.

It wasn't so easy for Bree and Azender.

The terrified squeals began soon after Druansha lifted off from Seilie Castle's terrace.

"Don't be frightened, Bree," I yelled over my shoulder. I'd hiked myself up into the flowing blue-purple mane, since that's where the wind could be the worst. I had to spit away loose strands of hair coming loose from my knot and blowing across my face. "Just hold tight, like I showed you."

"I know," Bree shouted back. "I'm not the one screaming."

Behind her I could see what she meant. Azender had hunched so low he had practically disappeared in the shaggy fur along Druansha's back, and his lips were stretched in an expression of utter fear. When Druansha banked gently to the left, he clenched and wailed again.

"She won't let you fall," I called back. "You'll be fine;

just hold tight."

The elder faun didn't answer so much as whimper, but there was little else I could do. Instead, I closed my eyes and tried silently to ask Druansha to take it even easier, if possible.

Just before sundown, the Brightlands Palace came into view. I turned back again to see if Azender was doing any better. He was still pressed against Druansha's hide and his eyes were closed, though they were clenched so tightly I knew he wasn't asleep.

"We're nearly there," I said to reassure him. "If you look, you can see the palace."

His fingers dug deeper into Druansha's fur, and he shook his head. "Tell me when we land."

Bree rolled her eyes. "It won't be long now. You've made it this far. I daresay you'll make it the rest."

"Easy for you to say," he groused. "You have the full strength of youth in your grip. Appreciate it while you can. It'll be gone soon enough, mark my words."

"You're hardly ancient, Mr. Azender," she said. "And you can open your eyes now. We're here."

When Druansha touched down on the open lawn behind the palace, I expected Azender to be the first to jump down to the solid ground, but Bree slid off first.

She moved below him and tapped the back of his hoof. "It's all right, Mr. Azender. You can let go now."

He pulled his head away from Druansha's back, but only far enough to peer over the side of her dragon haunches. When he noticed us watching him, he straightened. "Why, that was no trouble at all," he declared with sudden confidence. "I told you, Bree, hardly worth all your fuss."

"My fuss?" she shot back.

He ignored her, instead making a show of dusting himself off and composing himself.

I could see Bree had more to say, but she held it back.

"Stay close to him," I whispered. She nodded as I made my way down as well.

Once free of her passengers, Druansha swung back her head and held me with her dragon gaze. *You three go ahead.*

Why? Where are you going?

I want to check the grounds and see what Rhilasa has been up to. I'll find you soon. Go to your mother.

I nodded again and touched her cheek, where the deep blue fur extended like whiskers. I pulled back my hand, embarrassed that I'd taken such a liberty. "I'm so sorry. I shouldn't have done that."

It's all right. Truly. She followed the unspoken message with a sweet smile that crinkled her golden eyes.

Before I could thank her, she set off, flapping her grand wings, and rose back into the sky.

It was time to find my mother.

"How do we get to the passage you mentioned?" I asked Azender when I caught up to them.

The courtier searched the edges of the open field. "There's a gatehouse, an ancient thing, just beyond the lane. Perhaps you two should go ahead. I'd only slow you down. My limbs, you know, they aren't what they used to be."

"That's convenient," Bree mumbled.

"Convenience has nothing to do with it, I assure you," he spat back.

"We will all go together," I said. When he tried to argue, I cut him off. "No one is staying behind."

"Heartless," he muttered.

As we reached the edge of a grove, we spied a narrow tower nearly hidden among the trees. Azender perked. "That's it. I remember now."

He directed us to the simple stone building, which was not much wider than its door. I walked around it, searching for anything suspicious before trying the knob.

It opened easily, but when I poked my head inside,

there was nothing more than four bare walls. "You're sure this is it?"

"Of course, I am. But there should be a second door inside." He glanced down and touched his forehead. "Oh, gracious, I just remembered. The Queen used her Life Crystal to reveal it. I'd forgotten that."

Bree shook her head. "Did you really forget? Or has this been a trick from the start?"

She had good reason to be concerned, but I wasn't ready to give up. I lifted my Faytling from around my neck.

"What are you doing there?" The old faun peered over my shoulder.

"I'm trying something. Step back, if you would. Give me a bit of room." I touched the back wall with the Faytling in my hand and silently asked it to show me any hidden doors.

At that, a dot of fiery light appeared on the bare wall that grew into the shape of a door.

"What is that?" Azender demanded. "What did you do?"

I closed my fist around my stone. "It's a gift from Druansha."

"But it's not the Queen's crystal. It shouldn't have worked."

Bree had been right. He never thought we'd get this far. He thought we'd be stuck out here, unable to enter the palace. He probably expected we'd simply let him go free. There wasn't time to be angry, however. I pushed the door open to reveal a stairway cut into the bare earth that descended downward. "Is this the passage the Queen used?"

"It is." The answer was forced, and I was sure he would have lied again if he thought he could get away with it.

"Then we should hurry." I tightened my grip on my

Faytling and led the way down.

When I didn't hear anything behind me, I turned back. Bree and Azender were watching me from the threshold.

"Come on," I urged. "I can't do this alone."

"But are you sure it's safe?" Bree was tapping the earthen wall of the tunnel and looking at it like it might cave in at any moment. Finally, she stepped in.

Azender was another matter. He scratched his chin whiskers. "You no longer require my assistance, do you? I've gotten you to the tunnel. I've done my part." He backed away.

Bree grabbed his arm. "You said you'd take us to the Collection Room, and that's what you're going to do. Who knows where this tunnel goes. It could be a trap for all we know."

He tried to yank his arm back, but she was stronger.

"You misunderstand," he grumbled after he'd stumbled forward. "Of course I'll accompany you. I never meant to imply otherwise."

I was close to losing my patience, but Bree was right. We did need him. "Could we please hurry? Just get us to the Collection Room and we're done."

Bree didn't give him a chance to answer. She pushed him in front of her, and I stepped behind him, so he was in the lead. When Bree pulled the doorway closed behind us, total darkness enveloped us.

I lifted my Faytling and made it glow.

The pinkish light illuminated their faces.

"How does it do that?" Azender's curiosity was obviously piqued despite his grousing.

"I learned it from the Fayte Guardians."

His lips tucked into a dismissive sneer as we reached the final step, which was clear enough in the Faytling's light. "The Fayte Guardians, yes, I've heard of them. Druansha's people. The humans who believe those tiny drops of fae blood make them special. Do you even know what Fayte means?"

"I would imagine it's the name Druansha gave them." I raised the Faytling to illuminate the tunnel's width, which could nearly accommodate us walking side by side, but its ceiling was lost in the darkness above.

"Hardly," he said with an unkind chuckle. "It's the term for impure fae. Crossbreeds but even that seems too generous for what they are. They started with such a tiny bit of fae blood, and yet generation after generation, so many of them dilute it further by mingling with ordinary humans. Do any of them even have fae abilities anymore? I doubt it. You aren't really one of them, you know. You are far more than that. I'm sure that's why they have such need of you."

Did they have need of me? I suppose my father's fae lineage influenced my abilities, but even if more fae blood coursed through my veins, I was still a Fayte Guardian. Despite my gifts, I had so much to learn from Mrs. Crossey and the others.

"How they must covet your fae blood," he added.

"They don't." I didn't try to hide my irritation. "The Fayte Guardians hardly even need any magic. Druansha's prophecies are helpful, that's true, but the Guardians' true strength is their ability to move freely and unnoticed through the castles as servants. To hide in plain sight, you might say. We hear things and see things, and our sheer numbers make just about anything possible."

"Still, your Guardians, they are trying to be fae, are they not? With their spells and their potions and whatnot. It's sad, really."

"Is it?" It was difficult to keep my voice even and not betray the rage mounting within me. "Is that the way you feel? Serving a fae queen but not being fae yourself. Does it bother you that she's never shared a drop of her powerful blood with you?"

"Of course not! I would never ask for such a thing. It's

"It truly is a wonder," Azender added with unabashed admiration.

Bree was staring, too, her eyes wider than I've ever seen them. "It's not a wonder, Mr. Azender," she said. "That's our Spire Point Crystal!"

CHAPTER NINETEEN

BREE RUSHED PAST me to where the water's edge met the sandy soil. She dipped her fingers, creating concentric ripples that twisted through the color spectrum as they moved across the pool.

"Get out of there!" Azender shouted. "That's not for you. That's the Queen's pool."

Bree wheeled around. "Why is Spire Point's crystal here? It was intended for the King's memorial."

Azender's anger melted into something more like guilt. "Yes, that was to be its purpose before the Queen discovered its other qualities."

Bree lifted her hand and shook away the wetness.

Azender jumped back. "Don't fling that around. You can't fathom the water's power."

Bree glared at him. "But I do. This Spire served our village for as long as I can remember, as long as my grandmother can remember."

"That was before she..." Azender stopped midsentence. For a half-second, he looked like he wanted to grab those words and stuff them back into his mouth.

Bree's glare hardened. "Before she did what, old faun?"

"Something she learned from the old alchemist, no doubt. I've seen her dip her Life Crystal into that water. It makes the thing shine brighter than the sun."

Bree scoffed. "Of course. A crystal bath primes the stones. My grandmother and the other village sages took turns throughout the year. She always took whatever crystals we had in the house. She said it made them stronger. I'll show you. Give me yours."

She thrust her palm at me.

"What will it do?" I pulled my Faytling to my chest.

"Increases its power. That's all."

She thrust her hand at me again. Reluctantly, I placed the stone in her hand. She took it by the leash and held it over the water. It was already glowing, but when the stone touched the water's surface, it sent off a ring of light that nearly knocked me backward.

Bree steadied herself. "That's never happened before."

When she pulled the stone up, she examined it closely.

I peered over her shoulder. "Is something wrong? Do you see something?"

"It looks the same, but it feels different. Heavier." She raised it and lowered it again like a weight before handing it back to me. "The next time you use it, be careful."

Taking it back, I could feel the difference too. It was heavier. Not by a lot, but enough to notice.

"We shouldn't linger here." Azender ushered us around the water's edge.

That was fine with me. I wanted to see my mother. "How much farther is it?"

"Not far at all," he said. "This is it." He pointed to a round door carved into a solid black stone wall a few paces ahead. When he took the handle and pulled, it didn't budge. He patted around the edges, seeking a mechanism or latch. "I don't recall it being locked."

"May I look?" As I took his place at the handle, the Faytling brightened in my hand. Then the space above the handle undulated as if the rock had turned to liquid. The image of a dragon emerged.

I slid the Faytling over that image, and when it touched the dragon's mouth, it notched in, like the door locks of Balmoral Fayte Hall. At that instant, something moved deep within the wall. We heard a clank and a grind, then the door sprang away from the wall.

"How did you do that?" Azender's bushy eyebrows pulled together.

I pulled the Faytling back. "Another trick the Fayte Guardians taught me."

"Is it now?" He frowned and pushed his way through the open door.

He was annoying, but it didn't matter now. All that mattered was we were close. We had to be.

The old faun led us to a narrow corridor with stone walls as dark as the Collection Room with torches fixed at intervals. He lifted one from its holder and held it high.

"Are you sure this is the way?" I asked.

He turned and offered me the torch. "If you don't trust me, I'm happy to step aside."

"Sorry," I said. "I'm just eager to get there."

Bree leaned in. "Of course, we trust you. We never would have found this place without you." She glanced back at me, rolled her eyes, and mouthed the word ego.

The flattery worked. He resumed the trek upward without another gripe, and we fell in step behind him. After a bend in the corridor, the passage narrowed, forcing us to proceed in single file.

Azender brushed his fingertips over the glossy black walls on our right. "Hm, yes, this is the way," he muttered to himself. "There will be another staircase."

When the steps appeared, they were narrow and steep. At the top, Bree whispered at my shoulder, "Are you all right, mistress?"

"Just catching my breath." I fanned my hand in front

of my face to cool myself, then hurried to catch up to Azender.

He moved with the fingers of one hand holding the torch, and the others trailing along the wall. I didn't know what he was doing until he stopped and ran his fingers around a particular brick, twice, then three times. He was searching for something, and he'd found it.

Slowly, he pressed his whole hand against that brick and pushed forward. The movement triggered several others to move in unison, creating a small doorway.

"This is it," he said triumphantly before disappearing over the threshold.

Bree and I followed and found ourselves in a room full of cabinets and cages and scattered crates and jars. I recognized it was the Collection Room, but it was as if a hurricane had come through, and the heavy reek of smoke made it difficult to breathe.

With Azender's torch and my Faytling held high, we took in the damage. The cages that had been pushed against the walls were overturned and tossed across the floor. Shelves had been yanked from the walls and the contents of drawers strewn across the room.

I ran to the cage where I'd left my mother, but it was gone. I searched around and found it hurled several feet away.

"Mother!" I screamed the word, again and again.

"She is no longer here."

The whisper was so faint I wasn't sure I'd heard it at all.

"Who said that?"

From the shadows, a figure stepped forward. I recognized the shuffling gait and the drag of the cane. The alchemist.

"What happened to her? Where is she?" My voice sounded shrill even to my own ears, but I couldn't help it. I had to know before despair swept me away.

The old man slumped onto a stool. His robes scorched and blackened. His beard entirely singed away on one side, leaving burns and blisters from his cheek to his ear. "She begged me…" His weak voice gave out.

I moved closer with caution. "Begged you to what?"

His chest heaved and he raised those milky white eyes to me. "To give you… this." He lifted his left hand, which was wrapped around one of the diamond-shaped vials. Inside, ribbons of shimmery white swirled in a translucent liquid. A Sliver!

I took it with both hands and lifted it, examining it more closely. "Is it hers? Did this belong to my mother?"

"She said… you must… return it." His shoulders slouched forward, and his head bowed. Whatever was left of that man was gone in that final breath.

"Is it hers?" I demanded, knowing he wouldn't answer.

"What happened here?" Bree paced beside me like she was sleepwalking, her fingertips trailing over the charred surfaces of what remained.

When she passed my mother's cage, I saw something red and wet near the open door. Was it blood? I held the Sliver in one hand and used my teeth to tug off the glove on the other. I pressed a bare finger to the droplets. The room grew blurry and shifted beneath me. A vision was coming, and I braced for it.

When the haze cleared, I saw the room as it had been before the destruction. My mother was in her cage, as I'd seen her before, and Queen Rhilasa was there too, pacing. She was screaming, but the words didn't make sense. They were still muddled and unclear. I searched the room and saw the old man standing in the back corner. He was the object of her wrath. His chin rested on his chest and both hands wrapped around the cane planted in front of him. He was letting the Queen rant.

I focused on her. Why was she angry? I could hear a phrase here and there, but it didn't make sense. Then she wheeled around and came at him, her staff raised as though she meant to attack. He cowered, and I heard his words distinctly: "Behind the bowls."

She went to a shelf that held stacks of wooden bowls. With a sweep of her hand, she flung them to the floor, sending them tumbling in every direction. At the very back in a corner sat a simple brown pouch. She pulled it down gently. "Is it all here?"

He nodded. "All that you entrusted to me."

She set the pouch onto a table and pulled down a pitcher and a metal goblet. She took the pouch and dipped an edge, shaking it until a stream of gray powder poured into the cup. She added red wine from the pitcher and used a stirring stick to mix it.

"You know what to do?" she said to the old man, who seemed to shrivel where he stood.

"Yes, Your Majesty."

Then I watched as he walked the goblet to my mother's cage. When he unlocked the door and pulled her out, she jerked away. My mother fought him with all the strength she had left and forced her way to the shelves, where she groped for something. When she found it, she pressed it into the old man's hand. It was the vial he'd given me, and in that instant I knew what it was: Lucas's Sliver.

Then the vision stopped. I couldn't take any more.

I didn't need to see it to know what had happened next. I knew the alchemist had forced my mother to drink from that goblet then forced every living captive in that room to do the same. When he'd finished, the Queen had forced him to drink what remained. At the end, when the Queen was satisfied that her prisoners were dead, she cast a fire spell that incinerated what was left.

But where was she now?

Azender roamed the room, glass and ceramic shards crunching beneath his hooves. "But why? Why?" He shook his head, though more in confusion than serious disbelief.

The truth was there in every empty cage. In each one, a pile of gray ash remained. At my mother's cage, I could see the ghost of her—or I imagined I could—lying upon the floor as if she were sleeping.

I'd never speak to her again.

I'd never travel to her dream world.

I'd never feel her embrace.

Someone tapped my shoulder. It was Bree, behind me.

"I found a footman in the corridor. He told me the guards rushed to the room when they smelled the fire. When she saw them, she raised her crystal and disappeared."

At that moment, the Collection Room's door pushed open, and Troxell appeared with a host of Dwarven Guards. I slipped the vial holding Lucas's Sliver down the front of my bodice then grabbed a charred stool and held it in front of me, as if it offered any defense.

"Don't flatter yourself," Troxell spat at me as he approached. "I'm only here to deliver a message."

Azender, who had less than bravely taken a position behind me, poked his head over my shoulder. "Whose message?"

"The Queen's, of course," Troxell sneered. "She knew you'd come eventually, and she wants you to know this, half-breed: You may have fooled the Seilies' High Court, but you will still pay for all you have done. They may have saved your life for now, but she has other ways of making you pay, starting with the lives of those you hold dear. Your wretched mother was the first, but she won't be the last."

The twinkle of malicious amusement in his eyes made a knot of bile climb the back of my throat.

"Where did she go?" I demanded.

He shook his head. "That's the message, and I delivered it. I'll have nothing more to do with you, though

I doubt you'll be around much longer. The Queen knows you'll rush off to try to save whoever it is you think needs saving. So, who could it be?" He laughed, a terrible high-pitched laugh that was still ringing in my ears when he was out the door and down the hall.

"So, she's gone then? We're safe?" Azender was still cowering behind me.

I spun around to face him. "Is that all you care about? Your own safety?" I could hardly contain my rage. But who did the Queen intend to harm? Druansha? No, the Seilie Ministers would never allow it. Bree? She was the only friend I'd made in this horrid place. But she was here.

A terrible thought occurred to me. I rushed to the door and yelled after Troxell. "Is she still in the Brightlands? Is the Queen in this world?"

In the distance, he laughed again. "Who's to say, half-breed? Who's to say?"

It wasn't much of an answer, but it was enough. If she wanted to hurt me, truly hurt me as he said, she couldn't do it in this world. The faces of my loved ones flashed through my mind. Mrs. Crossey, the Bellingtons, Marlie, Lucas. They were all in danger. One of them, maybe all of them.

That meant I had to get back home. I had to stop her.

I found Bree hiding behind a scorched cabinet. She wiped away tears when she saw me.

"Is there something I can do, mistress? Any way I can help?"

"You can help by going back to your grandmother and staying as far away from here as possible."

Her tears stopped. "Come with me. We'll both go. Gran can protect you."

"No, even if she could, I can't stay here. I have to get back to my own world."

"But how?"

It was a valid question. I searched the burnt shell of the

Collection Room as if something among these ruins could help.

"I don't know, but there must be a way."

Azender, who was edging toward the door, turned back. "I'll probably regret this, but I can show you what to do."

CHAPTER TWENTY

AZENDER'S OFFER MADE me skeptical, to say the least. "You know how to get to the human world?"

He shuffled his hooves. "Not exactly. But I was there when the Queen made the crossing to bring you back. She used her crystal, and yours seems to hold similar power."

I touched the Faytling suspended around my neck. "I can use this?"

"I believe so."

I looked at Bree. "What do you think?"

She hiked her shoulders. A silent *Maybe?*

Where was Druansha when I needed her? I could go search for her, but that would give Rhilasa more of a head start. If she was already in my world, people were already in danger. I had to get home, even if it meant placing my trust in Azender. "What do I have to do?"

"Hold out your stone."

I did as he said. Already it glowed, as if anticipating the need.

Azender came close and peered at it. His squirrelly eyebrows rose and fell and twitched. He pinched his lips and bit his nails. "I'm trying to recall how the Queen did it.

I remember she made her crystal glow then she spoke to it. Yes, she spoke to it. Ask the stone to create the portal. Tell it where you want to go."

He looked unsure, but the method seemed sound.

"Open a portal," I said.

Nothing happened.

"Maybe if you were more specific," Bree said.

I straightened and tried again. "Open a portal to the *human world*."

We all stood, waiting and watching as the Faytling dangled from my hand. It was glowing so brightly I couldn't look directly at it, but still nothing else happened.

"What am I doing wrong?"

"Give me a moment, let me think." Azender scratched around his horns as he paced.

I pulled the Faytling up and closed my fingers around it, pleading with it for help. I thought back to the moment I first noticed the portal opening in the tunnel's antechamber outside Balmoral Fayte Hall. First a crack of turquoise light had appeared in the mist, then it widened until there was a space large enough for Rhilasa to step through.

Had it been the mist?

"Was the Queen near the crystal pool when she opened the portal?"

Azender frowned. "Yes, she went to dip her crystal in the water. She said she required the power it gave the crystal."

"And when she dipped it, did it create the mist as it did when I dipped my crystal?"

He nodded. "Yes, actually."

"That's what we must do. We need to go back there."

We raced back through the passageway and down to the secret crystal pool.

When I reached the water's edge, I pulled off my gloves, tucked the bulk of my skirt between my knees, and held it there to keep the fabric dry as I bent down and submerged my fingers, just as I would for the Convergence Ceremony. Icy shivers coursed down my spine.

At the center of the pool, the island of pink-hued crystals clouded, turning a dark violet color that imbued the entire pool with the same vibrant shade.

Behind me, Bree gasped. "How did you do that?"

I couldn't answer. I didn't know how I was doing it, any of it. I only knew that something within me was urging me to do it. The Faytling dangling on the cord around my neck and glowing the same shade of rosy purple confirmed it.

The blanket of mist grew denser and within that mist, pink wisps appeared. Dozens at first, then hundreds, and they coalesced until they became part of the dense cloud. I could no longer see Bree or Azender. I couldn't even see my own hands in the pool.

A strange tingling surged within me, starting in my fingers then rising through my limbs and spreading to every part of me. Everything pulsed with that unfamiliar sensation.

Was this the power Azender mentioned? I lifted one hand to the Faytling, gripped it tightly, and made the command: "Take me to Balmoral Castle."

As soon as the words were spoken, sparks appeared in the heavy mist that formed a thick column in front of me. At the very center of it, a narrow streak like a tiny lightning bolt cracked the air around it. It stretched then widened, just as Rhilasa's had.

This was the doorway that would lead me home, I had no doubt.

I stepped closer as Azender stumbled back, eager to stay away.

Bree rushed up beside me. "Are you sure it's safe?"

She touched my arm to make me pause, and the connection sent a flood of images through me. Her at the palace, her with her grandmother, her offering assistance from the moment we met. She had been a helpful handmaiden but also a trusted friend. How could I have done any of this without her? She had risked so much to help me. What would become of her?

I urged the images to show me. I wanted to know she would be all right.

But how? Despite Mrs. Crossey's training, I'd never been able to see the future as I could see the past. Still, I placed a bare hand over hers and focused my thoughts. I asked the visions plainly to show me her future.

The images swirled, and the ground seemed to shift beneath me. Then a distant, hazy image appeared as if it were a mile away. As I focused, the images grew closer, but they were still blurry, as they had been when I was with the Old Ones. I could see Bree, but there were so many versions of her, each layered over the others. She was a handmaiden in the Brightlands Palace, she was cook in the food hall, but in others she was in a simple dress, working in her grandmother's kitchen.

I focused on those images. In some she was frosting cakes, in others she was kneading dough. In several, she was either stirring cake batter or tucking loaves into an oven, with streaks of flour slashed across her cheeks and clumped in her hair with an unmistakable smile upon her lips.

In these images, she was happiest of all. A baker, just as she had planned.

The moments flashed by, but it was enough. I gripped her hand and locked on her gaze. "I'm going to be fine. And you are too. Keep baking. You'll reach your dream."

She blinked, confused. "How do you know that?"

"I saw it. You will be happy."

"You saw me in your visions?"

I nodded, eager to give her good news. Eager to give her hope. "Yes," I said, even though there were other possibilities. She would want this one, and I wanted it for her. If she believed it was true, maybe that's what would make it true.

The crack of light in front of me dimmed a shade. The portal was closing. Bree noticed too.

She tapped my hand. "You have to go."

"I know. But I want you to know how much I appreciate what you've done for me."

"I know. But you must go." Her nudges grew more forceful, but her smile told me she was sincere.

I turned back to Azender. "I also owe you a debt. Thank you for what you've done."

He nodded, and there was the glimmer of a smile on his face. "You are most welcome, Princess. If you ever come back, I do hope you'll remember me."

"Of course I will," I said. "When you see Princess Druansha, please tell her what happened. Please tell her why I had to leave. I can't let Rhilasa hurt my friends or my family."

The irony of the statement struck me. Rhilasa was my family too, but it wasn't the same. Family was more than blood. She'd made that clear enough. To her, I was an abomination, and that's all I would ever be. She had killed my mother to hurt me, and I knew she wouldn't stop there.

I only hoped I could find her before she hurt anyone else.

CHAPTER TWENTY-ONE

VIOLET, PINK, AND golden-white lightning shot away in chaotic streaks as the hole formed in front of me. I pulled back, wary of a magic so powerful it could tear the space between the fae world and my own. It was a wonder, to be sure, but Rhilasa could already be on the other side. So, it wasn't courage that propelled me into that unknown but fear that I was already too late.

As I stepped into the black void within those shimmering lights, it was as if I were again walking through the wall in Windsor Castle after Mr. MacDougall had locked me in the chamber. The slight tug. The sensation of walking through a syrupy pool.

It wasn't a feeling one tended to forget.

When I emerged on the other side, the darkness turned blindingly bright, far too bright to see, and the mist still surrounded me.

"Is that her?"

Marlie! How long had it been since I'd heard that cherished voice? A few days, though it felt like years.

"Do you see her, Mrs. Bellington? That is her, isn't it?"

"I see something, yes, but don't get too close."

I could hear them, but when I tried to answer, my lips wouldn't move. Neither would my feet or my fingers. My whole body was a stone, and it took every ounce of strength to drag air into my lungs and expel it again.

After a long moment, the mist cleared, and I could see their silhouettes. Slowly, their forms took shape. The moment I truly saw them—Marlie, Mrs. Bellington, Clara, and Ada—I wanted to cry out, to assure them I was all right, that I was home.

But as soon as they came into view, the darkness closed around me again. I reached for Marlie, because she was closest, but I only felt myself falling forward. An endless falling, then everything again went black.

Awareness returned in drips and dribbles. A soft, gray light at the edges of the black. There were muffled voices in the distance. Mrs. Bellington was scolding Marlie for hovering.

"I told you to give her room. The girl needs to breathe."

Only then did I realize she was speaking about me.

"I think she's waking up. Her eyelids are moving. Her fingers twitched too."

"Move aside!"

Someone who smelled like lavender and pine needles bent over me and peered into my face. I could feel the warmth of expelled breath.

"Can you hear me, dove? You're home. Thank the stars you're home! Open your eyes if you can. We were awfully worried about you." She leaned back. "Marlie, where's that tea you made? Pour a bit of it. Yes, just a dram."

I felt the cool press of a porcelain cup against my lower lip and the scent of Marlie's peppermint tea before a few warm drips slipped into my mouth. I had to shift to swallow.

"Yes, that's it. Here's a bit more."

Another tiny stream flowed into me, and I swallowed it

down. The spinning slowed, and Mrs. Bellington's wide, worried eyes and sympathetic smile came into view.

"Thank you," I said, though what tumbled out of me was a jumble of something that didn't sound like words.

"What did she say?" Clara leaned in over Mrs. Bellington's shoulder.

Her mother swatted her away. "She's trying to catch her breath. Give her some air."

I managed to move my hands so I could sit up. Surprised, Mrs. Bellington scooted back, giving me a wider berth.

Looking around, I could see we were in the antechamber to the Balmoral tunnel, the same place where Rhilasa had spirited me away. Boudica's chalice was in the center, probably still serving as the Fayte Guardians' makeshift divining pool.

I couldn't make my lips cooperate, but I could hold Mrs. Bellington's gaze.

"You are certainly a sight for sore eyes, my girl." With a wry smile, she guided a loose strand of hair behind my ear. "Welcome home."

Home. At last.

She checked my hands. "The gloves survived the trip, I see." She stood and offered a hand to help me up from the floor, where I was lying upon a blanket folded beneath me like a mattress. Once I was up, she helped me to a wooden chair pushed against the wall. Glancing around, I noticed changes to the space from the night of the Converging Ceremony.

The antechamber had been empty before, merely an extension of the tunnel, which had been blocked off by a row of chairs so no one entered for fear of further collapse. But now, two rough worktables and more chairs occupied it, along with two cots in the corner.

"There, there, dove," Mrs. Bellington cooed. "Don't try to speak. Save your strength."

I was too curious to be quiet. "What happened?" The words were dry and hoarse. I swallowed hard and tried again. "Is someone living down here?"

Mrs. Bellington glanced back at her daughters and Marlie, who were sitting at a table around a teapot. She patted my shoulder. "Never mind that now. Tell me how you're feeling. Would you like more tea? Does your head hurt? You took quite a tumble."

I shut my eyes and tried to sort through the questions and the hazy recollection of getting here.

Ada came up behind her mother. "She can only answer one question at a time."

Mrs. Bellington rose and ran her hands over the front of her gray wool dress. "Of course. I can't seem to help myself when I'm worried. Are you feeling all right, Jane?" She winced and touched her forehead. "Never mind. Just rest."

I managed to sit straight with some difficulty. "I think I'm all right. Did I faint?"

"That's putting it mildly," Marlie said. "The way you fell, I thought you'd split your noggin open."

"Marlie." The gentle rebuke came from Clara Bellington. "Is that necessary?"

"What?" Marlie glanced around, confused. "It's the truth. You said so your—"

She stopped at Clara's increasingly stern look.

Mrs. Bellington sat on the edge of a cot. "You must be tired. We can leave so you can rest, if you like."

Every part of me ached, and I felt like I could sleep for a week, but I didn't want to sleep. There wasn't time. "How long was I unconscious?"

"Not long," Marlie said, jumping up from the table and moving closer. "You came through about an hour ago. No more."

An hour. How much damage could Rhilasa cause in an hour? "Did you see anyone else? Coming through the portal, I mean." I tried to stand, but my knees nearly buckled beneath me. I moved to lean against the wall until the room stopped swaying.

Mrs. Bellington frowned. "*Should* there have been someone else? Perhaps you should sit, at least until you're a little steadier on your feet."

"There's no time, ma'am. She's probably already here. We have to find her."

Four sets of eyes locked on me, confused and wanting answers I didn't have. At least not yet.

Mrs. Bellington leaned forward. "Who, dove? Who do we have to find?"

"Rhilasa. The one who took me. She wants..." The room was spinning again. I touched my head and sat back in the chair.

"The fae woman who took you?" Marlie asked when no one else would.

Yes, they'd all been present when I was taken. They'd all seen her.

I nodded, but my head was still swimming. "She wanted to kill me because I killed Krol. She's his mother, Druansha's mother too. She's the Queen of the Brightlands."

Worried glances shot between them.

"A fae queen?" Mrs. Bellington said. "But if she meant to kill you, how did you escape?"

It took some time to explain about the Reckoning and the Seilie Ministers. I told them about the Brightlands Palace and the Collection Room, but I left out the cage and getting my memories back. If I told them that, I'd have to tell them everything, and I couldn't bring myself to admit my mother was gone.

"Why did this Queen destroy the Collection Room?" Mrs. Bellington asked, trying to make sense of my incomplete story.

"To destroy the evidence of her Slivering, I'm sure."

The Sliver! I sought the glass vial I'd slipped down the front of my bodice. Carefully I pulled it out. The glass was still intact. The shimmering white liquid still swirled in its mesmerizing way.

"What is that?" Mrs. Bellington stared hard at the vial.

I cradled it in my palm. The one thing I'd accomplished. "It's Lucas's Sliver," I said, still awed by it. "It's the part of him his father bartered away." At my father's command. "Can you fetch him? I'd like to return it to him."

They exchanged glances again, the four of them, but said nothing. I sensed trouble. "Did something happen to him? You must tell me."

Something darkened Mrs. Bellington's usually bright eyes. Something had happened. I didn't need a vision to tell me that.

I turned to Ada. She wouldn't spare my feelings. "Tell me, please. Is he here?"

"No, actually," she said. "He isn't."

What were they withholding from me? "Where is he?"

"He went to Windsor," she said sharply. "He got it into his head that Mrs. Crossey was better suited to retrieve you than we were." By the looks of it, Ada had taken that as a personal insult. Perhaps she had a right to, considering she was Balmoral's Scryer.

Mrs. Bellington stepped in. "The first few days you were gone, there was a lively debate about how to get you back. I, of course, along with Ada, Clara, and Marlie, thought it best to stay here. That it was more likely you would return to the place where you were taken. He, however, was of the opinion that since our own Sanctum was destroyed, Windsor was better equipped. In the end, we compromised. We would stay here and do what we could, and he went there to enlist Mrs. Crossey's help."

"He's there now?"

"Yes, he must be. He left more than a week ago,

though we haven't heard anything yet."

A week? Had I been gone so long? "You've heard nothing from him? Why not?"

"Under normal circumstances, it would be rather simple. But the Elders put a moratorium on Converging until this matter was sorted. The last thing we wanted was to give that monster another foothold in this world."

I understood the concern. How frightening it must have been to see my abduction and have no clue where I'd been taken or what had happened to me. They wouldn't even have known if I was alive or dead.

"But Druansha? Couldn't she tell you what happened?" In all this time, how had I not thought to ask her to send word to the Fayte Guardians? I'd been so wrapped up in my own problems, I hadn't spared a moment's thought for what they were going through.

Mrs. Bellington shook her head. "It was decided that we would not reach out at all. Considering that fae creature crossed into this world while we were trying to reach Druansha, it seemed best not to pursue any communication. But you're saying she has found a way to cross over anyway?"

"That's what her people told me. But if she didn't come here, I don't know where she went. She could be anywhere."

My aunt broke away and paced, absorbing this new information. "So, this fae queen, she's the Lady of the Fayte's mother and also the mother of the demon who nearly killed us all."

"Yes."

"And you believe she's come here to avenge the death of that demon?"

I nodded, eager for them to see the urgency of the situation. "Until we find her, you're all in danger. And Lucas and Mrs. Crossey, too. I truly don't know if anyone is safe."

Mrs. Bellington gnawed her lower lip. "There's been nothing to suggest she came here. I would imagine she would require the divining pool's mist, and there has been none of that. No one has reported anything strange or out of the ordinary. But there's been no contact with the Windsor Fayte. Is it possible she went there?"

"Anything is possible." My shoulders sank. How could we be so helpless?

Clara's eyebrows pulled down in a frown. "Mother, what about the pigeon you received from Windsor this morning?"

Mrs. Bellington returned a blank look. "Yes, from Mrs. Crossey. But there was no word of Lucas."

I perked. "What did it say?"

She pulled a slip of paper from her pocket and opened it. "She merely asks if there's been any word from our missing little bird." She glanced toward me. "She means you. And she concludes by asking for any news. See? It's all quite ordinary. That does remind me, though. I should send word of your return straightaway. They'll want to know."

"Yes, of course." I tucked the vial back into the crevice beneath my bodice. "I must make my way there as well, for Lucas's sake."

I expected Mrs. Bellington to argue, but instead she leaned back and touched her lips. After a long pause, she nodded. "And while Jane goes to Windsor, we shall remain vigilant here. I think our first order of business, however, shall be to inform the Elders. If that monster is already here, we're going to need every Fayte Guardian to be on alert, and we should establish contact with Druansha as soon as possible. Do we all agree?"

"Wholeheartedly," I said, and the others signaled their agreement as well.

"Good," the older woman said. "Clara, please fetch something for Jane to eat and bring her a change of clothes."

I glanced down and realized my dress was a muddy and tattered mess. I guess charging through tunnels and charred rooms had taken a toll. I ran my fingers over my head to smooth my hair, but I knew it would hardly make a difference.

Mrs. Bellington must have seen my distress because she added, "Marlie, be a dear and get some wash water and a hairbrush. Ada, you and I will get word to the Elders."

I sat straighter. I didn't like the idea of everyone running around on my behalf. "What about me? I can help."

The older woman nodded. "You will have a part to play. But the best thing you can do right now is rest and conserve your strength. We'll get a good meal into you and a good night's rest, so by tomorrow you'll be ready for a morning carriage to Windsor."

A carriage and a four-day journey, at best.

"What's wrong, dove? You don't agree?" Mrs. Bellington's eyes crinkled with worry.

"I just hope we're not too late."

CHAPTER TWENTY-TWO

LATER, WHEN THE others had retreated to their own rooms for the night, I sat in that underground room with Marlie, working my way through my second bowl of beef stew.

She planted an elbow on the table and watched me chew another chunk of potato. "What was it like, the Brightlands?"

I'd been expecting the question, but it didn't make it any easier.

When I continued to chew, she tried again. "You know, I never doubted you'd return. Some of the others feared the worst, but I knew you'd put up a fight. I knew you'd make your way back to us, somehow. Anyway, I'm glad you're back. We all are."

I dragged my spoon through the stew. "I'm glad to be back too. I wish I hadn't put you all in danger, though. Whatever it takes, I will make that right."

"It's not your fault. No one blames you."

I stared at the bits of meat and vegetables in my bowl. "I know."

She didn't move. She was still waiting. I knew she'd

wait as long as it took too, because that was the wonderful and exasperating thing about friends and family. They always seemed to know when I wasn't telling the truth, or even the whole truth. I still wasn't used to it. It wasn't me and my dragonfly alone against the world anymore. There were other people to consider, people I cared about who also cared about me.

I didn't have to keep secrets.

I peeked up at her. "Can I tell you something?"

She leaned back, deadly serious. "You can tell me anything."

"Can it stay between us? For now. I don't want to talk about it with everybody yet."

"Should I be worried?"

"I saw my mother."

Marlie stared at me. "Your mother was in the Brightlands? How?"

"I don't know exactly, but she was there. She was a prisoner, but now..." Pain knotted my throat.

Marlie leaned forward. I could feel her fighting the urge to embrace me and comfort me. That's what normal people did in difficult times. But like Rhilasa said, I wasn't normal. Only half of this world and half the other, and not truly fitting into either one.

"The fae queen killed her," I added, "before she came here. She did it to hurt me. She made sure I knew that."

Marlie covered her mouth. "Why didn't you tell us before? Why didn't you tell the others?"

The question left me numb. I swallowed hard and forced myself to answer. "Because I failed her. I had a chance to save her, and I didn't do it."

There it was. The horrible truth I'd kept locked inside was out, hanging in the space between us. I waited for the disgust on her face. I waited for her scorn.

Instead, her head tilted slightly to the side. "You think it's your fault?"

"Of course it is. I should have helped her escape as soon as I found her. But I let fear stop me, and I let others convince me that we'd be caught. But it was a mistake. I should have done something."

"Sounds to me like you would have gotten yourself locked up as well. How would that have helped your mother?"

"There was a village where we could have gone. People there might have protected us."

"Perhaps. But if that queen is as powerful as you say, wouldn't she have found you? Maybe if you'd done as you say, you'd both be dead."

She was trying to make me feel better, and I loved her for it, but she was wrong. "There must have been a way."

She was silent for a long moment, then she sighed. "Sometimes there isn't. Sometimes you have to accept the road you're given. You can't punish yourself for what you didn't know."

"But she's gone. I found her, and I lost her. It isn't fair."

"You're right. It isn't. But at least you found her. You spent time with her. Don't mourn the time you didn't have. Be grateful for the time you did have. Hold onto those moments. I wish I'd had more time with my parents too. We never want to let our loved ones go. The world gave you an amazing gift. Instead of wishing it was a better gift, maybe accept it for what it is. I know it sounds silly, but that's the only thing that helps me when I'm missing my parents. Sometimes I'm so angry that they aren't around anymore. I want to talk to them and be with them, but then I stop myself and remember that I'm fortunate to have had as much time with them as I did."

Maybe Marlie was right. Before I found my mother, I'd given up hope of ever seeing her alive. I should be thankful for that smidgen of time I spent with her and for the gift of getting my memories back. I could remember so much about our life together now and how she doted on me. More than I'd ever dreamed possible. If only I could shake the feeling that there was still a hole in my heart. One day, I might find peace with it, but at the moment, all I wanted was to stop Rhilasa from hurting anyone else.

As I sat with these thoughts, something buzzed around me.

"Do you hear that?" I rose and paced the room, searching for the source.

Marlie remained in her chair. Didn't she hear it?

Was I imagining it? No, there it was again, darting across the room, then it circled back and hovered inches from my nose. That tiny, familiar luminescent form—my dragonfly!

No, she wasn't my dragonfly, and she never had been, not really. She was Druansha in her dragonfly form, but it didn't stop me from squealing with delight at the sight of her.

Marlie's gaze raced around the room, following Druansha's flight. "What is that?"

"It's Druansha, our Lady of the Fayte."

"What? Are you sure?" Marlie frowned, confused. "Why were you staring at her that way?"

I looked at Druansha. Her silvery head dipped slightly.

Yes, you may tell her.

Thank you. I turned back to Marlie. "She can read my thoughts. Yours too, I'm sure. She's speaking to me that way."

Marlie stared hard at the glorious insect. "Truly?"

Your friend needs your help.

Druansha landed on the table between Marlie and me and danced back and forth. I sensed her impatience.

My mother has masked herself from me. I cannot find her, but the Old Ones sense danger. I've alerted Mrs. Crossey. She tells me Lucas Starwyck is there and that his health has taken a turn. I fear my mother may have something to do with it. He needs his Sliver at once.

My heart stopped. Was he Rhilasa's target? I told Druansha of the carriage being arranged in the morning.

The dragonfly's tiny legs stomped furiously. *That won't do. If we leave now, we can be there before dawn.*

Windsor was hundreds of miles away. But she was already reading my thoughts.

Meet me where you found me before. In the woods. Don't delay.

Without another word, she flew off before I could argue. I searched for her, but in a flash she was gone.

"What happened?" Marlie stared at me, utterly perplexed.

"I'm not sure." I relayed the news about Mrs. Crossey and Lucas, the urgency to leave, and the demand that I meet her in the woods. Before I was done, Marlie grabbed her coat from a peg on the wall.

"What are you doing?" I asked.

"I'm not letting you go alone."

"I don't think it's safe. I don't even know what she has planned."

Marlie buttoned her coat. "It doesn't matter. I'm going with you."

"But you—"

Her hand shot out. "It's not up for debate. If you're going, then I'm going. And here." She tossed me an extra coat. "Put that on and take my cap." She unpinned the white muslin from her head and handed it to me as well. "Keep your head down, and we'll take the back way out. No one else knows you're here, and if we want to get out without a fuss, we need to keep it that way."

There was no point arguing. I did as she said and followed her up the stone staircase to the hidden door in the pantry. When we reached it, she listened before inching it open.

Moonlight streamed through the high windows, illuminating everything in a silvery blue glow. We stuck to the shadows as we moved through the empty corridors.

"Where does she want us to go?" Marlie whispered when we reached the kitchen garden.

"She wants me—us—to meet her in the woods. There's a spot where I met her before."

Her lips thinned. I knew she had more questions, but there wasn't time for answers. We had to keep our eyes peeled for night guards.

We moved quickly across the western lawn where the mist hugged the ground and made the field look like something from a dream. The damp, cold air clung to my cheeks, and I prayed it wouldn't rain. In Scotland, rain was always a possibility.

When we reached the trees, I glanced back and searched the darkness.

"Do you see something?" Marlie scanned the landscape too.

"Something's different. Do you feel it?"

She rubbed her palms over her arms. "I feel cold. How long do we have to stay out here?"

I didn't feel the cold at all. We'd been moving so fast, I was starting to perspire beneath the coat. "You can go back. You don't have to do this."

"Nice try." She made a low snort. "You're not getting rid of me that easily."

"Suit yourself." I hid a smile. I wouldn't tell her, but when I was in the Brightlands, I'd missed her company. I was glad to have her beside me as we searched for Druansha.

"Is something moving over there?" Marlie pointed toward a boulder beyond the trees.

I was still listening for a dragonfly flutter when something rustled near the boulder. As I tried to make out what it was, the rock rose to reveal a dragon's head and shiny golden eyes. She blinked at us and exhaled a misty cloud from her nostrils.

"Whaaa…" The syllable dangled from Marlie's lips as she stared at the massive animal.

"It's all right." I stepped between her and the dragon, fearing Marlie might scream. "It's Druansha."

Marlie's shock turned to wild confusion. "She's a dragon?"

Sometimes.

I saw the surprise on Marlie's face as she stared at the giant, glistening eyes. She must have heard that silent word, just as I had.

I whipped back to Druansha. "You can speak to her? You could have done that all this time? Do you know how much trouble that would have saved us?"

Druansha's dragon shoulders shrugged. *It didn't seem necessary.*

She stretched her neck and wings for the sole purpose of making a spectacle of herself, I was sure. What an infuriating creature, in any form. How arrogant and… it didn't matter. There were far more important matters.

Exactly. We don't have time for your silly notions.

Had Marlie heard that? The way she was looking from me to the dragon and back again, I assumed she had.

"What's happening?" Marlie's voice was small and unsteady.

I turned my back on Druansha as if to say, *I will deal with you in a moment*, and attended to Marlie. "You know the Lady of the Fayte can transform into a dragonfly. This is merely another form."

One of many, thank you.

I tossed her a scowl. "Right, one of many. Don't let it alarm you. She's harmless."

To you, perhaps.

Marlie straightened. Her courage was returning.

"It's an honor, Your Ladyship." Marlie bobbed a curtsy.

Druansha gave me a look like my own manners were

falling short.

"Considering your form, I believe I know why you summoned us," I said.

Yes, I thought you might. Climb up, and we'll be on our way.

When she lowered herself to the ground, I went to her side and grabbed a fistful of her mane to hoist myself up. I glanced down at Marlie. "Please tell the Bellingtons what happened. Let them know I'll send a message as soon as I can."

Marlie shook her head and hoisted herself into a spot behind me. "They'll have to figure it out on their own. Like I said, I'm not letting you out of my sight. Wherever you're going, I'm going too."

Could she do that? I waited for Druansha to set her straight. Instead, she sighed and sent a plume of warm, misty breath into the cold, Scottish air.

Please get settled. We don't have much time.

CHAPTER TWENTY-THREE

THE MOON WAS low on the horizon when Druansha stretched out her dragon wings and glided down over the oak grove where Krol had commanded a tree root to attack me just beyond the Windsor Castle wall.

"We're home," Marlie whispered behind me. She'd been quiet for so long, I'd assumed she was asleep. Exhaustion weighed heavily on me too, but the air was so cold, I could barely feel my fingers or my cheeks.

"Who's down there?" Her hand shot out, near my elbow, pointing at something moving among the trees.

The dark speck grew larger as we neared, resolving into a round figure in a heavy cloak who was gazing up and… waving?

I told Sylvia Crossey to expect us.

Druansha touched down in the field beside her.

"Oh, my dears, you've made it," Mrs. Crossey said, her fleshy cheeks ruddy from the night's chill. She stopped in front of Druansha and clasped her hands together in front of herself. "Thank you, Your Ladyship. Thank you for bringing them home."

The dragon collapsed her wings, tucking them neatly

against her back as she made a sound deep in her throat, something between a purr and a growl. The way her cheeks twitched, I knew she was saying something to Mrs. Crossey that was meant for her alone.

Mrs. Crossey's head dipped sheepishly. "He's in the Hall resting, yes, but we should hurry. Come, girls, we have work to do."

I waited for Marlie to work her way down to the ground, then I did the same.

It was good to be back with Mrs. Crossey. When she'd arranged for me to visit Balmoral to search their archives for clues about my past, I never could have imagined the trouble that would follow me there or that my search would lead me to the Bellingtons. I could only wonder if Mrs. Crossey had suspected any of it herself.

After she embraced Marlie, she came to me and hesitated. She glanced at my gloves. I knew she wanted to embrace me too but worried about the vision it might trigger. It was the fear that always kept people at an arm's length.

With her help, I was getting better at controlling the assault of images and emotions, though they still overwhelmed me at times. I didn't care about that now. I rushed into her arms and buried my cheek against the rough weave of her cloak.

"Are you all right, dear?" she asked, more than a little startled by my embrace.

"I've missed you. That's all."

As her arms wrapped around me, the swirling closed in, but I focused on her touch, on her palm against my back, and her fingers touching the top of the braid that had come loose from its knot and fallen down my back. The sensation nearly overwhelmed me, but the more I concentrated, the more it lessened until it vanished altogether.

When I released her, she stared hard into my eyes.

"I'm all right," I said with a wide, goofy grin because I truly was.

If I may interrupt…

Druansha's gentle coaxing pulled me from our happy reunion and my little victory, back to the moment.

Mrs. Crossey smoothed the brown shawl that covered her. "Yes, there is work to be done. Much to do and little time in which to do it." She turned to Druansha again. "Thank you again for what you've done."

The stone embedded in Druansha's collar brightened and sent out tendrils of violet light that wound around her, forming a cocoon that stretched down to the ground and up to the tips of the trees surrounding us. When it faded, she was again her more familiar self.

"That's better." She stretched her arms and her neck as she settled into her womanly form. "Please tell me, has there been any sign of another Brightlander? Any indication of another of my kind at all?"

Mrs. Crossey pursed the thin line of her lips. "Another Brightlander? But I thought Jane had… I mean, wasn't he…?"

"My brother is no longer a threat. That is true. I'm speaking of my mother."

"Oh dear," Mrs. Crossey said. "Should we assume she's dangerous?"

"Unfortunately, yes. The young man is at particular risk."

I moved closer. "But we have his Sliver now. We can restore him."

"Yes, and the sooner, the better," Druansha said. "As long as he's in his weakened state, I'm afraid he's quite vulnerable."

Mrs. Crossey waved us back to the path. "Then let us make haste, girls."

I turned back to Druansha. "Are you coming with us?"

She shook her head. "I must resume my search for my

mother. She cannot ward herself forever. Call on me, if you need me. You know the way."

"Yes, Your Ladyship," Mrs. Crossey said. "We shall. Thank you."

Marlie and I waved goodbye to Druansha and followed Mrs. Crossey, but instead of turning back toward the castle, she headed deeper into the grove.

I hurried up beside her. "Why this way?"

"Too many eyes around Mr. MacDougall's office. The guards have increased their rounds. The back way is safer."

More tunnels. Lovely. I glanced down at the clean skirts Mrs. Bellington had given me and wondered how long before they were as soiled as the last.

Mrs. Crossey gestured to a giant yew tree, and when we neared it, she pulled her Faytling from beneath her collar and lifted the pendant and its leather cord over her head. She stepped up to the tree and held the amulet high. "In the name of the Order of the Fayte, I seek entrance."

When the center of the stone brightened, she touched it to the tree's trunk. At that instant, the tree's contours slithered to life, sliding and undulating against each other before pulling apart to reveal a passageway.

"Another hidden tunnel?" Marlie squealed, with more delight than I could muster.

Mrs. Crossey pulled back the Faytling and poked her head into the newly opened crevice before stepping in and motioning for us to follow. "Come on, then."

Marlie pushed past me. "Does it go to the Fayte Hall?" When she was inside, she spun around then stepped out again, marveling at the difference between the size of the trunk and the size of the passageway. "It's just like you said, Jane. The inside really is larger than the outside. How utterly marvelous."

"Marvelous, indeed," Mrs. Crossey said.

"Let us hurry. Young Mr. Starwyck needs our help, so pull out your Faytlings, and let's be on our way."

I tugged mine over my head and asked for the light, sending forth a far more powerful burst of light than I was expecting.

"What was that?" Marlie rubbed at her eyes and blinked, trying to bring normal vision back.

I clamped both hands around the stone to block the brightness. "It must be the extra power it absorbed in the Brightlands."

"Extra power?" Mrs. Crossey asked. "Would you care to elaborate?"

If I started to explain about the crystal pool and Bree and Azender, I'd end up telling her about the Collection Room and my mother and all the rest of it. I wasn't ready for that. I fought back the memory of the charred cage and the ash and the failure. I pressed it down to the deepest pit of my stomach until I could breathe again. I met Mrs. Crossey's curious eye and smiled. "I'll tell you everything, truly, but not yet. We must save Lucas."

~ ~ ~

Judging by the cobwebs and the intrusive root growth, the tunnel hadn't been used in decades. But as expected, Mrs. Crossey, Marlie, and I eventually emerged through one of the doors along the main tunnel that ran between the Fayte Hall and Mr. MacDougall's office.

Marlie grabbed a rock and scratched marks into the bricks beside the door.

"What are you doing?" Mrs. Crossey scowled at her.

Marlie dropped the stone and brushed the dust from her fingers. "I've looked everywhere for a map of these tunnels and found nothing. So, I thought I'd make one myself."

"Not a bad plan." Mrs. Crossey wiped away a smear of dust along her sleeves. "I've forgotten half of them, and I remember more than most."

"We're lucky you remembered this one. Ack!" Marlie thrashed and batted at her head, trying to remove a cobweb stuck in her hair.

"Can we discuss the tunnels and maps later?" I didn't care about the cobwebs or the muck that had soaked my hem. "We need to get to Lucas." I touched my chest with the hand that wasn't holding the Faytling, making sure for the hundredth time since we'd entered the tunnel that his Sliver was still in its place.

"Of course, dear," Mrs. Crossey said. "I know you're anxious, but he was fine when I left them. Only a bit under the weather, nothing to be alarmed about."

"Them? Who was with him?"

"Oh, what difference does it make? We're nearly there. Come on."

She spun around and headed toward the door so fast I had to run to catch up. "Mrs. Crossey, who is with Lucas?"

"Abigail. She was nearby when I got word from Druansha."

She knew how I felt about Abigail. I could see it in the way she stared straight ahead and didn't slow down. Marlie knew too. That's why she wasn't saying anything and was looking anywhere but my direction.

Why did it have to be Abigail? Lucas had been popular with many of the young maids when he'd been at Windsor before, and Abigail in particular made no secret of her admiration. I knew how he felt about me—at least I thought I did—but would that stop her ardent pursuit of him?

None of us said another word as we pressed on, not even when we approached the Fayte Hall's door. As soon Mrs. Crossey opened it, I rushed through, past the towering Library shelves, mostly empty now since the collection had been transferred to Balmoral. Fresh pangs of regret and loss pierced through me. So many of those old leather-bound journals and scrolls had been sent away for safer keeping only to end up buried in rubble after Krol brought that whole place down.

"Excuse me," Mrs. Crossey called after me. "Did you forget something?"

I grabbed the lump on my chest and turned back. Had the Sliver slipped out?

But no, she was holding one of the indigo robes that hung along the back wall. She'd already wrapped herself in one, and Marlie had too. Mrs. Crossey offered it to Marlie. "Take this to her, would you?"

I wanted to scream. Lucas's life hung in the balance, and she was concerned about a robe?

"Yes, I will insist on the robes," she said.

I winced. Reading thoughts hadn't been one of her talents before. Or had it?

She smirked, telling me she'd read that thought as well.

I grabbed the robe from Marlie and yanked it on, then hurried into the Sanctum.

Lucas was there, as Mrs. Crossey said he would be, but the sight of him nearly dropped me to my knees.

"Lucas!" I rushed to where he was lying akimbo behind the divining pool. Had he fallen? Had he been attacked?

He was on his back with his robe sprawled around him like angel wings. His tousled chestnut hair fell away from the rigid lines of his face, except for one curl that lay against his wide, smooth forehead and brushed the top of his eyebrows. His usually fair complexion and rosy pink lips had lost all color, leaving him nearly as white as the divining pool's stone. When I bent my ear to his lips, his breath was so shallow, his chest hardly moved at all.

Was it already too late?

Before I knew it, Mrs. Crossey and Marlie were beside me, hovering over him just as I was. Mrs. Crossey leaned her ear to his nose.

"He's breathing, but just barely." Mrs. Crossey looked around, searching for some explanation, some clue how he ended up this way. "Where is Abigail? Where is that girl? When I left, he was fine. Fatigued, he said, and a bit sore, but fine. I brought him some blankets so he could rest."

The blankets were still folded and stored beneath one of the tapestries that hung along the Sanctum's curved walls. A pillow sat on top, untouched.

"Why did you leave him with *her*?" It wasn't the most pressing question, at least it shouldn't have been, but I couldn't help myself. "Where is everyone else?"

Mrs. Crossey searched again and knitted her eyebrows. "That's a good question. I asked that girl specifically to stay with him until I returned."

"I'm here," a familiar voice said.

Abigail was at the entrance, pulling on a robe, and that wave of old jealousy swept over me again.

"Where were you?" Mrs. Crossey demanded as Abigail made her way toward us.

"He was getting feverish. I went to gather ice chips to cool him." She lifted a bowl, which must have been the chips.

"When did the fever start?" Marlie pushed forward. "Has he had an appetite? Any soreness or tingling in his limbs?"

I knew she was taking a mental inventory of symptoms in order to assemble a tonic or tea of her healing herbs.

She touched her palm to his forehead, "Oh, that is warm. Here, give me that ice."

Abigail pulled back the bowl and was about to argue before thinking better of it. She handed over the bowl.

Marlie took a chip and dabbed his forehead with it lightly. "He needs lemon balm and white willow bark. Abigail, is there any down here?"

"How should I know? I don't keep an inventory of every little—"

Mrs. Crossey stopped her with a look. "Go search the pantry. If you can't find any there, check with the scullery maids. They're resourceful when they need to be."

Abigail scowled, but she knew better than to disobey an order from Mrs. Crossey. We all did.

"Of course. Anything to help Lucas. I'll be back as soon as I can." She cast a lingering glance at him again. "Is he going to be all right?"

"Certainly, dear. We're doing everything we can."

Abigail didn't look convinced as she headed off to the errand.

When we heard the great door close, I bent down beside Lucas and brushed his hair from his forehead. Already a deathly pallor was stealing over him, forming shadows beneath his eyes and the hollows of his cheeks. Was I already too late?

I reached into the crevice beneath my bodice and grabbed hold of the Sliver's vessel. When I pulled it free, the shimmering opaque tendrils of light and liquid were no longer swirling in their lazy rotations but were all pressed firmly against the side of the vial aimed Lucas's direction, as if they sensed him somehow.

When I lifted the stopper and poured the contents into my hand, they drizzled down like syrup into my palm and formed a tiny ball, much smaller than the Sliver that had been taken from and returned to Queen Victoria.

Panic washed over me. I glanced up to Marlie and Mrs. Crossey. "Do you think it will work?"

Neither said a word.

A deep crease formed on Mrs. Crossey's brow. "I've no experience with Slivers, my dear. But we must hope for the best."

I stared down at Lucas's lifeless face. "Please let this work," I whispered as I lowered the Sliver to his forehead.

At that moment, my Faytling and his, both of them resting upon our chests, flashed with bright, blinding light. Simultaneously, the liquid and light tendrils in my hand rearranged themselves into a teardrop shape with the pinched end extending over my palm as if pulled by an invisible force toward his forehead.

When the Sliver's tip touched his skin, I expected it to rush into him like Queen Victoria's Sliver had.

But it didn't.

Instead, the light and liquid tendrils hovered above him, and the light from our Faytlings widened until they engulfed him completely.

"What's happening?" Marlie asked.

"I do not know." I opened my hands over the top of the hovering Sliver and pressed down, pushing the mass toward the space between his eyebrows.

Behind me, I heard Mrs. Crossey recite Gaelic words I didn't understand. As she muttered, fiery sparks formed within the shimmering tendrils swirling and dancing within his Sliver and slowly spread out around him until they wrapped around him completely. He twitched. First his nose, then his fingers and his feet.

A good sign? I didn't know, but my heart surged with hope. Then, in an instant, an explosion of light shot from his Faytling with such force it knocked Marlie and me backward.

For an instant, the world went black. My arms, my legs, my head, everything ached, and I was shaking. No, someone was shaking me. Fingers gripped my shoulder. With some difficulty, I opened my eyes, and someone was standing over me. A hazy figure, but it wasn't Mrs. Crossey. Not Marlie, either.

"Jane, are you all right?"

That voice! Tears welled, making the hazy figure even less defined. But it didn't matter. I knew that voice. I wiped away the tears, and then I could see him, hovering close.

Was it a dream?

No, I could feel the warmth of his breath and smell the citrus soap that barely masked the scent of wood lacquer that always clung to him. That scent that was so uniquely and wonderfully his.

His face lowered within inches of mine, and I reached up to cup his cheek with my open palm. The one person I could touch without fear. "I'm all right."

"Thank heaven." He wrapped me in an embrace. "You frightened me."

He pulled back too soon. But the shock of seeing him clearly, those inquisitive dark eyes and that tousled chestnut hair falling past his eyebrows and curling around his ears, it all nearly sent me back into a swoon.

"Lucas!" It was Marlie. "You're back!"

She struggled to get upright, and Lucas offered an outstretched hand to help.

Once she was up, he helped me up as well. That's when I saw Mrs. Crossey across the room, sprawled out upon the floor. I scrambled to her side and touched her shoulder. I shook her gently. "Mrs. Crossey, are you all right?"

Nothing moved. Nothing flinched.

I tried again. "Mrs. Crossey, say something. Please."

Still nothing.

Marlie scrambled to the other side of her and placed her fingers beneath her nose. "I can feel her breath. Faint, but it's there."

"What happened to her?" Lucas was still off to the side, rubbing his head as if none of this was making sense.

Dread dug a pit in my stomach and worked its way up. "What do you remember?"

He scratched his temple and squinted hard. "Standing by the divining pool, watching Abigail leave, then waking up."

I touched Mrs. Crossey's shoulder to rouse her. She still didn't move, not one whit.

Behind me, he whispered, "What can we do?"

My heart ached. All I wanted to do was sit with him,

wrap my arms around him, feel his heart beating against mine. If only there was time for that.

"I have so much to tell you," I said. "But Mrs. Crossey needs our help. I can't wake her up."

CHAPTER TWENTY-FOUR

LUCAS AND MARLIE helped me roll Mrs. Crossey onto her back.

Marlie examined her. "Did she hit her head?"

"Maybe." I checked for wounds. "Whatever hit us must have done the same to her."

"Her fingers moved." Lucas pointed to her right hand. "Did you see it?"

The older woman's eyes and lips twitched. She was regaining consciousness.

"Mrs. Crossey, can you hear me?" I leaned to her ear.

"What happened?" Mrs. Crossey's voice was thin and hoarse. Her eyelids fluttered.

"You're awake!" Marlie exclaimed. "Thank goodness."

The old woman's fleshy hand pulled from my own, and she batted me away. "What's the meaning of this? Oh!" She touched her forehead and glanced around. "What happened?"

Lucas leaned over. "You've had a tumble, Mrs. Crossey."

She stared at him in alarm. "You?"

"It worked," I said. "The Sliver is restored. He's whole

again. Do you remember?"

She touched her head again. "The Sliver. *His* Sliver, of course. I remember. And now I'm here." She slid her fingers over her cheeks and her neck.

"Are you hurt?" Marlie was still searching for wounds.

"It all feels quite strange," Mrs. Crossey said in a musing sort of way. "Very, very strange."

"Can we help you up?" I moved to take her hand, but she recoiled. "Sorry, did that hurt?"

She scowled at me then turned to Marlie and lifted her hands. "If you would be so kind."

How had I displeased her? I hardly knew, but I clearly had.

When Marlie had helped her to her feet, Mrs. Crossey leaned on her. "Thank you. Could we please leave this wretched room? I can't stay here."

"Of course." Marlie guided the older woman toward the door. "Shall I help you to your room?"

"My room? Yes, of course, my room."

Marlie turned to me. "Join us?"

Mrs. Crossey frowned, making it plain my company wasn't welcome.

Maybe Marlie saw it too, but she ignored it. "The stairs may be tricky, but with both of us, I'm sure we can make it."

"Give me a moment," I told her. "I'll be right behind you."

Marlie glanced at Lucas and nodded. "Certainly. Take your time."

As she and Mrs. Crossey hobbled away, I could feel the weight of Lucas's gaze on me.

I waited until they were out of earshot to speak. "Are you lodging in the mews?" That's where he'd stayed the last time he'd come to Windsor, when he was still operating under a false name and spying on me, thinking I was the threat to Queen Victoria. That might still irk me if

214

I hadn't been spying on him for the same reason.

"I'm sharing a room in the men's quarters. Mr. MacDougall asked me to help with furniture repairs while I'm here."

"Wasn't anyone curious why you disappeared then returned with a different name?"

He'd been introduced as Lucas Wyck originally, to keep his true identity and purpose secret.

He shrugged. "Fayte Guardians know the truth, and the others? No one has said anything directly, but I've heard some whispers. They're quite interesting, actually. Some believe my absence was due to illness, and that I'd been convalescing with relations in London. My favorite, however, is that I was fired for getting too friendly with a maid at the East Terrace fountain one night, but that I'd been given a second chance when they had to dispatch Windsor staff to Balmoral to cover the sudden vacancies there. The rumors don't really matter, though. After a while, they die down. People are always more interested in their own concerns."

That certainly was true for men. For women, who had their reputations to consider, it wasn't quite so simple. "And the maid you were supposedly caught with. Is it ever mentioned who she was?"

He pushed his fingers through his hair and laughed. "No, never heard a name. I believe her identity may still be a mystery."

"Is it?" I wasn't sure whether to laugh or not.

At the door to the tunnel, Marlie called back, "Jane, are you coming?"

I didn't want to leave, and the way he was looking at me, I didn't think he wanted it, either.

"Jane?" Marlie called out again.

Every part of me wanted to ignore her. All that mattered was Lucas, his hands dancing at his sides, his feet shifting like he couldn't stand still.

"I was thinking…" He pushed back a lock of unruly hair.

"Yes?" I winced at the eagerness in my voice.

"Jane!" Her voice was several octaves higher now, just in case I hadn't heard her before.

Lucas glanced at her, and I thought I spied a flush rising over his collar.

He sighed.

I wanted to tell him I had all the time in the world. That I would do anything to stay right there, basking in his warm, dark gaze. I wanted to feel those strong fingers entwined in mine, and my cheek pressed against his chest. But it was already too late.

We both knew I had to leave.

"Will I see you tomorrow?" I asked.

"Absolutely."

It took every ounce of strength I had to walk away from him. I wanted to stay. I wanted to throw my arms around him and bury my face against his neck. Instead, I forced one foot in front of the other, each one putting more distance between us. I'd see him tomorrow, I had to take solace in that. He was whole, and he was safe. We all were, at least for now.

~ ~ ~

Golden light seeped from the edges of the room's blue linen curtains and drove away a dream I didn't want to leave. I was back in my usual place in the Windsor kitchen, working alongside Mrs. Crossey, and I'd made her a batch of the cucumber and basil sandwiches Queen Victoria had enjoyed at Balmoral. I was bursting with pride as she took bite after bite and nodded with approval. I'd finally impressed her, and it meant the world to me.

But as the dream faded, and the real world set in, I held on to the hope that maybe it was a good omen. A prelude to how the new day would unfold.

"You're finally awake." Marlie sprang from her bed and grabbed a brush from the dressing table.

"Finally?" I pulled back the drape and was alarmed to see the sun had already crested the eastern hills. "Why did you let me sleep so long?"

"You looked like you needed it, so I let you." She pulled the brush through her long, honey-colored hair.

"It doesn't matter if I need it. There's too much to do." The last thing I remembered was sitting on my bed, staring out the window. It hadn't taken long for my thoughts of Lucas to turn to the Brightlands Queen. Fear had a way of doing that. I hopped off the bed and grabbed the work dress Marlie had left folded at the foot of my bed.

"I'm worried about Mrs. Crossey," Marlie said. "Did she seem off to you last night? She hit her head pretty hard. Should I tell the physician?"

"It couldn't hurt." Mrs. Crossey was still sour toward me when we left her in her room, but she had insisted to Marlie that she was fine. Still, I had my doubts, and until we found Rhilasa, I didn't want to take any chances.

Finding her, however, was proving a challenge. We'd thoroughly searched the Sanctum, where the divining pool could create the misty environment she'd require, and found no sign of her. The only other option seemed to be the foggy banks along the river. If she was there, maybe it was best to leave her there until we heard from Druansha.

But where was Druansha? Her continued absence could only mean she hadn't found her mother yet, but still, any news would be better than none.

As Marlie and I made our way to the kitchen, I was trying to decide how soon I could send that message to Druansha by way of the divining pool, but every time we passed a maid or a footman or a page, they stopped us to welcome us back from Balmoral. As far as most of them knew, Marlie and I had been helping out at the Scottish castle. Those who were Fayte Guardians knew of my abduction but had every reason to believe my return was a happy ending to unfortunate events. And they were the hardest to shake.

Under different circumstances, the attention would have meant the world to me. Not so long ago, not a soul in the castle would have given me a second glance, let alone stopped to chat. But right now, I missed that old anonymity. It would have made it much easier to get where I needed to be and do what I needed to do.

Every wasted minute was another minute Rhilasa could strike.

I couldn't ignore their kindness, however, so I tried to explain that Mrs. Crossey was expecting us and that we were already running late. It wasn't exactly the truth, but it wasn't quite a lie, either. At least it didn't feel like one.

As we approached the kitchen, I could hear a ruckus and smell the plethora of simmering sauces, roasting meats, and baking cakes and breads. That's when I realized these little delays weren't my biggest problem.

These were not ordinary preparations.

We'd arrived too late to see if the Royal Standard was flying atop the Round Tower, and I'd assumed our sovereign and her family were still at Balmoral Castle. But this amount of commotion and activity had to mean Queen Victoria was here. And if she was, she was in danger too. That thought stopped me cold.

I had brought a monster to Queen Victoria's doorstep.

"Are you all right?" Marlie whispered.

I'd stopped dead in my tracks, frozen by this new fear. "I need to speak to Mrs. Crossey," I said, snapping out of my stupor. "She has to warn the Queen's guard."

Marlie started to shake her head, then the danger dawned on her too. "You're right. We must tell her straightaway."

We rushed into the kitchen, weaving past tables where

maids were chopping vegetables and cooks were rolling dough. When we tried to push by the roasting station, a pudgy, red-haired cook named Martin thrust out his hand and forced us to stop.

"About time you showed up," he said.

"It is?" I glanced at Marlie. I'd never exchanged words with Martin before, so it was odd to be addressed by him now.

"Will you be wanting any of the roast left from last night's household dinner? Mrs. Crossey said I should ask you."

"Why me?" I asked.

He rolled his eyes to the ceiling. "She said you'd be taking care of the servants' dinner, I would imagine."

Marlie and I exchanged confused looks. I searched for Mrs. Crossey at our usual worktable, but it was empty. "Where is she?"

"How should I know?" He turned back to the lamb shank he was roasting. "She said you'd be taking care of everything until she returned."

"Is there a problem here?"

Mr. MacDougall's deep baritone voice sent a cold drip down my spine.

"No, sir." The cook looked at me. "Unless she thinks so."

I squared myself to the House Steward slowly, too numb and surprised to say anything.

Marlie stepped in. "Everything is fine, sir. We arrived back late last night, but there seems to be some confusion about tonight's dinner service."

"Ah, yes," he said with a skeptical air. "Jane, may we have a word in my office?"

Having a word with Mr. MacDougall was the absolute last thing I wanted to do, but I was sure I didn't have a choice. Although his role in the Order of the Fayte had been diminished by his involvement—willfully or not—in

Krol's conspiracy against Queen Victoria, his standing as Windsor's House Steward remained unchanged.

In the kitchen and elsewhere in the castle—anywhere beyond the Fayte Hall, really—his rank required he be treated with respect, whether I trusted him or not.

And I still, decidedly, did not.

"Of course," I forced myself to say. "I'll grab an apron and be right there."

"Do not make me wait. Miss Carlisle, you may return to your duties."

I shot her a don't-make-me-go-alone look.

She bowed her head. "Yes, sir. But I was helping Jane."

His gaze pinned me over that hawkish nose of his. "Do you require help?"

He was daring me. I clasped my hands behind my back. "No, sir. I'm quite all right."

His disapproving look swept over me. "Good," he growled before making his way back to the corridor toward his office.

"Will you be all right?" Marlie whispered once he was gone.

"Who knows?" As I made my way down the corridor, the butterflies in my stomach reminded me that not so long ago a summons to that office meant certain trouble. I grabbed a fresh kitchen apron from a nearby hook and tied it on as I went to Mr. MacDougall's door and knocked.

"Enter." The command sounded as ominous as ever.

With an overpowering sense of dread, I let myself in.

"Close the door behind you, and take a seat."

I did as he instructed. Although I'd told Marlie I would be fine, I wasn't sure of that at all, not with those razor gray eyes staring at me from the other side of that massive desk. The mantel with the carved dragon heads, mouths gaping and fangs exposed, reminded me this was not a man to be underestimated.

Beneath my leather gloves, my palms grew warm and

slick with perspiration as he glared at me from where he sat behind his desk, his skeletal hands folded on the surface in front of him.

"You look well, considering your ordeal." Those wiry eyebrows pulled low over his nose.

Was that a trick question?

"I'm not sure what you mean." I gripped the folds of my skirt, afraid to look at him for fear of giving anything away if he did not already know the details.

He tilted his head with a smug grin. "You needn't play coy with me. Mrs. Crossey informed me that you were returning to us. Unharmed, it seems."

I tried to keep the panic off my face. "I didn't know she had shared the particulars."

He pushed back his chair. Was he surprised or insulted?

"I assure you she has. I was surprised, however, to hear her telling that dimwit cook that you were in charge of the servants' meals today. When I asked her about it, she seemed a bit… I suppose the best way to describe it would be distracted." His thin lips rolled inward and all but disappeared. "So I ask you, Jane, is there anything I should know?"

He glared at me and, again, I feared a trap.

"I don't know what you mean." And truly I didn't have the foggiest idea what Mrs. Crossey had in mind.

He reached his long arm across his desk to adjust the slant of the pen resting in its pot. "I see. Well, there seems to be nothing more to say on the matter, so let me just add this: If anything is amiss, or if there is any assistance I may provide, I hope you know you have only to ask. I misjudged you before, and it pains me to know the trouble that caused."

There were no daggers aimed at me in those hooded eyes now, only regrets. Was he apologizing to me? I wasn't sure what to make of it. He was the last person I'd consider an ally, but he was a Fayte Guardian. And still a ranking one at that. Without Mrs. Crossey, who else could I turn to? I swallowed hard and blurted: "As it happens, I do need help. As you must already know, the Brightlands Queen is here—I think she's here—and I believe she intends to do harm."

He tilted his chin slightly to the side, and his brow wrinkled. "Excuse me, the what?" His confusion appeared genuine.

"The Brightlands Queen," I said more slowly this time. "She's the one who took me. I believe she intends to kill people close to me to make me suffer for killing her son. Mrs. Crossey, Marlie, the Bellingtons, Mr. Starwyck…"

He lifted his hand. "Yes, I get the idea." His voice was calm, but there was terror in his eyes.

I bit my lip. "Did Mrs. Crossey tell you any of that?"

He mastered himself and shifted in his seat. "Do you think it may be possible our Lady of the Fayte has betrayed us?"

"Absolutely not." The words jumped from my lips before I could think better of them. "She's never been more committed to our cause. She's searching for her mother too, just as we are."

"Her mother? This vengeful creature is her mother?"

Oh goodness. "What exactly did Mrs. Crossey tell you?"

He frowned. "Enough." He rose from his desk and paced the floor, his hands clasped behind his back then folded across his chest. After a deep sigh, he turned back to me. "I'm afraid it might be possible Mrs. Crossey has taken this business upon herself, either out of pride or a sense of responsibility."

"Is that why she's gone off today? Is she working on something?"

He sighed again. "I wish I knew. We crossed paths while I was taking my morning walk. She wasn't exactly forthcoming about where she was going, but I saw her carriage turn toward the village. Considering the time, it must have something to do with this business. She isn't usually about at that hour. She didn't mention anything, but you know how stubborn she can be."

"Yes, I'm afraid I do." I bristled. Was I siding with Mr. MacDougall against Mrs. Crossey? "What I mean is, she always has a way of putting others before herself."

"Yes," he said, "rather annoying but true." He tapped his lip with his sinewy forefinger. "Without the Lady's aid, I don't see how we can find this creature. Gaining her assistance must be our top priority."

I stiffened in the chair. He was saying the very thing I was thinking. Yet this was the man who accused me of being a mortal threat to our own dear Queen, the same man who conspired with those who meant her harm. Of course he said he'd been unaware of their motives and he'd apologized and tried to make amends. Mrs. Crossey believed he could be trusted, but I still had my doubts.

At the moment, Mrs. Crossey's behavior was more baffling. Her frosty reaction to me after the ordeal in the Sanctum and now this. "Why do you think she went into the village?"

"I've been wracking my brain for an answer to that question, and I can only think of one reason: to seek counsel from her sister, Miss Trindle."

The name triggered a cascade of old memories. I hadn't seen Miss Trindle—or Headmistress Trindle, as I knew her—since the day she'd delivered me to the servants' entrance more than a year ago, bringing an abrupt end to my years as her student at Chadwick Hollow School for Orphan Girls. Mrs. Crossey rarely talked about her sibling, which made me wonder why he thought she would confer with her now.

Yet these were extraordinary times.

"Even if you're right, I still believe we need the Lady of

the Fayte," I said.

Mr. MacDougall sat back and folded his arms. "I'm inclined to agree."

"Once the meal is done, I can slip away without being noticed, and I hope by then Mrs. Crossey will have returned."

His gaze clouded, but he nodded. "It's a sensible plan." He planted his fingertips on the desk. "In the meantime, if you see anything or learn anything that might shed light on this matter, please bring it to me. We're treading uncharted waters here. It's best to proceed with extreme caution."

"I understand. I'll feel better about our chances once we hear from the Lady." I rose and made my way to the door. I was about to turn the knob when he said my name. I turned back.

He was staring at my gloved hands. "Do they still afflict you?"

I held them up to inspect them. "Yes, but I wouldn't call it an affliction so much. Not anymore. I've become used to them. I can control the visions better now. One day, perhaps I won't even need the gloves. I hope so, anyway."

"I do as well," he said. "Thank you, Jane."

I wasn't sure why he was thanking me, but I took it as my cue to leave.

When I returned to the kitchen, Marlie was still at my worktable, sorting through a bowl of vegetables. "Is everything all right?" She seemed braced for bad news.

"I think so. He's concerned, as we are. What's going on here?" I glanced at the carrots, celery stalks, and onion bulbs.

She pulled the last onion from the bowl and set it with the other two. "I thought you might need some help. I pulled these from the pantry for a stew, and there seems to be more than enough beef left over from the Queen's dinner last night."

I examined the ingredients, removing a skinny carrot and celery stalks that were so limp they draped over the onions. "You can take these back. They're good for stock, not much else. Also, if you can, bring back a dozen or so potatoes. Maybe some green peas. I'll see about the meat, but I think we can do better than stew."

"You won't be trying something fancy, will you? We're on our own, remember?"

"Nothing fancy." I shooed her away to the pantry.

By the time she returned, I had procured a hearty portion of meat and was working on a short crust pastry.

She frowned. "It's to be pasties, then?"

I could see her panic as she calculated how long it would take to form so many individual pies. "Not pasties, no. Raised pies. Five or six about yea high should be sufficient."

She blinked hard. "Molded pies like Chef makes for the royal dinners?"

"Of course not. Chef would never hand over his copper molds. But the pie dollies should do just fine. They won't be as pretty, but they'll taste just as good. Thyme! We'll need a good deal of thyme and black pepper and a few bay leaves too."

"That's still more trouble than stew. Why the bother? It's not even Sunday."

I glanced away. I suppose I was making more of a fuss than I probably should, but we were stuck here at least until Mrs. Crossey returned. "It's just something I've been wanting to try. What's the harm?"

Marlie grimaced, but her glance darted away. "Well, look at that. Where do you suppose he's going?"

I followed her gaze to Mr. MacDougall striding through the kitchen and pulling on his great coat.

"I hope he's off to collect some help."

A few hours later, when the first batch of pies had come out of the oven and were cooling on racks, Mrs.

Crossey strolled in with a smirk. "Look at you, working so hard. All well in hand, I see?" She turned to leave again, but Marlie cut her off.

"Off again so soon? May we see you later, then?"

Mrs. Crossey frowned. "What on earth for? I mean, it's been a long day, and last night was so…" She let the words trail off.

"But there's much to do," I said, my voice pleading.

Her forehead wrinkled. "You're doing fine."

She was acting like she didn't even know what I was talking about. Had that strike to her head been worse than I thought? "Can we meet later? Perhaps it's better to discuss it then."

Mrs. Crossey sighed, annoyed. "Fine. Come to my room when you're finished here."

"Could we meet down below?" I whispered.

"Below? What…" She winced and touched her forehead. Her face twisted in pain.

I moved toward her, afraid she might faint. I touched her shoulder. "Are you all right?"

She recoiled at my touch, and her expression went blank. "Right, what were you saying?"

"May we meet with you down below? At the usual hour?"

"Yes. That will be fine." She turned and hurried toward the door.

We stared after her.

"Something is wrong with her," Marlie whispered.

"Something is definitely wrong." I muttered the words even as my mind raced for answers.

CHAPTER TWENTY-FIVE

MARLIE AND I found the Library alight when we entered the Fayte Hall soon after the kitchen cleared from dinner service. We thought we'd be the first to arrive, but Lucas was already there, robed and hunched low over a scroll spread out before him. Several others were piled alongside. He was so deep in thought, he didn't look up.

I pulled on a robe and was fastening it beneath my Faytling when I approached. "I looked for you at dinner."

Marlie had made herself scarce, trying to give us some privacy, no doubt. For most of the day, I'd managed to keep my mind on work, but in those stray moments when I wasn't fretting about Rhilasa, I'd caught myself daydreaming about seeing him again. I'd imagined rushing into his arms and being swept away by a kiss. I'd imagined gazing into his eyes and losing myself there. I'd imagined all sorts of ridiculous things, but now that he was only paces away, I couldn't even bring myself to say hello.

I only stood by, watching him and the way the firelight played across his unruly curls and caught on the reddish strands that wove through his dark hair. I watched his thumb rub along those full, pink lips. The lips I could almost feel upon my own.

He glanced up from his study and caught my eye. I tried to look away, but that smile told me he knew I was staring. My neck and cheeks burned.

"Come look at this," he said. "I found an early blueprint of the Balmoral Fayte Hall among the scrolls up there." He pointed a finger at the upper shelves of the bookcases that encircled the Library. The wheeled brass and wood ladder was parked behind his chair. "It even has my father's early sketches of the hydrometer. Now that I see how he hooked up the water pipes, I believe I have an idea what needs to be done to restore it. Once the area is cleared out, of course."

I leaned over the table to see the drawings myself. There were views of the contraption from different angles and magnified panels depicting the most intricate instruments. "It looks incredibly complicated, but if anyone can restore it, I'm sure it's you. You've already done it once."

He sighed. "My father did it, mainly. But I believe it will be possible to re-create it. All the details seem to be here."

I wasn't looking at the drawings anymore. I was staring again at the wistful way he gazed at that marvelous machine. A profound sadness filled those toffee-brown eyes of his. If I could take that pain away, I would do it in a heartbeat. At that moment, I would have done anything for him.

He looked up again. "I wouldn't be here if you hadn't found my Sliver. I don't know if Marlie or the others told you, but after you left, something changed. I could feel myself slipping away. I fear what would have happened if you hadn't brought it back when you did. How did you even manage it?"

"I was lucky, I suppose." I stared off and focused on the flicker of the flame burning in the dragon head sconces embedded in the walls and watched it play among the shadows.

"I'm sorry," he hurried to say. "I wasn't trying to be nosy."

"It's not that. It's just, I don't really deserve the credit. It was my mother's doing."

His face changed. "But I thought… She's there? That's wonderful."

"It was. She was a prisoner of the Brightlands Queen." All at once, the memory of her in that cage rushed back.

No. No. No. Don't remember her that way.

I thought of her standing against the watercolor sky and the burbling green-blue stream. That's how I wanted to remember her.

"The Brightlands Queen killed my mother, and it was my fault."

He rose and touched my arm. "I'm so sorry. I didn't know."

I welcomed his hand upon my elbow and the simple comfort of human contact, a comfort only he could offer since his touch alone had no effect on me. It was a relief that hadn't changed now that he had his Sliver.

But why hadn't it change? If he was restored, shouldn't his touch affect me now?

An awful thought struck me: Had the Sliver failed?

He noticed me staring at his hand and pulled it back. "I'm sorry. Is something wrong?"

When I'd left him in the Sanctum, there'd been plump in his cheeks and a sparkle in his eyes. But now there were hollows and shadows. "I was only thinking that your touch should trigger something now, if you truly are restored, but maybe these things take more time."

"I feel better, so something worked," he said. "We can be thankful for that."

That cheerfulness broke my heart because I knew he was lying. He was struggling to hold back a cough, and when he moved his hands, I noticed them tremble.

He was trying so hard to keep me from noticing, I forced myself to smile and play along. "You're right. We should certainly be thankful for that."

He took my hand and pulled me close again, and all those worries faded away. When he gazed into my eyes and smiled, there was nothing but him. No Mrs. Crossey. No Marlie. No Rhilasa or the Brightlands or Fayte Guardians. Just my heart beating for him and him alone.

"I can't tell you how good it is to see you, Jane. When we're done here tonight, would you like to join me for a walk? We could talk…"

I thought he was going to say more, but he let the sentence dangle unfinished. It made the offer even more appealing.

"I'd like that." My cheeks burned, but I didn't care.

I thought he'd drop my hand then, but instead, he raised it to his chest. All the books and scrolls and even the Library walls fell away. Nothing existed but him and me, and the way his lips were drifting closer to mine.

The main door flew open and brought the world crashing back around us.

His chin dropped to his chest. "Of all the…" Again, he left the sentence unfinished.

I slipped my hand from his and stepped away as though nothing had been happening, certainly not an almost-kiss that left my knees weak and every other part of me tingling.

"Good, you're here," Mr. MacDougall said as he yanked on a robe. "I was hoping we could have a word before—"

He was interrupted by the door flying open again. Mrs. Crossey sauntered in.

"Ah, you made it," Mr. MacDougall declared with something less than enthusiasm. "I trust it was no trouble getting here?" He was speaking to Mrs. Crossey, but he sent me an odd glance, as if to be sure I was listening.

"No trouble," she said, scanning all four corners of the chamber. "Is this all there is? Only you four?"

"I thought we agreed it would be best not to call a general assembly, under the circumstances," he said.

"Ah, yes. Of course." She moved into the Library and gazed up at the mostly barren shelves. She seemed on the verge of asking a question then seemed to think better of it.

Marlie appeared from behind a bookcase and grabbed a robe, which she offered to Mrs. Crossey. "You won't want to forget this."

Mrs. Crossey glanced at the rest of us and seemed to note that we were wearing robes before she took it from Marlie. "Yes, thank you. Shall we get started? There really isn't time to waste, is there?"

"Yes, the sooner the better." Mr. MacDougall proceeded toward the Sanctum, though I could tell something was bothering him.

Mrs. Crossey followed quickly after him.

I fell in step beside her. "Did the physician pay you a visit?"

She smirked. "Yes, but I told him I was fine. I've never felt better."

"Very well." Mr. MacDougall cleared his throat. "I believe we are ready."

As we settled in around the divining pool, I caught Mrs. Crossey staring at the tapestries, but her gaze looked a million miles away.

"It's such a shame what happened to the Balmoral hangings," I said. "Do you think they can be restored?"

She narrowed her eyes on me. "The Balmoral hangings? Hm, yes, I suppose so." She took a place between Marlie and Lucas at the pool.

"Here's your place, Mrs. Crossey," Mr. MacDougall said as he tapped the empty spot beside him.

"Of course it is. I'm just making sure all is as it should be." She completed the circumference, hastening the final few steps before taking the Master Scryer's position.

"We're ready, whenever you'd like to get started, Mrs. Crossey," Mr. MacDougall added.

The woman looked again upon the image of Druansha placing her hand on Queen Boudica's head, the bright light indicating the moment the fae maiden bestowed her gifts on the human warrior.

"Mrs. Crossey," I said gently.

When there was no response, I tapped her arm. She turned, startled, but she wasn't disturbed. Her expression was oddly blank, almost confused.

"Are you ready?" I gestured to the pool, where everyone was eyeing her.

"Oh, yes." She straightened and placed her hands on the rim of the white alabaster basin.

I removed my gloves and tucked them into my skirt pocket.

Mrs. Crossey stood utterly still and silent. Was she waiting for something?

"Whenever you're ready," Mr. MacDougall prompted.

"Right." She glanced around the pool to see the others had placed their fingers into the pool, then submerged her own in similar fashion.

In unison, our Faytlings began to glow, a soft pink that slowly became a deeper violet. At the same time, the clear water turned a milky white and the mist rose from the surface and over the sides of the basin wall, obscuring our feet in the cloudy mass.

Though our eyes were to remain closed, I peeked to see Mrs. Crossey swaying but saying nothing.

Why wasn't she uttering the incantation? And I wasn't alone. Marlie and Lucas were peeking as well. Even Mr. MacDougall was sending a worried, sidelong glance her direction.

What was wrong with her? She must realize we needed Druansha's help to find her mother. When I finally lowered my own fingertips into the cool water, the white mist turned a deep, dark purple. Darker than it had ever turned before.

Was that Mrs. Crossey's doing?

Instead of waiting for her to begin the incantation, I delved into the darkness myself to seek Druansha.

Are you out there? Can you hear me?

I waited for a response. When there wasn't one, I attempted a phantom walk, but that failed as well. Was my concentration lacking? Had my time in the Brightlands changed me?

That thought sent a cold spike of fear through me. Was that why I hadn't had a vision when Lucas touched me? After working so hard to control my visions, had I managed to lose them entirely?

Mrs. Crossey lifted her hands from the water and shook away the droplets. "It would appear our dear Lady of the Fayte is not interested in communicating with us. Quite unfortunate."

Why was she giving up too soon? There was still a chance. But when I opened my eyes, she had already stepped away from the pool.

"Please don't go," I begged. "It's the only way we'll find the Brightlands Queen. Druansha is the only one who can do it."

Her eyebrows spiked. "The only one? Are you sure?"

How could I make her understand? She didn't know how malicious Rhilasa could be. She didn't know how terrifying. "Please, let us try once more. I almost felt the connection. You must have felt it too. Where's the harm in one more try? Don't you agree, Mr. MacDougall?"

His shoulders hunched as though he were trying to make himself smaller than his lanky six-foot frame. "I believe there is merit to trying again."

233

"Yes, absolutely. We should keep trying," Marlie added.

Mrs. Crossey shook her head and walked away from the pool. "I assure you, it's a waste of time. I know how disappointing it is, but there's simply nothing more to do." She threw up her hands and returned to the Library. "It's quite late. I think we could all do with a good night's sleep. Everything will look better in the morning. Don't fear. I'll come up with something. Never fear." With a cavalier smile and a wave, she sashayed toward the door.

The rest of us stood in stunned silence.

"Did that seem odd to you?" Lucas asked.

"Terribly odd," Marlie said. "What do you think, Mr. MacDougall?"

"If you'll excuse me." Mr. MacDougall hurried away from the basin. "Perhaps Mrs. Crossey is right, and everything will look better in the morning."

The rest of us watched him leave. Was he going after her? Or was he just avoiding our questions? I watched him put away his robe and hurry out the door.

Marlie shook her head. "Should we go too?"

"You can," I said, "but I'm not going anywhere. Rhilasa is out there somewhere, and we have to find her, with or without Mrs. Crossey's help. I'm going to keep trying to reach Druansha. Even if she doesn't know where her mother is, she might know how to draw her out. We need any help we can get."

"I'm staying too," Lucas said. "I won't leave you down here alone. If she comes for one of us, I think we have a better chance if we stick together."

Marlie was looking at the door.

"You don't have to stay," I said.

"Oh, I'm staying. I was just thinking there might be something in one of the older texts. We sent most of the archives to Balmoral, but I know Mrs. Crossey held back some things. I'll see if there's anything about that fae queen that might be helpful. She must have a weakness. If you need me, I'll be in the Library."

She darted off, leaving Lucas and me by the pool.

He inched closer to me. "Do you get the feeling she's leaving us alone on purpose?"

My cheeks heated as I stared hard at my toes. "I'm afraid I do."

He moved closer again and said in a whisper only I could hear, "Remind me to thank her."

~ ~ ~

The crescent moon peeked through the gap between the bedroom curtains, giving the room a soft, silvery glow. It was still too dark to see if Marlie was awake, but I could hear her breathing, low and rhythmic. She was probably still asleep.

I, on the other hand, had been awake for hours. "Did it seem to you like she didn't even want to reach Druansha last night?"

After a groan and some rustling, she said, "Who?"

"Mrs. Crossey. She gave up so fast. It wasn't like her."

After more rustling, Marlie mumbled, "That doesn't make sense, though. She knows we need to speak to Druansha if we're to have any luck finding the Brightlands Queen."

"I think she knows something she's not telling us." It was the theory I'd been turning over in my mind for the last hour. "Maybe she already knows where Rhilasa is."

Silence, then something that sounded like a sigh.

"You're probably right," I said, interpreting the sigh as disagreement. "Maybe she doesn't know where she is, but she must know something. It would explain her odd behavior."

"Do you think she's trying to protect us?" Marlie's words were distorted by the cotton sheet pulled up to her nose. "She can be a bit of a mother hen."

She certainly could. The woman had become like a second mother to me during my time in the castle, and I'd grown to love her as one. Before I discovered the truth about my parents, she was the closest thing I had to family.

But that wasn't it. It didn't feel right. "It seems like she's preoccupied," I said. "Do you think she might be looking for Rhilasa alone?"

"I sure hope not. But she wasn't like this when you were gone. She kept to herself more than usual, but she and Mr. MacDougall seemed to be getting on better than they had in a long time. Maybe it's something else. Maybe a family situation. Perhaps that's where she went yesterday when she disappeared."

Headmistress Trindle. That had been Mr. MacDougall's guess too, and it certainly was possible. I hopped out of bed and grabbed a clean dress from the wardrobe where we kept our clothes.

"What are you doing?" Marlie squinted at me in the darkness. "It's nowhere near first bell yet."

I rebraided my hair as quickly as I could and pinned it on top of my head. "I know. But I think you might be right. Will you do me a favor and tell Mrs. Crossey I may be a little late this morning?"

She sat up and swung her legs to the floor. "Why? Where are you going?"

I slipped on my stockings and grabbed my boots. "It's time I pay Miss Trindle a visit myself."

CHAPTER TWENTY-SIX

THE GOLDEN GLOW of dawn brushed the tops of the eastern ridge as I headed down the lane toward the Windsor mews.

By the time I saw Mr. MacDougall out for his daily stroll, it was too late to turn back. He'd already changed course to intercept me.

As he approached, he pulled his tweed cap from his head. "Jane, what brings you out so early?"

"I couldn't sleep, to be honest. I'm worried about Mrs. Crossey."

He scratched at the bushy blond and silver whiskers along his jaw. "Yes, that was a troubling business last night."

"I can't help but worry, sir. I'm afraid she is pursuing"—I glanced around cautiously—"*things* on her own. I'd never forgive myself if something happened to her. We should be sticking together."

Across the field, a crow squawked, and a horse in the stables neighed. He stepped closer and lowered his voice. "This is not something we should discuss here. Shall we go to my office?"

He was right about the need for discretion, of course. But there wasn't time to take the conversation elsewhere. "I'm afraid I cannot, sir."

He wheedled his walking stick into the ground, and his lips pinched and twisted. "I understand your concern," he said when he looked up again. "But she is the Supreme Elder now. It is not my place to question her, nor is it yours."

"I'm not questioning her. However, I don't think a visit to my former headmistress is out of line. In fact, I think it's long overdue. If, over the course of that visit, Miss Trindle can shed some light on this matter, all the better."

"That's where you're going now? To Chadwick Hollow?"

I nodded and held my head high. "Who better to know Mrs. Crossey's mind than her relation?" He could try to forbid me from going, but it wouldn't work. I'd already decided that nothing would stop me. I did hope, however, it wouldn't come to that.

"I'm not sure that visit will be as fruitful as you hope. I've gotten the impression over the years that the two are not close. I don't think they've even spoken more than a few times since you arrived, and only then because Miss Trindle was eager to hear of your progress."

She was? The woman had overseen my care and guided my education, but she had seemed so eager to be rid of me. Not once had she even contacted me since I'd been here, so I was surprised to hear she had inquired about me at all.

My mother had entrusted her with my care, though. And now that I had my memories back, I remembered all the kind things my mother had said about Miss Trindle and the genuine affection she'd had for the woman. My mother might have believed she was placing me in Miss Trindle's care for only a few days, but she had been confident I would be well treated.

How much easier those earliest days might have been if I had known that at the time. But now that I did know, I truly did owe Miss Trindle my thanks. Her care and guidance had been a blessing, yet I'd given her so much grief. The more I thought about it, it wasn't just my thanks she deserved. It was time for an apology too. I didn't share that with Mr. MacDougall, but it was true just the same.

As a dairy cart approached, Mr. MacDougall gave it a long look before turning back to me. "How do you intend to get there?"

"I have enough to hire a coach in the village. It shouldn't take long. Marlie said she would cover for me in the kitchen until I return."

He nodded, but I couldn't tell if he agreed with me or not. As the cart passed, he raised his hand and shouted for the driver to stop. He ran up to speak with him, and I tried to listen, but the breeze carried away his words. I watched Mr. MacDougall plunge his hand into a front pocket, pull out something, and offer it to the driver. When the House Steward returned to me, he appeared rather pleased with himself.

"Mr. Donovan has a delivery to make then he's willing to take you to Chadwick Hollow and bring you back when you're done."

The gesture surprised me. "You hired him for me? Thank you, it's very generous." It was beyond generous. It was downright thoughtful.

He tipped his hat again with a weak smile. "You see, I'm not so bad, Miss Shackle. Consider it a bit of recompense for past events." Then he and his walking stick set off toward the castle.

As I watched him go, I was still marveling at what he'd done. He was genuinely trying to help me. If I was going to ask Miss Trindle to forgive me, perhaps it was time I forgave him.

I considered it as I strolled down the Long Walk as I

waited for the cart's return. I was nowhere near the end of the mile-long lane when I again heard the rumble of those wooden wheels.

The kindly old man offered a jaunty salute as he came up beside me. "Good day, lass." He was missing a front tooth, and there was green, hand-stitched patch on top of his brown cap. "MacDougall says yer needing a ride to Chadwick Hollow."

"Yes, if it's not too much trouble."

"No trouble at all." He hopped down and came around the side to give me a hand up. "Old Midge and I will be happy to see you there. Won't we, girl?" He rubbed the gray mare's rump, making her nicker and stomp. "Oh, that's enough of that. You don't want to scare our guest, now."

I settled onto the bench. "You needn't worry."

"No, I suppose not," he said as he went around to his side of the cart. "I can see that by the look of you. Now, do you work here at the castle or are you visiting?" He hopped back onto his perch, grabbed the reins, and set the horse off at a canter.

"I work in the kitchen."

"Should have known. MacDougall said they would double next week's dairy order if I returned you before eight. I suppose that's his way of keeping the place running smooth."

"Yes, I suppose it is."

"I'm not sure how long you were intending to spend at the school, but if it's all the same to you, I sure could use that extra order."

"Certainly. I was planning to make it a short visit, anyway."

The grin on his face grew distinctly wider, and he gave the reins another snap to urge the horse to pick up the pace.

I spent most of the ride planning what to say to Miss

Trindle, but by the time we rounded the bend that brought Chadwick Hollow into view, my stomach was in knots.

"My goodness. I haven't seen this place in so long. It seems smaller than I remember."

"Consider where you've been, lass. A grand castle like Windsor is enough to change anyone's perspective."

I suppose he was right. Chadwick Hollow was a respectable and well-tended home on the outskirts of a respectable and well-tended part of the village, along a lane dotted with elm trees at the front and a stream running along the back. A fence and hedges formed a tidy border around the place that the groundskeeper always kept trimmed per Miss Trindle's strict instructions.

The gray paint looked a little more worn than I remembered, and there was a loose shingle from the pediment over the front door, but it was still a lovely Georgian house that had once belonged to a London merchant who had built it with the intention of starting a large family. When his new bride died from the pox during their first winter together, he couldn't bear to stay and had returned to London to nurse his grief. He'd told his solicitor to sell it off as quickly as possible, and Miss Trindle had seized the opportunity.

When we pulled up to the front gate, it was still too early for the students to be stirring, but there was a light in the westernmost window on the ground floor. That was Miss Trindle's office, and I wasn't surprised to see her already at work.

As I stared at my old home, I still hadn't decided what exactly to say when I knocked on the door. Yet before the driver even helped me to the ground, the door opened, and the willowy figure of Miss Trindle appeared.

Suddenly bashful, I yearned to climb back into the cart but forced myself through the iron gate and up the flagstone path.

"Hello, Miss Trindle." I waved, though my hand felt

like a sack of potatoes. "I hope I'm not disturbing you."

She touched her chest. "Jane Shackle? Is that really you?"

Her smile soothed my jangled nerves. I threw out my arms. "It's me."

She stepped back and ushered me in. "What an unexpected pleasure. Wait, has something happened? Oh goodness, are you all right?"

"I'm fine. Everything is fine. I've been meaning to come by for ages."

Miss Trindle quirked an eyebrow. A sure sign she sensed trouble. She peered back at the cart sitting at the side of the lane. "Is that Mr. Donovan from the dairy farm?"

I waved back at him. "He was kind enough to give me a ride. I hope it's all right for him to wait."

"Certainly. I don't remember you being such an early riser. Castle life has changed you, yes?"

"I suppose it has." The entryway was exactly as I remembered it. The navy flocked wallpaper. The grand double doors to the classroom on one side, the single door to Miss Trindle's office on the other, and the dark, polished staircase that ascended to the dormitory rooms where the girls slept. Where I had slept not more than a year ago. I focused on the warm light spilling out of the office.

Miss Trindle closed the front door softly then lowered her voice. "We are alone, Jane. You may tell me why you're really here. Are you in trouble?"

Of course, she had seen through me. In a way it was comforting to know I couldn't fool her. I took a deep breath and dropped the pretense. "It's not me, Miss Trindle," I said. "But I am worried about your sister."

"Oh? You've certainly piqued my curiosity. Shall we discuss it over tea?"

She ushered me through her spartan office and into the

cozy parlor where she extolled the merits of adoption to childless couples and paraded my schoolmates before them. While she fetched the tea, I settled at one end of the burgundy settee, a seat I'd never been allowed while I lived under her roof.

As I waited, I couldn't help but remember all the times I'd watched that ritual from afar. Observing the parade but never being included in it myself. At the time, it had devastated me.

Was I unfit? Unworthy? Unlovable?

Every time, I told myself I didn't want to be adopted anyway, so I was glad to be excluded.

Every time, it had been a lie.

The truth was, I didn't want to admit to myself or anyone that I could simply be unwanted.

That had been my fear, but now that I had my memories back, I knew the truth. My time here should have been temporary, and Miss Trindle had to believe my mother could return. She also knew I was a Fayte Guardian and had another path to follow, even if I didn't know it yet.

Being in this place brought back so many of those old memories and opened so many old wounds. Yet, despite everything, I had ended up with the Fayte Guardians, where my mother wanted me to be all along.

When Miss Trindle returned, she held a tray with a teapot, cups, cream and sugar, and a small platter of biscuits. She poured the tea into the waiting cups. "I wasn't aware that Mrs. Crossey shared our relation with you."

"She did, but not at first. I admit I was surprised."

Her fingers tightened on her teacup. "Before we discuss my sister, I'd like to hear about you. How have you been?"

"Quite well, thank you."

She tilted her head. "Is that all? After all this time? My

sister says you have thrived, and I want to believe it. You were unhappy here, I know that. It pained me, but I didn't know how to help. I always hoped I'd done the right thing by taking you to Windsor. I believed that's what your mother would have wanted."

"It was what she wanted."

Miss Trindle's eyebrows shot up. "You've spoken to her?"

How could I explain all that had happened? There simply wasn't time. "We reconnected, and I remember everything now. The memories that were blocked are restored."

A warm flush swept over my cheeks. I hadn't intended to disclose so much, but there was still more that had to be said.

"I want you to know how thankful I am for all that you've done for me. Mrs. Crossey has guided me, and she helped me discover the truth about my family. I've even found my aunt and cousins."

Miss Trindle touched her chest, and I thought I caught the shine of tears welling in her eyes. "I'm so glad to hear that."

"So all of that is to say, I know how much you helped me. You didn't have to, but you did, and I'm so grateful."

I tried to explain what I could about Krol and his plot against our Queen, about the conspiracy at Balmoral that nearly destroyed the Order, and my ordeal with the Brightlands Queen.

"Goodness!" she declared at intervals, and each time looked more distraught than the last. When I was finished, she shook her head. "How have you managed?"

"That's the thing. I'm better than I've ever been. But I'm worried about Mrs. Crossey. She disappears for long periods, and I am afraid she's trying to find the Brightlands Queen on her own."

"Hasn't the Lady of the Fayte offered to help?"

"She's searching too, but we've heard nothing beyond that. I'm starting to fear the worst."

"And you believe my sister is in danger?"

"I believe she's trying to protect the rest of us, and I'm afraid she may get herself hurt." Or worse, but I didn't want to frighten Miss Trindle any more than I already had.

"My older sister does tend to put herself in harm's way more often than not," Miss Trindle said. "But I'm afraid I won't be of much help. I haven't seen or spoken to her in weeks. The last time was just after you left for Balmoral. She came for tea and filled me in on your progress." She dipped her chin. "I hope you don't mind that she's kept me apprised since you left. I only wanted to know that you were doing well."

I didn't mind at all. It was a comfort to know she cared so much. "It's funny, actually. All this time, I thought you were glad to be rid of me. I was so difficult. I didn't realize it back then, but I see now what a terror I was, and I apologize for it."

"Don't be silly," she said sweetly. "You were never a terror. Quite the opposite. I worried about your tendency to keep to yourself. I suppose that was to be expected, though, considering your challenges. I wish I could have been more forthcoming with you at the time. I do regret that. I was trying to honor your mother's wishes."

"I know, and I understand completely. Now you know why my mother was so secretive. She feared my father, and rightly so. I thought my father's death would be the end of the nightmare. I never dreamed it could get worse."

"I hope you know you aren't alone."

"I know, but thank you." I sipped my tea and thought about that. No, I wasn't alone, and I never had been. My visions and the loss of my memories made me feel so isolated for so many years, but the truth was, there had always been people—and a fae princess—watching out for me. I just didn't know it.

"It's hard to imagine what's happening at the castle. These are perilous times for the Order, to be sure. But I'll tell you something: You are a remarkable young woman, and no one is better equipped to help the Order weather this storm."

I dodged her gaze and sipped again. Hadn't Azender said the Guardians only valued my fae blood? "Yes, I suppose my gifts make me well-suited to these challenges."

"No, it's more than your gifts. They are not the source of your strength. That comes from within you. It's your confidence in yourself and your conviction. You are your own best counsel, and you always have been. That's why I knew it was no longer necessary to wait for your mother. You made yourself ready to be a Fayte Guardian. Some might have helped you along the way, but you are your own light in the darkness. Never forget that. Trust what's in your heart, and you will never be misled."

Her words stunned me. I never expected such praise from her. "Thank you. I hope one day to deserve that high opinion." I hid my embarrassment behind another sip of tea.

"As for my sister, I wish I could help, but I don't know her mind."

A knock at the door stopped her.

"Yes," she called out. "You may come in."

A young girl with a bright blue ribbon wrapped around a dark ponytail opened the door and blushed at the sight of me. "I'm sorry, ma'am. I thought you were alone." She stepped back and pulled the door closed before Miss Trindle told her to stop.

"What is it, Lidia? You may speak. Miss Shackle is a former student. She's come for a visit."

The girl stared up at me in surprise. "The Miss Shackle?"

Miss Trindle rested a reassuring hand on the girl's shoulder. "The one and only."

I smiled at the child. "Hello, Lidia. It's a pleasure to meet you. Do you know, I think I was about your age when I came to live here."

"You were?" The girl's eyes grew wide. "And now you live in the castle with the Queen!"

I tried not to laugh. "I do live in the castle, that is true, but not exactly with the Queen. I work there."

Little Lidia turned her wide brown eyes on Miss Trindle. "She really does live in the castle, just like you said."

Miss Trindle's lips twitched, and I suspected she was trying to keep a straight face too. "Yes, just as I said."

"Do you think I might work in the castle one day?"

Miss Trindle brushed her palm over the girl's head in a motherly fashion, and it brought back another wave of fond memories. So many times she'd done the same thing to me and the other girls. "Of course, if that's what you set your mind to do."

Little Lidia turned to me, and in a conspiratorial tone, she asked, "How'd you do it? How'd you get there, Miss Shackle?"

"I'll tell you how she did it," Miss Trindle interjected. "She was a very good girl who ate all her supper and was always tidy and worked hard on her schoolwork and never wandered away from the play yard when no one was looking."

The girl's smile faded. "I do that too. Mostly."

"Mostly?" Miss Trindle challenged.

The girl dipped her head. "I think mostly, but maybe I could do better."

Miss Trindle tapped the girl's back. "Go call the other girls to the schoolroom. I think it's time we get started."

"Yes, ma'am. It was awfully nice meeting you, Miss Shackle. I do hope you'll visit again." She beamed a smile before retreating.

"Was I ever so small?" I shook my head, not believing

it could be possible.

"The truth of the past is never exactly how we remember it," Miss Trindle said.

"Certainly not in my case," I said. "Thank you for making time to see me. I do hope I haven't overstepped."

"Of course not. I appreciate you bringing this to my attention, and I am glad to see how well you're doing. I always knew you were destined for great things, Jane. Please don't ever hesitate to ask if there's anything you need. Now, you better get back before Mr. MacDougall sends out a search party."

She walked with me to the door and waved as I made my way back to the cart, where Mr. Donovan helped me up to the bench.

"Was it a nice visit, Miss?" he asked after I made my final wave, and he spurred the horse down the lane.

"It was," I said. "Very nice indeed."

CHAPTER TWENTY-SEVEN

WHEN I ENTERED the kitchen more than an hour after my assigned start time, I was almost surprised to see Mrs. Crossey was there, stirring the morning porridge.

"Well, well. Nice of you to join us," she said without looking away from the pot.

"Good morning," I said cheerfully, ignoring her sarcasm. "I hope Marlie told you I'd be late."

"She did. She was a bit vague on the particulars, however."

I'd been thinking how to explain my absence the whole ride home, and I'd decided to be honest. "After everything that's happened, I was feeling a bit homesick. I wanted to pay a visit to Chadwick Hollow."

"Chadwick Hollow? And why would that be?"

Was that genuine concern or more sarcasm? "I wanted to apologize, I suppose, for being such a difficult child. All the injustices I thought I'd suffered, I see now they were nothing of the sort. Miss Trindle had only been doing her best to keep me safe. I wanted to thank her."

She jutted her chin at our worktable, where a pile of

potatoes filled a large bowl. "Get to work on those, if you would."

That's when I knew she was angry. Not that I expected to be promoted to junior cook straightaway, but I'd been working in that capacity for weeks at Balmoral. Didn't that qualify me for something more than peeling potatoes? "Are you sure you wouldn't prefer I make the biscuits?" I asked. "Or, I could finish the porridge for you."

"No, just the potatoes. Then start on those there." She pointed at the other basket.

"The leeks?" I asked.

"Yes, the potatoes and leeks."

She was definitely angry with me.

We didn't speak again for more than an hour. When she was finished with the porridge, she had me carry it to the Servants' Hall while she disappeared out the back door.

When she returned sometime later without a word where she'd been, she told me to prepare some carrots and celery. A half-bushel each. I was about to complain when Mr. MacDougall entered the kitchen. He gave me a long look, then turned to Mrs. Crossey, who had barely noticed him as she fussed with the placement of two pans and a stew pot on the stove.

"Might I have a word with you in my office, Mrs. Crossey?" he asked.

She ignored him.

"Mrs. Crossey?"

Still nothing.

He tapped her on the shoulder. She whipped around and regarded him coolly. "Oh, you're speaking to me? Of course." She turned to me. "Get the stew started. You can do that, can't you?"

At least it wasn't more potatoes. But before I could assure her I was more than capable, she was already following after Mr. MacDougall.

Several minutes later, when she returned, she appeared

distracted.

I handed her the wooden spoon I was using to stir the simmering pot. "Is everything all right?"

"Fine, I suppose." She took the spoon and gave it a vigorous turn. "That headmistress of yours dropped in, wanting to know about your progress."

"Miss Trindle?"

Mrs. Crossey shrugged. "Yes, I believe that was her name. She's certainly an anxious woman. Anyway, it seems some people don't have enough to keep them busy, so they make excuses to interrupt those of us who do. Rather irksome."

"Irksome? Yes, I suppose it is." Was she angry at her sister? Or had she truly forgotten who Miss Trindle was? "If you don't mind, I'd like to pop in and say hello to her."

She frowned at me. "Fine, but don't dawdle. We don't have all day."

"Understood." I made my way to the corridor as quickly as possible, hoping she didn't notice my trembling hands or the swirling panic that threatened to swallow me whole.

~ ~ ~

"It isn't her," I said when I shut Mr. MacDougall's office door and slumped against it. My knees were so wobbly, I kept hold of the knob to be sure I wouldn't collapse.

My outburst caught Mr. MacDougall and Miss Trindle in a quiet huddle beside his desk. Slowly, they pulled apart, but the worry was plain on their faces.

"That is not her," I added, breathless and chest heaving.

They exchanged a careful glance, and Mrs. Trindle offered the House Steward a subtle nod.

"Please keep your voice down." He was straining to

keep his composure. "But, yes, we've come to the same conclusion. The question is, what do we do about it?"

"What—" I pulled away from the door, then lowered my voice. "What can we do about it? Is that even Mrs. Crossey or...?" I couldn't finish my sentence. The alternative was too painful.

"To be honest with you," Miss Trindle stepped forward, "we don't know, but the longer she's in this state, the more likely it is to become permanent, if it isn't already."

I couldn't feel my hands. I couldn't feel anything. "What can we do?"

"I was telling Mr. MacDougall about some of the books I recall from my early lessons in the Library that might offer some help."

His lower lip protruded, and he nodded, agreeing as an academic might to some abstract theory. I wanted to scream. They wanted to consult old books? "Marlie, Lucas, and I already scoured the Library and found nothing helpful. If there was anything that could help down there, it must have been sent to Balmoral with the other archives."

"You might be right," Mr. MacDougall said. "But Mrs. Crossey held some volumes back, and there's a chance we might see something you missed."

"A chance?" I wanted to scream at them because the truth should have painfully obvious: If that creature wasn't Mrs. Crossey, it had to be Rhilasa. We'd been so busy trying to find that fiend that we didn't notice she was under our noses the entire time.

But I wasn't going to say that. I wasn't going to say anything. I knew what I had to do.

"Do whatever you think best, but I'm going to get Mrs. Crossey back."

"I wouldn't recommend—"

Mr. MacDougall was still warning me not to be rash as

I slammed the door behind myself and hurried back to the kitchen to save my friend.

I paused only briefly in the corridor before returning to the kitchen. It wouldn't do any good to look as panicked or frenzied as I felt or to let the monster that was parading around as Mrs. Crossey know how terrified I was.

I pulled my Faytling from beneath my collar, removed a glove, and held it tightly in my bare palm. *Please help me save Mrs. Crossey. Please, Faytling.* With a deep, bracing breath, I tucked it back beneath my collar and rounded the corner, ready to face the impostor.

She wasn't at our worktable. She wasn't anywhere on the kitchen floor. Not the ovens, the pantry, or the washing room.

Then I spied her, slipping through the door beyond the Servants' Hall. She glanced back, and our eyes met. The way hers widened, I knew she understood the ruse was up. She pushed through the swinging door and disappeared.

I shot after her. When I reached the corridor, I saw her duck into another hallway. I ran, ignoring the disapproving looks from the footmen and maids appalled by my undignified behavior.

When I emerged in the Grand Vestibule, I saw no sign of her, but then there were footsteps echoing up the staircase. When she turned back and spotted me, she hiked her skirts and hastened her pace. I hurried after her.

At the top landing, two footmen stood idle.

"Stop her!" I gestured at Mrs. Crossey. "Don't let her pass!"

One pointed at Mrs. Crossey and frowned, not understanding or believing why I could be hailing them to stop a cook. As Mrs. Crossey passed them, she pointed at me and whispered something that made them nod, then she continued on her way.

"Stop her!" I begged again.

But it wasn't Mrs. Crossey they were eyeing. It was me.

They descended the staircase and blocked me as I tried to pass.

"Are you feeling all right, Miss?" one of them said, taking a position in front of me as the other moved alongside. "Mrs. Crossey says you've been feeling out of sorts. Perhaps we could call a doctor?"

"I don't need a doctor." They were treating me like a child, like I was half out of my wits.

Perhaps they weren't far off. I was about as frantic as I could be. My heart thundered against my chest. I wanted to tell them she was the threat not me, but there was no time. Even if I did explain, they wouldn't believe me.

How could they?

That left me with only one option. I stopped, let my shoulders slump, and gave up the chase.

Of course, I was only pretending.

With furtive looks, I waited until their guard was down and their attention distracted, then I bolted past them.

I didn't look back to see if they were chasing me. I didn't even care. The impostor had widened the gulf between us. She was already far along the red-carpeted South Corridor of the Long Gallery and nearly at its bend. If I slowed down, I'd never reach her. So, I ran with no regard for dignity or propriety.

But there were voices. Men's and women's voices. No, only one woman's voice, and it rose well above the others.

Her Majesty Queen Victoria.

I slowed to a brisk walk and kept my eyes locked on the impostor, who was eyeing the huddle that was emerging from one of the side chambers. An assortment of advisers and officials surrounded the Queen, a diminutive figure dressed in a tailored blue bodice trimmed with drapes of gossamer lace at her throat and wrists over a matching skirt that swayed like a ringing bell as she ticked off her commands.

"I will address the House of Commons. Not next

week, not later this week. Tomorrow. Tell Denison I will not be put off, and if he insists on being difficult, it will not go well for him. Tell him that."

The impostor stepped to the side as the group neared, and only when she saw a maid emerge from another chamber and dip into a curtsy did she follow suit. As she drew one foot back, she swayed out of balance.

She glanced up as if to check if anyone caught that awkward move. When she saw I was the only one, she sent me a wicked grin before making a show of wobbling and swaying in an exaggerated way. Her arms flailed, trying to right herself, then she stumbled directly into the Queen's path.

It all happened so fast no one could stop the collision that sent both women and three of the men tumbling to the floor and leaving them sprawled unceremoniously upon the carpet.

One of the advisers still standing was trying to peel the impostor off the Queen when I reached them. Neither woman was moving, however, and I nearly stopped breathing myself.

The adviser finally managed to roll the impostor over, and I saw her eyes twitch open. She looked around with an expression of pure confusion. The adviser helped her to her feet and maneuvered her to the nearest chair. I moved close, ready to step in should she try to attack the Queen again.

The others attended the Queen, who wasn't moving at all. One man, a senior adviser with a bushy white mustache and beard, held her hand in his and tapped it gently. "She's breathing, but she isn't moving. Oh, ah, there you go. Your Majesty, you've had a bit of a fall. Are you able to move? Are you in any pain?" He glanced up at one of the men standing around. "Charles, collect the physician. She's most certainly been hurt."

The one who must have been Charles tore away,

leaving me a better view of the Queen. Her eyelids fluttered then opened wide. "Don't sit there," she barked. "Help me up. This instant."

"But, Your Majesty, I'm not sure that's a good idea. We're fetching the physician. Perhaps we should—"

"Bah," she said. "I'm quite all right."

As she struggled to lift herself, he offered an extra hand, and a gentleman on the other side did the same to help her to her feet.

She brushed her hands across her skirts and her sleeves then touched her cheeks. When she glanced at me, her lips curled with malice.

That's when I knew it was no longer the Queen. Not my Queen, anyway.

"Perhaps you should sit and wait for the doctor," the anxious man beside her urged. The impostor shook her head.

"A little mishap nothing more. You there," she motioned to me, then pointed to Mrs. Crossey, who was slouched in the chair with her head in her hands. "See to that poor woman." She splayed her fingers then curled them back in a flourish.

As she did, a turquoise light flashed on Mrs. Crossey's chest beneath her blouse then disappeared. When I glanced back at the impostor, her fingers were closed around something in her palm.

I could no longer see her crystal's turquoise glow, but I knew it was there, in her fist, filling her with its power.

"Come, gentlemen," the woman announced, as though nothing had happened. "We have remarks to prepare." She set off toward the staircase with her confused but obedient advisers in tow.

Mrs. Crossey was still motionless, but she groaned softly. She needed help. The doctor appeared at the far end of the corridor, his pace quickening when he spied us.

"The physician is coming, Mrs. Crossey," I whispered

close to her ear. "He's going to take care of you."

She nodded. It was nearly imperceptible. "Go," she whispered. "You must get her."

That was all I needed to hear. I shot off toward the impostor.

When she paused at the staircase, I thought I had a chance to catch up, at least until she glanced back and saw me bridging the distance between us.

She frowned and called over the footmen who had tried to stop me before. She leaned close and whispered. When the Queen pulled away, they came for me.

"Her Majesty wishes for you to stay with that sick woman while the doctor examines her."

"You don't understand." I wanted to tell them that wasn't our Queen, that it was a monster, that they were making a terrible mistake if they let her get away.

But even if I said it, it wouldn't matter. I'd sound like a madwoman.

As I watched the impostor glide down the stairs surrounded by her unwitting accomplices, she gave me one last glance over her shoulder, and her lips twisted into that wicked smile.

She had won, and she knew it.

CHAPTER TWENTY-EIGHT

MRS. CROSSEY, THE real Mrs. Crossey, stood with stern authority at the head of the divining pool, watching as dozens of Fayte Guardians adjusted their indigo robes, shuffled into the Sanctum, and murmured back and forth, wondering why they'd been summoned to this emergency midnight gathering.

I knew that aloof demeanor was only a facade. Standing beside her, I could see her knuckles turning ghostly white as she gripped the pool's rim. The woman should be recovering in bed, but even I knew how much we needed her.

"Are you sure you can do this?" I whispered before anyone else joined us at the pool.

"I'll be fine. It's our dear Queen you should worry about, not me."

She was right, and I was worried. The image of that grinning charlatan striding away in Queen Victoria's form had vexed me all day. Witnessing the transference had answered two important questions, however. One, that Rhilasa was inhabiting bodies, not altering her own physical appearance, and, two, that the Queen was still in that body too. If her experience was anything like Mrs. Crossey's, she would almost certainly have little awareness of what was happening until Rhilasa left.

The question that remained was how—or even if—we could compel Rhilasa to leave Victoria's body. She had left Mrs. Crossey of her own volition, and not even Mrs. Crossey knew if there was anything that could have forced her intruder out.

Although Mrs. Crossey had rallied soon after Rhilasa's departure and was able to stand and walk with some assistance back to her quarters, she didn't remember anything about how Rhilasa had invaded her or what had transpired while Rhilasa controlled her.

At first, she hadn't even believed she'd been under Rhilasa's spell until I'd dragged Mr. MacDougall to her bedside to confirm my story.

"I suppose there's one silver lining to all of this nonsense," she'd said as she sat against her stacked pillows and stared out her window. "We at least know where she is, so we can turn our attention to removing her."

Unfortunately, that was proving to be easier said than done. No one had any idea how to do it, but we'd decided, the three of us in that spartan little room that overlooked the northern hills, that the best place to start—the only place, really—was to reach out to Druansha and hope our previous attempt had been sabotaged by Rhilasa.

We couldn't afford to fail again, so it was decided that we'd gather every available Fayte Guardian. All that combined power, we hoped, had to improve our chances.

As much as I still distrusted Mr. MacDougall, I had to give him credit. He'd quietly gotten the word out to the Fayte Guardians about the gathering.

I caught sight of Marlie coming through the door and motioned her over. "Did you find Lucas? Is he coming?"

She scanned the faces beneath the indigo hoods. There

had to be thirty, maybe forty Guardians in the Sanctum. "I explained everything. He said he was planning to be here, but he wasn't looking quite like himself."

"What do you mean?"

"He seemed incredibly tired. All these late nights must be taking a toll. He may need a good night's sleep."

Had my expectations about returning his Sliver been too high? I hoped it meant his recovery was just taking more time and not that his Sliver was failing. "Yes, he probably needs to rest. I'm sure you're right."

"Of course, I am. Besides, look at all these Fayte Guardians. That Brightlands Queen doesn't stand a chance."

It was always heartening to see the Guardians gathered together. In the castle we worked alongside each other without acknowledging the bond we shared or our common purpose. Sometimes I even forgot there were so many of us.

But here, with our Faytlings proudly displayed and no fear of revealing Fayte secrets to outsiders, it was different. I'd missed the monthly Convergings, when we could speak openly and commiserate and enjoy the camaraderie of carrying on the Fayte Legacy. It reminded me, every time, what an honor it was to be one of their number.

Mr. MacDougall approached Mrs. Crossey on the other side and whispered into her ear. She nodded and turned to the crowd as he took the place beside her. "Gather 'round, Guardians," she called out. The hoarseness of her voice was the only indication that she still wasn't in tip-top shape. "Fingers into the pool, if you would."

The Guardians complied, with a few side glances and tense murmurs. When Mrs. Crossey recited the incantation calling upon the Lady of the Fayte and the soft lavender mist rose from watery surface, I could feel some of the tension in the room release. This was more familiar territory.

As Mrs. Crossey continued to recite her ancient Gaelic words, I mentally sent Druansha a plea of my own. *Please come, if you can hear us. Please, we need you.*

At that instant, the Sanctum's air turned thick, the way it does when a storm's approaching. Even before I opened my eyes to see the violet sparks flashing in the mist, I knew Druansha was near. Tiny sparks coalesced into long ribbons of light that stretched and swirled until they formed a brilliant misty column.

From the center of that column, Druansha appeared.

Like everyone present, I held my breath waiting for her to emerge and for the that gaping hole between our worlds to close.

When the shimmering light dimmed, she stood before us in her elegant, gossamer gown. My heart flooded with relief.

Finally, she was here. Did she already know what her mother had done? Could she help us? I had so many questions, we all did, but she was not interested in questions.

She offered none of her usual greetings, but instead headed straight for the door. Was she leaving? Another question I was too afraid to ask as I watched her pause at the tapestry nearest the opening. A gentle frown creased her forehead as she touched the violet crystal hanging from her neck then brushed her fingertips over the tapestry's weave.

That touch transformed the tapestry in an instant. The pastoral scene of Guardians working in a garden disappeared, replaced by a golden triangle with an open side and three slashes along its base sitting upon a solid purple field.

When the transformation was complete, she moved to the next tapestry and did the same, and so on, until she had changed every tapestry in the room, bestowing upon each a unique golden rune resting on a field of brilliant purple.

Not a single Fayte Guardian spoke as she worked. No one even seemed to breathe. I don't know if anyone else knew what she was doing, but I did. Those were the runes that protected her bedchamber in the Brightlands Palace, and as they appeared upon the tapestries they radiated with orange-yellow light.

That same glow sparked elsewhere as well, revealing those symbols in the inlaid stones beneath our feet and the woven braids chiseled into the walls, even hidden in the bookshelves' ornamental trim. They were everywhere, and somehow she was making them even more powerful against the Brightlands Queen.

Only when she'd finished with the last tapestry did she speak. "My mother hid herself so well from me, I'd begun searching in the other realms. Now that her presence is no longer in question, we must act decisively and with haste. These runes will enhance the protection around the Sanctum. As long as we're within this circle, we are safe. But you must still take care not to repeat anything we discuss here. I don't know her strength, so we should assume she can read our thoughts. Are there any questions?"

She paused for a response but was met only with confusion.

"I know this is distressing," she continued. "But your Queen is in grave danger. We must work quickly if we're to release her from my mother's hold."

Panic filled the Sanctum. Many, apparently, had been unaware of the danger to the Queen. A Guardian standing behind Marlie began to wheeze and slumped to the ground in a dead faint. Two others quickly bent to revive him and helped him to a chair in the Library.

As the commotion died down, Mrs. Crossey tapped the edge of the divining pool. "This is why we've gathered you all here. I know you have questions, and we'll answer as many as we can. But as the Lady has said, we must act quickly."

"If an Ancient One has already taken Her Majesty, haven't we already lost?" shouted a Guardian lurking in the back.

Mrs. Crossey lifted her chin with defiant determination, making her appear as regal as any Queen. "We may be at a disadvantage, but we have been at a disadvantage before. Fayte Guardians are resourceful, are we not?"

Those around me nodded and muttered a weak, "Yes."

"We are cunning, are we not?" she pressed more firmly.

The group replied with a heartier, "Yes."

"And we are ready to stand strong and carry on with the duties handed down to us by our ancestors, are we not?"

Now the Sanctum filled with vigorous cries of "Yes" and "Yeah," enthusiastic nods, and fists pumping into the air.

Satisfaction spread across Mrs. Crossey's face. "Good. Do I hear any suggestions?"

Mr. MacDougall cleared his throat, and all eyes turned to him. "Might it still be possible for our Lady to appeal to her mother and persuade her to end this vendetta?"

Attention shifted to Druansha. Her elegant chin dropped.

"I'm afraid it is not," she said. "My assistance to the Fayte Guardians over the years has not endeared me to my mother. If I were to seek her benevolence on your behalf, I'm afraid it would worsen the situation."

Marlie stepped forward. "If these runes protect us from her, couldn't we use them to protect Queen Victoria, or anyone for that matter?"

Again, Druansha frowned. "Your plan might work if we could hold her in a single place long enough to get the runes around her, but she would likely realize what we were doing before we succeeded. And again, that might cause her to retaliate or cause more harm."

With each dashed idea, the hopeful spirit in the room died away. Even Druansha seemed to be giving in to despair, which tore at my heart.

"I have an idea."

I glanced around, as surprised as anyone that the words had passed my own lips. It was rash, and I didn't really have an idea, only a fragment of an overheard conversation.

"Yes?" Mrs. Crossey said, urging me on.

Although I didn't have a fully formed thought, I couldn't remain silent, either. "I was there when Rhilasa took Her Majesty. Before it happened, I heard our Queen telling her officials about a visit to Parliament tomorrow. Could that help us?"

Druansha and the others remained silent. Were they considering it?

"I suppose it does help us," Druansha offered. "It tells us that we must do something and fast, because if my mother intends to leave this castle as Queen Victoria tomorrow, there may be no limit to the destruction she could cause."

CHAPTER TWENTY-NINE

MARLIE BIT INTO her buttered bread slice as she held open the door to Windsor Castle's East Terrace.

"How can you eat?" I brushed by her and into the gray, misty morning with my gloved hand lingering on my stomach over my overcoat, trying to calm the bee swarm churning there.

Of course, it didn't help at all. Once I'd told the Fayte Guardians and Druansha what I'd overheard, Mr. MacDougall had asked the Master of the Stable about the time she was expected to set off and how many coaches would be in the party. When the man answered that a single coach was scheduled to depart near dawn, our plan quickly came together.

I'd gone to bed in a fog of euphoria, convinced the scheme to rescue the Queen would work.

But now, in the burgeoning light of day, I wasn't so sure.

"There wasn't time for a proper breakfast," Marlie replied with her mouth full. "What else was I supposed to do? You can't expect me to capture a Queen on an empty stomach."

My finger flew to my lips. "*Shh!*" I knew no one was around, but hearing the words aloud only raised more doubts.

As we rounded the southern corner and made our way toward the King George IV Gate, the bees in my midsection buzzed up a new storm. Had something gone wrong? Where was everyone? A trio of gardeners were trimming the rose bushes, but otherwise the grounds were empty.

I bent my head toward Marlie. "This is where we're supposed to be, isn't it?"

"Don't worry. We're fine."

"But I don't see anyone." How could she be so calm? Druansha had warned that if Rhilasa made it to London, we might never stop her. If she took a mind to, she could decimate Parliament, or worse. Who knew how much damage she and that terrible turquoise crystal could do to the Empire?

My heart thudded like a stampede of wild horses.

"Have you learned nothing since you've been a Guardian?" Marlie sent me a sharp, sidelong glance. "This is what we do. We can be invisible when we choose to be, remember?"

She was right. I tried to ignore my rankled nerves as we continued on. I didn't recognize the two guards at the gate, but surely they were Guardians. And several yards down the lane, three workmen were replacing a cart's broken wheel as another man held the horse's reins.

"Are they Guardians?" I whispered as we passed them, walking with determination so we wouldn't look suspicious if they were not.

Before she answered, I heard a long, low whistle from the trees.

"There," she whispered back. "Head that way."

When we crossed into the shadows of the tall oaks and

elms, we found Mr. MacDougall and a half-dozen of the Guardians, mostly footmen and stable hands I recognized from the night before, crouching behind tree trunks and shrubs.

"Mrs. Crossey's on the other side with another team," Mr. MacDougall said when he noticed me searching for others. "But I doubt we'll need the help."

He had such a smug look on his face, I knew he was waiting for me to ask why, so I did.

"The Master of the Stable assured me he could make a few changes to the Queen's coach assignments. It should give us the advantage."

In the distance, rumbling wheels silenced us.

"Is that her?" Marlie leaned low behind a bush but still tried to see down the lane.

"Quiet!" Mr. MacDougall urged. "And keep hold of your Faytling, like the Lady said."

The coach emerged through the gate, making my heart thunder again as it approached.

"I think it's time," Mr. MacDougall whispered to me.

For a moment, I wasn't sure I could do it. If I moved even a muscle, I feared I'd faint. What if I failed? What if the whole plan failed?

"You can do this," Marlie whispered. "And we're all here. You're not alone. Remember the plan. Just get her out of that coach."

Right, we had to move quickly before she sensed the danger, and seeing me alone, she'd hardly consider me a threat. While I distracted her, the others would surround her.

I repeated the plan to myself as I made my way to the center of the Long Walk lane. The coach slowed as it neared, but it didn't halt.

When it was nearly upon me, the others hurried from their hiding places to form a line, forcing the coach to stop.

The driver perched atop the gleaming black carriage tipped back his head, and I thought I saw a hint of a smile. Yes, he was one of us.

Still, he had to play his part. "In the Queen's name, remove yourselves," he hollered down.

"We will not," I shouted back.

After a moment's hesitation, a liveried man from the back hopped down and pulled open the door with the royal insignia emblazoned in gold. He held out his hand to help Rhilasa, masquerading as our monarch.

She took her time fussing with her black taffeta skirts and overlarge sleeves before lifting her glaring scowl to me. "Do not do something you'll regret, child. Allow me to pass before someone gets hurt."

I glanced at the Fayte Guardians on both sides of me and hoped she was so focused on us that she didn't notice the line of Guardians forming a line silently behind her.

Her smug grin told me she thought she had the advantage, and that grin was all it took to turn my fear into white-hot rage.

My fingers curled into fists, straining the seams of my gloves "We won't let you do that," I called back.

Her arrogant smirk became something far more menacing. She waited a breath, then two, then said, simply, "Is that so?" She turned to the footman holding the door and flicked her wrist, summoning him forward.

But no, it wasn't the footman she called. Someone inside the coach rustled. A scrappy black boot appeared on the first step, and then a head of unruly chestnut hair.

Lucas stood tall beside her. Shoulders pulled back, chin lifted, and eyes staring blankly ahead. There was no expression on that precious face. Not anger or fear or confusion. Absolutely nothing.

The sight of him like that nearly brought me to my knees. "What have you done to him?" I shouted, knowing it was the wrong thing to say. Knowing I was giving her the fear she desired.

I didn't care. This was Lucas. This was my beloved. It was all I could do not to run to him and throw my arms around him.

Rhilasa ran her hand from his elbow to his shoulder before turning back to me. "We have a special connection, he and I. He was my first host here in this world. Did you know? I learned from my dear son's mistake. He came to this world in his own form, and it made him vulnerable and weak. We are not accustomed to this world, as you well know. However, there are other ways that make your bothersome dry air no bother at all." She ran her fingers along his arm again. "All that is required is at least a bit of fae blood, and this one made it so easy with that gaping hole in his soul. He would have been the perfect hiding place if you hadn't meddled."

"You're lying," I shouted, though I knew she wasn't. It was another dagger in my heart.

"Oh, yes." She knew she was striking a nerve. "I had great plans for him, which you ruined by restoring that old and shriveled Sliver." She stretched her neck and rolled the Queen's rounded shoulders, as if that form didn't quite fit. "You didn't really think that desiccated thing would save him, though. Did you?"

"Leave him alone," I shouted.

"Or what?"

I glanced at Marlie beside me and Mr. MacDougall. They stood tense and ready, waiting for the moment to strike. But what were they waiting for? "Do something," I rasped. Why weren't they moving in on her? They should have had her in a circle by now.

"Oh, no." Rhilasa chuckled. "They won't be doing that. In fact, watch this." She lifted her right hand and swiveled her wrist. A brilliant turquoise light flashed, and suddenly her crystal was in her hand. She muttered a low incantation as she lifted the stone high over her head. Turquoise lightning streaks shot from it, striking Lucas and everyone around me, even the coachmen and the driver—every Fayte Guardian, it seemed. Each one slumped where they stood or sat.

I dropped to the ground beside Mr. MacDougall and took his wrist. The pulse was faint and his breathing shallow. He was unconscious but alive. All of them were.

I stared, horrified. How had she done it? Why was I unaffected?

"I wanted you to see it all for yourself," she said with a sneer. She thrust her crystal high in the air again, and another burst of turquoise light shot out.

It plunged into me like a searing hot knife.

Then it was gone.

Rhilasa watched me. A deep, angry crease formed between her eyebrows. She'd expected me to go down like the rest. She'd expected to overpower me as she had overpowered even Druansha that day in the Throne Room.

But nothing had happened.

It took a long moment for the realization to sink in. "Your power doesn't work against me." The words tumbled out, half question, half statement. "That's it, isn't it? You thought it would work on me just as it worked on the others, but it doesn't."

At that moment, I couldn't see Queen Victoria's wide cheeks, her rounded jaw, or anything that made that royal visage the polar opposite of Rhilasa's true form. The Queen's natural blue gaze burned into me just as Rhilasa's had the day she'd dragged me from this world and dropped me on her Throne Room floor.

"You're different," she spat. "Why are you different?" She straightened and turned to the trees and scoured the shadows. "You're there, Druansha. I know you are. Do not hide from me."

We'd decided, all of us in the dead of night, that

Druansha should remain in the warded Sanctum, so her presence wouldn't alert her mother to our plans. Perhaps Druansha had grown impatient or sensed our predicament. I didn't care. I was thankful to see her striding from trees and across the low grass.

"Yes, Mother," she said, eyeing the Queen. "I am here, and I can assure you that what you fear is true. I took Jane to the Old Ones, and they received her. She is beyond you now."

The Queen's face bloomed red with rage. "They took her? I don't believe it!"

"They Turned her," Druansha said. "Their roots entangled with hers. They showed her the visions. They welcomed her."

Rhilasa flinched with each word. "They refused me all these years, and they took her? A half-breed?" The rage passed, and she composed herself. "It doesn't matter. It doesn't change anything."

"But it does," I said. It was clear to me now. She couldn't win. I wouldn't let her. "Release every one of these people, give us back our Queen, and leave this place."

"I think not," she said, almost laughing. "I rather like this situation." She stretched her arms again and brushed an approving gaze over her gleaming coach and my handsome beloved.

"If you don't," I said, "I'll tell everyone what you really are."

She tossed her head back and laughed, a deep, desperate laugh. "Here you are only a maid! You're nothing. No one will believe you."

Druansha raised a finger in the air. "They will believe her, because I will tell them it's true. I will tell them everything."

Rhilasa's sneer faded. "You wouldn't dare."

"I would, and I will," Druansha said. "But tell me,

Mother, your newfound love of this world has nothing to do with your fear of returning to the Brightlands, does it? Are you afraid the Seilie Ministers will hold you to account for the stunt you pulled at the Reckoning?"

"I do not fear the Seilies. They can hold Councils and Reckonings and whatever they want, but they will never take my throne. Do you know why? They want nothing to do with the Brightlands. They never have. Ruling is a messy business, and they don't want to get those delicate, immortal hands dirty."

"If that's true and you aren't afraid to return, then take me," I said. "I'll accept whatever punishment you see fit. I'll go willingly and without a fight. But leave this place, and let these people go free."

Rhilasa turned the turquoise crystal in her hand, over and over again, mulling the offer.

"You don't have to do that, Jane," Druansha said. "She won't win."

The dozens of bodies lying lifeless along the lane didn't support her argument.

"Is this another one of your tricks?" Rhilasa said.

"My offer is sincere. I don't care what you do with me, but you must release the Fayte Guardians, every one of them, as well as Queen Victoria."

She mulled it another moment, then said, "Fine, I'll take you to the Brightlands. It's what I wanted, anyway."

"Good," I said, surprised and relieved but still shaken. It was for the best. It was the only way. "Wake everyone up, and let's return to the castle."

Her eyes narrowed on me, and her fingers wrapped more tightly around her crystal. She was plotting something behind those blue eyes. "No. They'll wake up once we're gone."

"But what of Queen Victoria?"

"She'll remain." Then without another word, she reached out the crystal and a thin blue light sliced through the air in front of her. It lengthened at both ends then pulled apart. I tried to see where it led, but the center was utterly black. Where was she taking me? I didn't know, and I couldn't ask.

But did it matter? I'd made my decision.

I turned to Druansha. "Please help them. Get them back safely."

She took my hands in her own. "You are stronger than you know," she whispered.

I knew she would have spirited me away somehow if I asked, but that would leave the others in peril. I had to do this. This was my purpose. I had the power to save them. I gave them all one last look. Marlie, dear Marlie, slumped beside me. Mrs. Crossey on the other side of the lane. Mr. MacDougall, who had earned my respect. And, Lucas, my beloved. I closed my eyes. That pain struck deepest of all.

"Please," I whispered to Druansha, "tell them it was the only way."

CHAPTER THIRTY

I HIT THE Throne Room's polished stone floor with a resounding *thud*. But this wasn't like the last time. I was conscious and completely alert. I knew where I was, and I knew why.

What I didn't know was what Azender was doing on the throne, frozen in the act of plucking a purple berry from a platter held by a liveried attendant at his side. As the faun courtier's head swiveled my direction, the soft light from the Lumen stone walls glanced off something metallic lodged beneath his stiffly curled pompadour.

I looked more closely and saw they were silvery strands woven together, encircling that big, round head of his, just beneath the base of his small, pointed horns.

Either my eyes were deceiving me, or Azender was wearing a crown.

He frowned at the sight of me, making that crown dip low toward the slope of his nose.

At the sound of footsteps behind me, I turned to see Rhilasa in her own form, striding toward the throne, the long tail of her pale-blue bodice swishing across the floor, covering the matching pair of fitted trousers. The sharp heels of gray boots beat a rapid tattoo as she crossed the room.

"Your Majesty!" Azender jumped from his seat.

Her seat.

"What a delightful surprise!" His glance shot to the Dwarven Guards holding positions along the wall. There were only a few, not the full regiment Rhilasa had kept. He kept the broad, happy grin on his face, but his fingers furiously twitched at the guards, urging them forward.

Not one of them did. Instead, they cast surreptitious looks at each other and tightened their grips on their spears.

"Get off my throne, Azender." Rhilasa ignored me as she passed.

"Well, technically"—he shifted and stammered a bit—"when you left, the throne was abdicated. No one thought you were coming back." He turned to the handful of guards and attendants on one side and then the handful on the other. "Someone had to step forward to lead—"

"I will not say it again." Rhilasa was upon him now, and though he stood on the throne's platform, she stared him straight in the eye.

He searched around, hoping, it seemed, to find someone, perhaps anyone, to help him defend his claim. Every eye cast downward or away. Not a single one looked his direction.

Only Rhilasa.

She extended an open palm.

As he lifted the crown off his head, I glanced over my shoulder. The portal had closed, and I could see the tall double doors were pushed wide open. There were two guards standing alongside, but if I made a run for it...

"You will get nowhere."

I didn't have to look to know Rhilasa was speaking to me. She could read my thoughts here. This was her palace, still protected by her wards. But the urge had been fleeting, anyway. There was no escape from her here. I'd known that before I stepped into the portal, and I'd accepted it.

It was enough to know that Queen Victoria was now free from Rhilasa's grasp and the Fayte Guardians, too. Druansha would make sure of it, and she'd be sure those I loved were safe. I hoped, perhaps above all else, that there was some way she could help Lucas where I had failed. He'd suffered so much. He deserved to be restored fully, not suffer for the rest of his life because of the treachery of our fathers.

A knot caught in my throat. Of course, I'd wanted a different outcome for us. That had been the secret wish I kept wrapped in my heart. It had sustained me. It had given me hope when I thought I had none. Perhaps it had even helped me realize I could do something that truly mattered.

That's what I was doing now.

I was so lost in these thoughts, I hardly noticed Rhilasa and Azender had fallen silent. They were turned, both of them, toward the door, listening to the approach of marching boots.

When a troop of Dwarven Guards appeared, I recognized Troxell at the front, glaring from beneath a polished metal helmet. Behind him, in similar battle dress, were four columns of guards standing in formation.

"Are you here to welcome me back, Troxell?" the Queen said, Azender's crown now firmly in her grip. She quirked a smile, but her jaw tensed.

The Master of the Guard lifted his head, making the white feathers atop his helmet sway. "Your Majesty," he called out, "you are under arrest."

The thin line of her lips twitched in amusement. "By whose authority? His?" She jutted her chin at Azender, who was maneuvering behind the throne, as if putting that alabaster stone between him and Rhilasa could save him.

Troxell ignored the question and pulled to the side, a cue that made the four columns merge into two. Down the center of them appeared two taller guards—fae, by the look of them—bearing white banners emblazoned with the seven golden crowns entwined by vines and roses. The Seilie Sigil.

When they parted, a single figure strode forward. I recognized him as well, even without the long crimson cloak that had marked him as the Court's Voice. When he pushed that long, black hair over his shoulder, it moved like liquid silk, hugging the curves around his teardrop ears and flowing over the wide shoulders that stretched the limits of his snug sage-green doublet and blended, almost imperceptibly, into the black silk cloak that fell to his knees.

As he approached, the smooth line of his jaw hardened like stone, and those onyx eyes fixed on Rhilasa. If his appearance worried her, however, she did a fine job of hiding it behind that contemptuous glare.

"To what do I owe the pleasure, Minister?" She held the forfeited crown with one hand and tapped it against the other.

The Seilie stopped in front of Troxell, so close to where I stood I could smell the fresh earth scent of him, as rich and fragrant as a garden after a rain. "It is not for pleasure's sake, I assure you, Rhilasa."

Not Queen? Not Your Majesty? That detail was noted with raised eyebrows throughout the chamber.

It was no doubt noted by Rhilasa as well. She lifted the crown she'd taken from Azender and settled it upon her head before straightening to her full height. "I understand you perfectly. Restitution must be made. My behavior was rash, I admit it, but I'm sure we can come to an agreeable accommodation, as we always have."

His deep, dark eyes turned to me, but I could not read his expression.

I knew you would return. We've been waiting.

It was his voice, but how was it possible with the Queen's wards?

She is powerful, yes, but not more powerful than me, child.

"Are you speaking to her?" Rhilasa's voice rose with her rage. She descended the platform and stormed toward us, looking from him to me and back again, trying to detect our unspoken words. She thrust her right hand forward, and instantly her staff appeared with her turquoise crystal flashing bright and sending off turquoise sparks. "I demand you stop it. This instant."

It's all there, in your crystal. Ready when you need it. She is not more powerful than you.

He held out his hand to me. As I moved to take it, Rhilasa held her crystal toward me, and lightning streaks burst from it.

My hands shot up to block the blast. With eyes squeezed shut, I braced for the impact of her magic.

But nothing happened.

I peeked out to see why. My eyes shot open, shocked at the sight of my hands surrounded by a ball of turquoise light. I marveled at the shimmering color and sparks. Then, from my fingertips shot ribbons of lavender and violet that swirled and danced with the turquoise.

The Seilie Minister watched too, his face too calm to read. Rhilasa stared as well, but her horror was plain to all.

I wiggled my fingers within that ball of light to be sure I could, then I heard the echo of the Seilie's words. She is not more powerful than you.

Rhilasa recovered herself and, with her crystal in both hands, she strode toward me, slowly at first and then gaining speed.

Was she going to strike me with that crystal? Or beat me with her own hands?

As I braced, the turquoise and violet ribbons wove more tightly together, forming a smaller, denser ball between my palms. My only thought was to protect myself. When I hurled that ball at her, my only intention was to stop her in her tracks.

What happened was so much more.

Rhilasa thrust her crystal into the lightning ball, stabbing its very heart. But the instant the crystal entered the glowing sphere, it flashed with the brilliance of the sun and exploded into a million glassy shards that scattered around us like so many stars. I watched them glitter and twinkle as they fell, their light fading, until they disappeared altogether before they ever reached the floor.

"What have you done?" Rhilasa's scream contorted her face into a macabre expression. Lips peeled back against her teeth, eyes webbed with throbbing red veins.

But there was more at work than rage alone. There had to be. As I watched—as we all watched—Rhilasa's cheeks stretched and thinned till there was nothing but gaping holes between her cheeks and jaw, and the skin of her neck shriveled away to nothing, leaving only sinewy tendons. Even her fingers, those devastating talons that had terrorized me, were now nothing more than crooked, brittle sticks, until they, like the rest of her, finally shattered into a thousand tiny fragments, leaving only tiny sparks that quickly diminished to nothing at all.

"She's gone?" Azender stood over the crumpled heap of gray silk that Rhilasa had worn only a moment ago, staring at it in astonished disbelief.

"Is she…?" I didn't know what to say. I didn't understand anything that had just happened.

"She is gone," the Seilie Minster said calmly, watching us both and raising his hand to quiet the murmurs coming from the guards and attendants.

"For good?" Azender pressed.

When the Seilie nodded, Azender bent to pluck the silver crown from the top of the pile. He held it, admiring it with renewed fire in his eyes.

"You may give that to me." The Seilie held out his hand.

Azender gripped the silver coronet in both hands and pulled it to his chest. For a moment, he seemed ready to fight for it.

But that moment passed. His shoulders slumped as he walked across the room and offered it up.

The Seilie Minister accepted it, and the first hint of a smile played upon his lips. "Thank you, Sir Azender."

Azender's head shot up to meet the Seilie's gaze. "*Sir* Azender?"

One of the Seilie Minister's sharp eyebrows quirked. "Duly earned, I would say. A suitable title for the Master of the Palace, if you will accept the role."

"Master of the Palace." Azender savored the words. Then he pulled one hoof behind him and bowed deeply. "Immortal liege, it would be my honor." He rose, and added, "But, who then—?" He stopped and glanced at me.

The Seilie Minister's head swung to me as well. "It is Seilie Law that a monarch's defeat in battle accords the victor full rights and privileges."

Azender pivoted fully to me and bowed again. All around the room, every guard and every attendant did the same.

The Seilie Minister strode toward me, holding the crown. Again, I smelled the scent of wild blossoms wafting from him. With a flick of his finger, my hair fell from its knot into waves down my back. Then he lifted the crown and placed it upon my head.

It was no heavier than a summer bonnet, yet I could feel every inch of the metal pressing against my head. Where it touched bare skin, the metal sent shivers cascading through me.

My gloved fingertips slid gently along its shiny curves and contours. So many metal strands bound together, like so many paths, so many possibilities bound into one. A single perfect circle.

"Queen Jane."

Even as Azender uttered the words, I knew they were wrong. The whole thing was wrong. I lifted the crown from my head and handed it back to the Seilie.

The calm in his expression cracked. "What's this?" The question wasn't angry but confused. "It belongs to you."

I thrust it at him again. "No, it doesn't, or at least it shouldn't. I cannot rule, and I don't want to. This crown rightfully belongs to Druansha."

The thought settled on him, then he took the crown. "If that is your wish, it shall be done. But…" He stopped and his lips stretched into thin, determined lines. "The realm owes you a debt. Is there anything we might offer?"

There was something. There had always been something. The thing I truly wanted. "Is it possible… I mean, do you think you might help me do something for a friend?"

His chin dipped to his chest as he reached for my shoulder. His fingers remained there for a long moment. I looked up into his wide, charcoal eyes, and it was as if I could see a millennia of wisdom staring back at me. When he pulled away, he said simply, "The answer is within you."

I took a breath. "Yes, I see it now." This was my destiny. This was my path.

CHAPTER THIRTY-ONE

DRUANSHA STOOD BEFORE me, waiting as I stepped through the portal the Seilie had conjured between the Throne Room of the Brightlands Palace and Windsor Castle. Behind her, the Sanctum's tapestries still held her protection runes.

"Is it true? Is my mother gone?" Her eyes fluttered with hope or trepidation, I wasn't sure which.

"I didn't mean for it to happen." I didn't know what else to say. How can you apologize for killing someone's mother, even in self-defense?

I braced for anger but only sadness darkened her eyes, though it wasn't sadness for her mother. When she glanced back into the Library, where familiar faces gathered around a table, I knew it was something else. In the gaps between the onlookers, I could see cushions and blankets, then an arm. I didn't have to see his face to know it was Lucas.

The Seilie had showed me a glimpse of my beloved's decline when his hand rested upon my shoulder, a tender warning to prepare me for what I'd find when I returned to Windsor Castle.

Yet the sight of him lying there was almost more than I could bear. His cheeks and lips were pale and so much thinner than last I saw him. Beneath his linen shirt, his chest rose and fell in slow, unsteady repetition.

"We're doing everything we can," Mrs. Crossey said when I rushed to join them. The others—including Marlie and Mr. MacDougall—pulled aside to make a place for me. "Everyone else recovered from that monster's hold when she took you, but he never quite came out of it. We thought it might be her influence, so we brought him to the Sanctum. The wards should have severed any connection that remained, but there's been no change."

Druansha came up behind us. "I've tried to reach him, to guide him back if she's pulled his spirit away. But when I touch him, I sense nothing. I cannot find him."

"We're not out of options yet," Mrs. Crossey insisted. She dipped her Faytling in a bowl of oil beside his head that smelled strongly of cinnamon and lavender, then she touched his temple with it and glided it across his brow. "Marlie found a recipe in the old scrolls for an ointment that protected the earliest Guardians from angry fae influence. We've re-created it as best we could."

"You needn't bother," I said.

"Don't give up, dear," Mrs. Crossey urged gently.

"I'm not, not ever." I took Lucas's bare hand in my gloved one and squeezed it. I whispered into his ear. "Can you hear me?"

Around me the others drew silent, but I paid no attention to them. I concentrated on Lucas. There was no movement on his face, but his fingers twitched in mine.

"Did you do that?" I asked softly.

Another twitch and a brief, weak squeeze.

My heart swelled with hope. This was why I was here. This is what I was meant to do, but there was still uncertainty. Still a risk. The secret the Seilie had shared with me could save Lucas, but it would come at a cost.

Before I went further, I had to know if Lucas wanted this too. It would only work if his heart was with me.

I squeezed his hand, leaned closer to his ear, and whispered: "I can heal you, but we will be united as one. When it's done, it can never be undone." I paused, feeling the weight of the words as heavy on myself as they must be to him. "Shall I continue?"

The final word had barely left my lips when I felt the twitch of his fingers. The rim of thick, dark lashes upon his cheeks fluttered, then his eyes opened. The golden flecks in his hazel gaze flashed and held me with an intensity that warmed me to my toes, then he nodded.

I touched his cheek and nearly choked with relief and joy and every ounce of the overwhelming emotion I felt for this incredible man. My friend and my love. Quickly, I removed my gloves, lifted my Faytling over my head, and held it tightly in one hand. With the other, I touched the place between my eyebrows in the way Krol had touched Queen Victoria to remove her Sliver. I focused on the part of myself that felt most like myself.

Almost instantly, every part of me, down to the very tips of my toes, tugged toward my forehead. When my fingertip tingled, I pulled it gently away, extracting the tiny white strands of my soul. My Sliver.

The Seilie had warned me to take no more than a finger's length and to swirl it in a tiny circle to sever the connection.

As I followed his instructions, gasps erupted around me. I heard Mrs. Crossey utter, "What in the ever-loving world...?"

"It is the Shadow Rite," Druansha said softy.

I heard their words, but it was as if Lucas and I were a million miles away. There was only him and me and the Sliver that we both watched intently as it flickered up like a white flame from my fingertip before I lowered it to his forehead. As it neared, his eyes closed and the flame dipped, as if naturally drawn to the empty place it could fill.

Slowly, I turned my hand so my whole palm hovered above the Sliver, but once it touched his skin, just between his eyebrows, it slipped into his soft flesh and disappeared. His back arched and his chest heaved with a massive breath, then his eyes grew wide and bright.

In a single, easy motion, he sat up and touched his chest. "It's there," he mused. "I can feel it. My heart, it's so full. The emptiness is gone." He reached out and brushed my cheek, then pulled me closer.

I threw my arms around his neck and buried my face in the warm hollow of his neck. His arms wound around me, one at my waist and the other at the back of my head, where his fingers stroked my long, loose hair.

He whispered so only I could hear, "I can feel you there, my love."

I pulled back and his gaze locked onto mine. Those eyes were like a whole world, one I wanted to slip into and never leave. Then he pulled me closer, and I tilted my head up, welcoming those soft, full lips against mine.

His arms tightened around me, and every part of me came alive. I leaned into his embrace, both of us yielding to the other. Nothing existed now but us two, our hearts and souls perfectly entwined.

Mrs. Crossey cleared her throat, and when we didn't part, she did it again, more loudly and touched my shoulder until I pulled away. Lucas took my hand and held it tightly.

"Yes, very good," Mrs. Crossey said, a bit flustered. "We're all very glad that worked and that you two seem to have come to your senses—"

"About time too," Marlie interjected.

I cut her a sharp look, but her giddy grin was too infectious. Even I couldn't keep a straight face.

"But I admit I am confused," Mrs. Crossey continued. "If you are now Slivered, as Lucas was, won't you suffer the same as he did?"

I squeezed Lucas's hand. "It was a much smaller Sliver I gave him, enough to sustain him but not enough to harm me. It does unite us, though. It makes us one."

Druansha remained apart from the others, and I could see she didn't approve.

How could you do it, Jane? You know how it destroyed my parents.

Of course, that was her worry. It had been mine too. But the Seilie Minister had showed me how Rhilasa's greed had corrupted the Shadow Rite that saved her life. She'd plucked out her own Sliver and placed herself in King Kravol's path, knowing his kind heart would take pity on her. She used the connection the Shadow Rite forged between them to control him and steal his power.

Lucas and I would be different. We were different. Our hearts were already entwined.

I wish the best for you, both of you, truly.

Mrs. Crossey, however, was still bristling at my intimate proximity to Lucas. "Perhaps if you'd just move over here, dear." She took my arm to guide me away, then yanked it back. "Oh, dear. I'm so sorry. I wasn't thinking."

But it was too late. She'd held my bare wrist. I braced for the onslaught of a vision.

I waited a full minute before grabbing Marlie's hand.

"What's wrong?" My friend's eyes widened. "Are you hurt?"

I shook my head and considered placing a bare palm on Mr. MacDougall but thought better of it. I grabbed the hand of one of the maids instead.

Still absolutely nothing.

I asked Lucas, "Did you feel anything?"

He shook his head. "Only you."

I locked gazes with Druansha. "Are my visions gone?"

She gave me a half-smile and shook her head. "I don't know. The Seilies have not shared those secrets with me. I shall inquire, however, when I return."

I stared at my bare hands and suddenly remembered something important. Something I'd completely forgotten to tell her. Sheepishly, I said, "You'll want to visit the palace soon. They're expecting you."

Her lips quirked. "Oh? Is there something you wish to tell me?"

I knew I should explain her new status and that performing the Shadow Rite wasn't the only life-changing decision I'd made today.

"Don't fret." She mocked me with her smile. "I knew the moment you arrived. I was curious how long it would take you, though. And you're right. I should be going, now that I know you two are all right."

I gazed up at Lucas again. "Are you all right?"

He grinned, making his eyes and nose crinkle in the most adorable way. "As long as we're together, I think I'll be just fine."

Mrs. Crossey threw up her hands. "I suppose there's nothing for me to say. What's done is done, and all seems well. I shall like to discuss this with you further, young lady, once we're more settled. I still have questions."

"Of course you do." I threw my arms around her and whispered, "Anything for you. I owe you everything."

She squeezed me back so hard, I thought she'd crush my ribs, but I'd never felt so loved in all my life. "I just want you to be happy." She pulled back. "I do hate to break up this happy moment, but I'm afraid I made a promise to Her Majesty that I'm obliged to keep. She came to the kitchen yesterday looking for you."

The chamber went silent.

I touched my chest. "For me?"

"I told her you were visiting with a relative, which was near enough to the truth. She insisted I convey her appreciation to you for the deeds that were carried out on her behalf and which she says she has very little recollection. Also, she'd like what she called 'a little chat' upon your return."

"Yes, of course," I said. Despite the amazed looks from the others, I couldn't help but smile. The Queen and I had had enough of these little chats for me to predict how it would go. So far, she'd taken my surprising disclosures and the explanations of our escapades in stride, but how was she going to react when I told her these most recent events could only have transpired if fae blood ran through her very own veins. Yes, that would be an interesting chat indeed.

CHAPTER THIRTY-TWO

BEHIND ME, THE castle door scraped open, disturbing my solitude.

"I thought I might find you out here."

Lucas stepped out and joined me on the stone bench as I watched the morning fog roll over the hills beyond Windsor's outer walls. Already the summer sun was warming my cheeks and would soon burn the mist away.

"Did Mrs. Crossey send you to collect me?"

He kicked at the pebbles at his feet. "You can't blame her for being concerned. She thought you would be pleased with the promotion."

The promotion. I'd been hoping for more responsibility since I returned to the kitchen two weeks ago, but still, when Mrs. Crossey and Mr. MacDougall had announced this morning that I would receive the title of junior cook, along with a stove and worktable of my own, I'd been as surprised as anyone.

"I am pleased," I said. "I only hope I don't disappoint them."

"So, you're worried. Is that why you're sitting out here

alone instead of settling into your new situation?"

"That situation is barely five feet from Mrs. Crossey's stove, where I've spent the better part of a year." Had it only been that long? Ten months ago, that's when I'd arrived at this castle. An eternity, it seemed. So much had changed.

I had changed.

He settled into the space beside me and nudged his leg against mine. I closed my eyes and welcomed the warmth of him, feeling it seep through my skirts and petticoats, through my skin and all the way down to my blood and bones.

Had anyone seen us, it might appear he was taking a scandalous liberty, but he knew my heart. If there had been any question of it after our souls became one, the golden band with the glimmering opal at its center removed all doubt. He'd been so terribly nervous when he surprised me with it on a moonlit walk. I'd accepted it gladly and kissed him, long and hard, with love shining bright in his eyes, even brighter than the stars.

I knew my past, and now he knew it too, all of it, but all I cared about was the future we would navigate together. The two of us as one.

He gave my bare hand a gentle squeeze that made me thankful all over again I no longer required gloves since his was now the only touch that affected me. Our silent communication was so much easier than speech. No uncertainty. No secrets.

You must see why she'd be concerned. She's afraid she's upset you.

I smiled at his kindness. *Of course I'm not upset. I'm so thankful for it. A cook is all I've ever wanted to be.*

Not a Scryer, like Mrs. Crossey?

Or like my mother? Yes, I'm happy she made me an Apprentice Scryer as well. I cherish all of it.

The Elder Council, I'd been told, had intended to place

me in the role upon my return to Windsor after Krol's attack.

But…?

I only wish I could share the news with her.

Druansha.

Yes, Druansha.

He nodded. There was nothing more to say.

I hadn't seen our Lady of the Fayte since the Shadow Rite. She'd returned to the Brightlands and communicated with us only briefly during the last Converging Ceremony. She said the Brightlands would require more of her attention, but that the Fayte Guardians were in good hands. That if it became necessary, the Old Ones could send word to me directly.

So far, we were managing. The Fayte Guardians shared information with each other through the divining pool, and it was making us stronger and more observant. As long as any new peril came from this world and not another, I was confident in our ability to protect the Queen and her family.

The scrape of the door opening behind us made Lucas pull away.

His parting thought: *Soon, it won't be necessary. Not after the wedding.*

I could feel the smile on my lips all the way down to my toes. *Yes, our wedding.*

"What's this, then? Mr. Starwyck, I sent you to collect her, not to gaze into her eyes."

Lucas glanced away in a guilty fluster, but she winked when I tried to explain I had kept him.

"The truth is," she continued, "I'm intrigued by this ginger cake you've been promising. Perhaps we can give it a try this afternoon?"

"I'd like that. I've been experimenting with the ratio of ginger to treacle, and I think I've got it just right."

My first attempt had been far too rich and the second

too bland. If the next one didn't hit the mark, I was determined to find a way back to Spire Point to beg Grinella Obble for her secret.

"Glad to hear it," Mrs. Crossey said. "Now come along, we have jobs to do and a Queen to serve. We don't have all day."

She held the door, waiting as Lucas and I filed by, him on his way to the carpentry shop he'd fashioned from an unused storeroom and me to the kitchen with Mrs. Crossey. His fingers brushed mine once more, not a goodbye but a promise to meet again after the evening meal for our nightly turn around the garden.

A sound across the lawn made me turn back. "Did you hear that?"

"What, dear?" Mrs. Crossey peered over my shoulder. "Must have been the wind."

A breeze was picking up and rustling the leaves, but that wasn't it. I knew that familiar buzz, that soft flutter of tiny wings. Even in the distance and even after all this time. I knew I could count on her, my friend, my companion, my sweet dragonfly.

The End

———————

Jane's journey has reached its end, but the magical adventure continues with *Guardian of the Realm: The Queen's Fayte Book Four*, set in ancient Britain at the dawn of the Fayte Legacy.

Learn more at www.DDCroix.com/guardian-of-the-realm.

DEAR READER

Thank you for taking time to read *Shadow Rite: The Queen's Fayte Book Three*. Writing these books has been an amazing adventure. I've enjoyed every minute of Jane's journey, and if you have too, please consider leaving a review at Amazon or Goodreads.com. Good reviews and positive word of mouth are immensely helpful and always deeply appreciated.

FREE BOOK

To get a free copy of *Memory Thief*, a prequel story about the events preceding Jane Shackle's arrival at Windsor Castle, and to be notified of new releases, join the Readers Brigade at www.DDCroix.com/Readers-Brigade.

ABOUT THE AUTHOR

D.D. Croix is an award-winning author who writes delightfully dark fantasy with hopeful and bright ever afters. Under another name, she also writes award-winning romance and historical novels. When she isn't plotting new adventures for her characters, she oversees Orange County Writers, a network of published and aspiring authors based in Southern California.

If you'd like to be notified of new releases and have access to exclusive content, giveaways, and other fun stuff, please join the Readers Brigade: www.DDCroix.com/Readers-Brigade.

If you'd like to send her a message, please contact her at dd@ddcroix.com.

To connect on social media, you can find her at the following:

Facebook: www.facebook.com/DDCroix
Twitter: www.twitter.com/DDCroixWrites
Instagram: www.instagram.com/DDCroixWrites
Pinterest: www.pinterest.com/DDCroixWrites
Goodreads: www.goodreads.com/user/show/77702468-d-d-croix

ACKNOWLEDGMENTS

What a wild journey this has been. As *Shadow Rite* makes its debut, the COVID-19 pandemic is finally beginning to recede, and what feels like a long hibernation seems to be coming to an end. During these unusual times, I've been so grateful for the comfort of escaping into the magical Fayte Guardian world. I've loved immersing myself in Jane's adventures and getting to know her extraordinary friends (and foes). They have brought me so much joy, and I hope they do the same for others.

Through the writing of this book, I've also been grateful for the steadfast camaraderie of Orange County Writers. During the lockdown, it has been such a blessing to be able to stay connected, even if it was only through social media and virtual meetings when we couldn't meet in person. I'd especially like to thank Greta Boris, Kristy Tate, Barb DeLong, Cee Cee Wakefield, Megan Haskell, Casey Dorman, Barbara Neal Varma, Marissa Dunham, and Andrea Lewis because they are not only wonderful writers, but generous humans who give so much of their time and talent to make our writing tribe thrive.

I'm also profoundly thankful for all the reader angels who have supported this series, especially Shannon Cramer, Michelle Jones, and Amy Carpenter for their kind words and gentle nudges to write faster.

Creating *Shadow Rite* was a team effort, and I was lucky to have two remarkable teammates. Karri Klawiter of Art by Karri created the extraordinary cover art and design, and Katrina Roets is the eagle-eyed editor who added her professional touch to the manuscript.

Nobody deserves more appreciation, though, than my husband and my daughter. Their love and encouragement mean the world to me, and I love them more every day.